The Abbot's Agreement

Master Hugh hopes you
enjoy this tale.

Mel Starr

The chronicles of Hugh de Singleton, surgeon

The Abbot's Agreement

The seventh chronicle of
Hugh de Singleton, surgeon

MEL STARR

LION FICTION

Published by Lion Fiction
an imprint of
Lion Hudson plc
Wilkinson House, Jordan Hill Road,
Oxford OX2 8DR, England
www.lionhudson.com/fiction

ISBN 978 1 78264 109 4
e-ISBN 978 1 78264 110 0

First edition 2014

Acknowledgments
Scripture quotations taken from the Holy Bible, New
International Version, copyright © 1973, 1978, 1984
International Bible Society. Used by permission of Hodder &
Stoughton, a member of the Hodder Headline Group. All rights
reserved. 'NIV' is a trademark of International Bible Society. UK
trademark number 1448790.

A catalogue record for this book is available from the British
Library

Printed and bound in the UK, July 2014, LH26

For the reverends R. C. Morrell, Henry Steel, G. H. Bonney, Don Bastian, William Cryderman, Dean Parrott, Dwight Knasel, Ralph Cleveland, Michael Hambley, Bruce Rhodes, and Craig Watson.

"Respect those who work hard among you, who are over you in the Lord and who admonish you. Hold them in the highest regard in love because of their work."

1 Thessalonians 5:12–13

Acknowledgments

In the summer of 1990 my wife Susan and I discovered a lovely B&B in the village of Mavesyn Ridware. The proprietors, Tony and Lis Page, became friends. We visited them again in 2001, after they had moved to Bampton. I saw then that the village would be an ideal setting for the tales I wished to write. Tony and Lis have been a wonderful resource for the history of Bampton. I owe them much.

When Dan Runyon, Professor of English at Spring Arbor University, learned that I had written *The Unquiet Bones*, he invited me to speak to a fiction-writing class about the trials of a rookie writer. Dan sent some chapters to his friend Tony Collins. Thanks, Dan.

And many thanks to Tony Collins and the fine people at Lion Hudson for their willingness to publish an untried author. Thanks especially to my editor, Jan Greenough, who excels at asking questions like, "Do you really want to say it that way?" and "Wouldn't Master Hugh do it this way?"

Ms. Malgorzata Deron, of Poznan, Poland, has offered to maintain my website. She has done a wonderful job. To see the results of her work visit www.melstarr.net

Glossary

Abbot: the leader of an abbey, generally elected by monks of his abbey with the approval of the bishop of the diocese.

Angelus Bell: rung three times each day; dawn, noon, and dusk. Announced the time for the Angelus devotional.

Ascension Day: forty days after Easter. In 1368, May 26.

Balloc broth: a spiced broth, used most often to prepare eels or pike.

Banns: a formal announcement, made in the parish church for three consecutive Sundays, of intent to marry.

Beadle: a manor official in charge of fences, hedges, enclosures, and curfew. Also called a hayward.

Calefactory: the warming room in a monastery. Benedictines allowed the fire to be lit on November 1. The more rigorous Cistercians had no calefactory.

Candlemas: February 2. Marked the purification of Mary. Women traditionally paraded to the church carrying lighted candles. Tillage of fields resumed this day.

Castile (soap): a mild soap imported from Spain.

Chapter: the monks of an abbey met each morning. During the meeting a chapter of the Rule of St. Benedict was read. Therefore the place of meeting was the chapter house, and the assembled monks were the "chapter."

Chauces: tight-fitting trousers, often of different colors for each leg.

Choir: the east end of the abbey church where monks' stalls were located. Here they gathered to celebrate the canonical hours and daily mass.

Compline: the seventh and last of the daytime canonical hours, observed at sunset.

Coney: rabbit.

Corpus Christi: the Thursday after Trinity Sunday. In 1369, June 15.

Cotehardie: the primary medieval outer garment. Women's were floor-length, men's ranged from thigh-length to ankle-length.

Cotter: a poor villager, usually holding five acres or less. He often had to work for wealthy villagers to make ends meet.

Cresset: a bowl of oil with a floating wick used for lighting.

Daub: a clay and plaster mix, reinforced with straw and/or horse hair.

Demesne: land directly exploited by a lord, and worked by his villeins, as opposed to land a lord might rent to tenants.

Dexter: a war horse, larger than pack horses and palfreys. Also, the right-hand direction.

Dower: the groom's financial contribution to marriage, designated for the bride's support during marriage and possible widowhood.

Dowry: a gift from the bride's family to the groom, intended for her support during marriage and widowhood, should her husband predecease her.

Explorator: a monastic official whose duty was to ensure that an abbey or priory was secure for the night. Also called an a roundsman.

Farthing: one fourth of a penny. The smallest silver coin.

Franklin: a medieval English landowner of free but not noble birth.

Gloucester College: the main Benedictine house in medieval Oxford University, now Worcester College.

Groom: a lower-rank servant to a lord, ranked between page and valet.

Guest-master: the monastic official in charge of providing for abbey guests.

Habit: a monk's robe and cowl.

Hallmote: the manorial court. Royal courts judged free tenants accused of felonies; otherwise manorial courts had jurisdiction over legal matters concerning villagers. Villeins accused of homicide might also be tried in a manorial court.

Hayward: also called a beadle, he served under the reeve. Usually a half-yardlander or a mid-level villager.

Horn dancers: men wearing deer antlers who danced in the town marketplace at Michaelmas. Probably derived from an ancient pagan hunting custom.

Infirmarer: the monastic official in charge of the abbey infirmary and the health of the monks.

King's Eyre: a royal circuit court, presided over by a traveling judge.

Kirtle: the basic medieval undershirt.

Kitchener: the monastic official who was in charge of preparing abbey meals.

Lammastide: August 1, when thanks was given for a successful wheat harvest. From Old English "Loaf Mass."

Lauds: the first canonical service of the day, celebrated at dawn.

Lay brother: not a monk, yet he had taken vows and was considered a member of the community. Chiefly responsible for agricultural and industrial work to ensure the self-sufficiency of the house.

Liripipe: a fashionably long tail attached to a man's cap.

Madder: a plant the roots of which were used to make a red dye.

Martinmas: November 11; the traditional date to slaughter animals for winter food.

Maslin: bread made with a mixture of grains, commonly wheat and rye or barley.

Michaelmas: September 29. This feast signaled the end of the harvest. The last rents and tithes for the year were then due.

Midsummer's Eve: June 23/24.

Misericord: the Rule of St. Benedict prohibited eating flesh, except for monks who were ill. In 1336 Pope Benedict XII permitted Benedictines to eat meat four days each week so long as it was not served in the refectory or during a fast season. A special place called the misericord was the site of these carnivorous meals.

Muntelate: lamb stewed with onions, egg yolks, lemon juice, and spices.

Nones: the fifth canonical office, celebrated at the ninth hour of the day (about 3 p.m.).

Obedience: a monastic office. The Precentor, the sacrist, the almoner, the infirmarer, and the kitchener were among the obedientiaries holding an obedience.

Page: a young male servant, often one learning the arts of chivalry before becoming a squire.

Palfrey: a gentle horse with a comfortable gait.

Pannaging: allowing pigs to forage in a forest upon payment of a fee to the lord.

Parapet: the upper level of a castle wall.

Pottage: anything cooked in one pot, from soups and stews to simple porridge.

Precentor: the monastic official who directed the church services.

Prime: the second office of a monk's day, an hour or so after lauds.

Prior: the second in authority in an abbey; the leader of a priory.

Reeve: the most important manorial official, although he did not outrank the bailiff. Elected by tenants from among themselves, often the best husbandman. He had responsibility for fields, buildings, and enforcing labor service.

Refectory: the monastery dining hall.

Reivers: Scottish raiders who often pillaged the northern counties of England.

Reredorter: the monastery toilets.

Retrochoir: the area immediately behind the monks' choir, occupied by the sick and infirm, and also often by novices.

Sackbut: an early form of trombone used in Renaissance music.

Sacrist: the monastic official responsible for the upkeep of the church and the vestments, and also time-keeping.

St. Catherine's Day: November 25. St. Catherine was the most popular female saint of medieval Europe. Processions were held on her feast day.

St. John's Day: June 24.

St. Stephen's Day: December 26.

Salver: a tray for serving food or beverages.

Scriptorium: the copying room in a monastery.

Sext: the fourth of the canonical hours, celebrated at midday.

Shilling: twelve pence. Twenty shillings made one pound, but there was no one-pound coin in the fourteenth century.

Tenant: a free peasant who rented land from his lord. He could pay his rent in labor service or, more likely by the fourteenth century, in cash.

Terce: the third canonical office of the day, celebrated about 9 a.m.

Toft: the land surrounding a house, often used for growing vegetables.

Trebuchet: a medieval military machine which could hurl rocks with great force.

Twelfth Night: the evening of January 5, preceding Epiphany.

Venial sin: a sin which is relatively slight or committed without full reflection and so does not deprive the soul of saving grace.

Vespers: the sixth canonical office, celebrated at the approach of dusk.

Vigils: the night office, celebrated at midnight. When it was completed, Benedictines went back to bed, but Cistercians and Carthusians stayed up to begin the new day.

Villein: a non-free peasant. He could not leave his land or service to his lord, or sell animals without permission. But if he could escape his manor for a year and a day he would be free.

Whitsuntide: "White Sunday." Pentecost, seven weeks after Easter Sunday.

Yardland: thirty acres. Also called a virgate or, in northern England, an oxgang.

Bampton

1. Galen House
2. The Church of St Beornwald
3. Blacksmith's Forge
4. To St Andrew's Chapel
5. The Ladywell
6. Bampton Castle
7. Cow-Leys Corner
8. The Mill

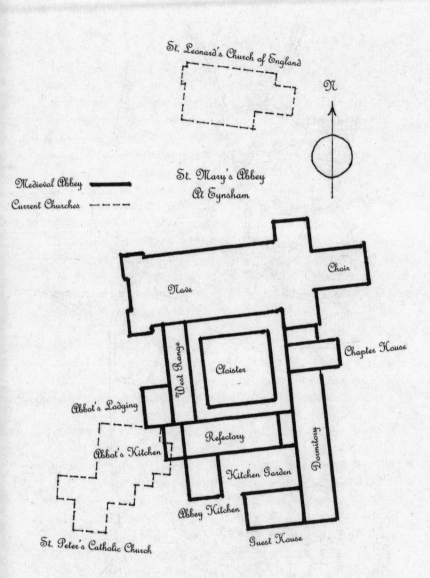

St. Leonard's Church of England

N

Medieval Abbey

Current Churches

St. Mary's Abbey
At Eynsham

Nave

Choir

West Range

Cloister

Chapter House

Abbot's Lodging

Refectory

Dormitory

Abbot's Kitchen

Kitchen Garden

Abbey Kitchen

St. Peter's Catholic Church

Guest House

Eynsham Abbey

Chapter 1

My life would have been more tranquil in the days after Martinmas had I not seen the birds. But I am an inquisitive sort of man, and the noisy host caught my attention. It is said that curiosity killed the cat. It can prove hazardous for meddlesome bailiffs as well.

I was on the road near Eynsham, on my way to Oxford. I did not travel muddy autumn roads for pleasure, although I thought some joy might follow, but to seek an addition to my library. In the autumn of 1368 I owned five books: *Surgery*, by Henri de Mondeville; *Categories*, by Aristotle; *Sentences*, by Peter Lombard; *De Actibus Animae*, by Master Wyclif; and a Gospel of St. John which I had copied myself from a rented manuscript while a student at Baliol College.

I sought a Bible, if I could find a fair copy for no more than thirty shillings. Such a volume at that price would not be lavishly illuminated, but I cared more for the words upon the page than some monk's artistry. If no such Bible was to be had, I would be content with a New Testament, or even a folio of St. Paul's letters.

When I told my Kate of my intentions she demanded that Arthur accompany me to Oxford. A man traveling alone with thirty shillings in his purse would invite brigands to interrupt his journey, did they know or guess what he carried. Or even if they did not. Arthur is a groom in the service of Lord Gilbert Talbot. A sturdy man, he would make two of me, and has proven useful in past dealings with miscreants. He does not turn away from a tussle, and who would if they generally dispatch any foe? A felon who sought my coins would reconsider if he saw Arthur start for him with a cudgel in hand.

I am Hugh de Singleton, surgeon and bailiff to Lord Gilbert Talbot on his manor at Bampton. I am the husband of Katherine, and father of Bessie, now nearly two years old, and, the Lord Christ merciful, will be father to a son, perhaps, shortly after

Twelfth Night. Kate is well, so I have hope she will be delivered of our second child safely. Her father, Robert Caxton, is a stationer in Oxford, and 'twas to his shop I intended to go first. That was before I saw the birds.

The road had passed through a wood, then entered fields cultivated by tenants of Eynsham Abbey. No men were at work this day, or not where they could be seen. But within barns and kitchens men and women were at bloody labor, for Arthur and I traveled on Monday, the thirteenth day of November, the time when men slaughter those animals they will be unable to feed through the winter, so that the beasts will rather feed them.

A pair of crows, chattering magpies, and a flock of rooks perched in the bare branches of a large oak, cawing and occasionally flapping from their places to circle down to the ground near the base of the tree. As some birds left the tree, others rose from the earth to alight in the naked branches. This oak was at the very edge of a fallow field where a flock of the abbey's sheep grazed, unconcerned about the raucous chorus above them. Sheep are not much concerned with anything, being dull creatures.

I reined my palfrey to a stop and gazed at the noisy birds some hundred and more paces distant. Arthur, who had been speaking of the return of plague and his own loss, fell silent and turned in his saddle to follow my gaze.

The man did not remain mute for long. "Birds," he said. "Somethin' dead, I'd guess."

I thought the same, and said so. "Whatever it is," I added, "must be large. A dead coney would not attract so many."

"Pig, maybe?" Arthur said. "Swineherds been settin' their hogs to pannaging to fatten 'em up."

"Could be, but would a pig-man not seek a lost hog before birds could find it?"

Arthur shrugged. I dismounted and led my beast to a convenient hawthorn which grew beside the road and proclaimed its presence with many red berries. I tied the palfrey there and set off across the fallow field toward the birds. Arthur followed.

An old ewe raised her head, watched my approach suspiciously, then snorted and trotted away. The flock briefly hesitated, then followed.

Whatever it was that the birds had found lay in the dappled shadow of the bare limbs of the oak, so I was nearly upon the thing before I recognized what the birds were feasting upon. And the corpse wore black, which aided the shadowy concealment.

I was but a few paces from the body when the last of the birds, perhaps more courageous than his companions, lifted his wings and flapped to safety in the branches above.

A man lay sprawled upon the fallen leaves, dressed in the black habit of a Benedictine. Whether he was old or young I could not tell, for the birds had peeled the flesh from his face nearly to the skull, after plucking out his eyes, which they love most of all. The monk's nose and lips and cheeks were gone, and he grinned up at us while the birds protested our arrival from the limbs above us.

"Holy mother of God," Arthur said, and crossed himself. "What has happened here?"

I spoke no answer, for I did not know. All that was sure was that a monk, likely of Eynsham Abbey, had died half a mile from his monastery and his corpse had gone undiscovered by all but birds.

The abbey must be informed of this, of course. I told Arthur to return to the road and his horse and hurry to the abbey. There he must tell the porter of our discovery and ask that the abbot or prior come to the place with all haste. I would remain with the dead monk, to keep the birds away, and to learn what I could of his demise.

The monk was not old. He wore no cowl, and I saw no grey hairs upon his scalp. He was not tonsured. Here was no monk, but a novice.

He lay upon his back, arms flung wide, palms up. The birds had been busy there as well. I stood and looked about the place. Few leaves remained upon the trees. Indeed, most had fallen some weeks past. If the corpse was dragged here from some other place the leaves might mark the path. But they lay undisturbed in all directions.

How long had the novice lain here? No fallen leaves covered the youth. But the squabbling birds might have brushed leaves aside. And how long would it take the scavengers to do the injury I saw before me? Not long, I guessed.

I examined the novice's habit but saw there no mark or perforation or bloodstain which might betray a wound. Perhaps such a laceration was under the body. I would wait to turn the lad until folk from the abbey arrived.

My eyes fell upon the novice's feet. They were bare, and the birds had not yet discovered his toes. Would he go about in November with unshod feet? Some monks might, seeking penance for a sinful thought or deed, but it seemed unlikely that a novice would do so. If the youth died of some illness or accident, I was not the first to find him. Some other man did, and took his shoes. If the novice was murdered, the man who slew him may have taken more than his life.

It was a loathsome business to turn the faceless head. I thought to see if the back of the novice's skull might reveal some injury, as from a blow. I found nothing, and as I stood over the corpse I reflected that, if a man was felled by a blow from behind, he would likely fall face first into the leaves.

I heard agitated voices and turned to see Arthur leading half a dozen Benedictines toward me. When near the road they approached at a trot, their habits flapping about their ankles, but as they crossed the field and glimpsed what lay at my feet they hesitated.

Arthur, too, held back, and only one monk came close and stood with me, looking down at the body. He gazed down upon the mutilated features and said softly, "'Tis John."

This monk crossed himself as he spoke, and his fellows did likewise. I saw them exchange glances as they did so. I am not clever at reading faces, but it seemed to me I saw neither shock nor sorrow, merely acceptance of the fact.

"Who are you?" the monk asked.

"I am Hugh de Singleton, bailiff to Lord Gilbert Talbot on his manor at Bampton."

"Ah, Abbot Thurstan has spoken of you, and the business of Michael of Longridge and the scholar's stolen books. When Abbot Thurstan heard this news he would have come, but he is aged and frail and I dissuaded him. We all knew who it must be that you have found here."

"Who is it?" I asked. "You named him 'John.'"

"'Tis John Whytyng, a novice of our house. I am Brother Gerleys, the novice-master at Eynsham Abbey. When your man told Stephen Porter of this death, and Abbot Thurstan was told, he sent me."

"Had the lad been missing?"

"Four days. Abbot Thurstan thought he had returned to Wantage."

"Wantage?"

"His father is a knight of that place."

"John was not enthusiastic for his vocation?" I asked.

"Nay. Oh, he was quick enough at his lessons, and seemed to enjoy study. Perhaps too much. But he found no joy in silence and prayer and contemplation, I think."

"Too much joy in his studies? What do you mean?"

"I mean that John was more interested in intellectual pursuits than the meditative life of a monk. The abbey has two other novices, Osbert and Henry. Neither is as clever as John... as John was."

"Only three novices at Eynsham?" I said.

"Aye. When I was a novice an abbot could pick and choose from lads whose fathers wished to find a place for them in a monastery. Younger sons who'd not inherit, and would have no lands... unless they wed a widow or the daughter of some knight who had no sons.

"But now the great pestilence has come a third time, there is much land available, and a habit has less appeal than when I was a youth. John was a handsome lad. Maidens, I think, found him appealing. Although," he added, "you'd not know it now."

"And he enjoyed the company of a lass?"

"Aye. So I believe. There is no opportunity within monastic

walls to observe whether or not this is so, but he was often incautious when he spoke of fair maids."

"Did you send word to his father at Wantage when he disappeared?"

The novice-master shook his head. "To what purpose? He was not happy with us, and he'd not be the first novice to reject a calling. We assumed he'd gone home, and that his father would send us word of where he was.

"What has caused this death?" Brother Gerleys asked. "Your man told me that you are trained as a surgeon."

"I cannot tell."

"The pestilence, you think? Two of our house have been struck down since Lammastide... although none since Michaelmas. We pray daily the sickness has passed. We are now but fourteen monks and thirty-two lay brothers. If plague takes any more we shall not have enough to continue, I fear."

"I awaited your arrival to turn the corpse, so you might see it as we found it. I see no sign of struggle or wound; nor is there any sign that the pestilence killed him."

"Very well, then."

I knelt beside the body to roll it so as to expose the back. No monk stepped forward to aid me, and when Arthur saw their hesitation he did so in their stead. A moment later the cause of John Whytyng's death was evident. So I thought.

In his back the novice had suffered several stab wounds. I counted three perforations in his habit. The novice-master saw these also.

"Stabbed," he said softly.

I looked down upon the fallen leaves which the corpse had covered, then knelt again to examine the decaying vegetation which had lain directly under the wounds. I stirred the leaves gently, but did not find what I sought.

"What is it?" Brother Gerleys asked.

"There is no blood here. No clots of blood upon his habit, nor upon the ground. If he died here his blood would have soaked the leaves, but there is none. There has been no rain these past

22

four days to wash blood away, and even had there been the lad's body would have shielded any bloodstains from the wet."

I touched the dead novice's habit and felt some moisture there. Indeed, the wool was nearly as wet as if he had a day or so earlier been drawn from a river. I lifted the edge of one of the cuts in the wool of his garment. The wound was also clean. Little blood stained either flesh or habit.

"What does this mean?" Brother Gerleys said.

"He died elsewhere, I think, then was moved to this place."

The monk looked about him, then spoke. "Why here, I wonder? He was not well hidden, and so close to the road and abbey it was sure he would be found."

"Aye," I agreed. "Which may mean that whoso slew him did not much care if the novice was found, so long as the corpse was not discovered in the place where the murder was done."

"How long has he lain here, you think?"

"I cannot tell," I shrugged. "But there is perhaps a way to discover this."

Brother Gerleys peered at me with a puzzled expression, so I explained my thoughts.

Abbey tenants and villeins would have butchered many pigs in the past days. I had in mind that the novice-master obtain a severed boar's head and set it upon the forest floor somewhere near this place. Then he could daily visit the skull and learn how long it would take birds to find and devour the flesh to the same extent as the injury they had done to the novice. Brother Gerleys nodded his head, agreeing to the plan.

Two of the monks who accompanied the novice-master had carried with them a pallet. Brother Gerleys motioned to them and they set the frame beside the corpse and rolled the body onto it. This left John's mutilated, eyeless face upraised again to the sky. One of the monks saw this and retched violently into the leaves. I sympathized. The novice's ruined countenance brought bile to my own throat.

I knelt beside the corpse again, and touched the black wool of the habit. It was dry, or nearly so. Why was the back of the garment so damp? Dew would wet the upper side of the habit, I thought.

I, Arthur, and Brother Gerleys led the way back to the road and the horses. The monks, of course, had come afoot to the place.

"Your man," Brother Gerleys said, "told me that you were bound for Oxford when you saw the birds and found John."

"Aye. This business has delayed us, but we will still be there by nightfall if we do not dally."

"Abbot Thurstan asked that you call upon him. He wishes to know what befell John."

"I cannot tell. But you might do as I suggest with a pig's head and that may tell you how long past the novice was left in the wood."

Abbot Thurstan was an ancient fellow. He was elected to his position when the pestilence struck down Abbot Nicholas nearly twenty years past. It was no longer necessary for the monk to be tonsured fortnightly. He had but a wispy fringe of hoary hairs circling his skull above his ears.

I left Arthur to water the horses and followed Brother Gerleys to the abbot's chamber while other monks took John Whytyng's corpse to rest before the church altar.

The abbot's chamber door was open when we approached, Abbot Thurstan dictating a letter to his clerk. The aged monk saw our shadows darken his door and looked toward us. As he did so I heard the sacrist ring the passing bell.

The abbot swayed to his feet as Brother Gerleys announced my presence. It took some effort for the abbot to do this, and I was cognizant of the honor. An abbot need not rise from his chair when a mere bailiff calls upon him.

Abbot Thurstan coughed, looked from me to the novice-master, then spoke. "It was John?" he said.

"Aye," Brother Gerleys replied.

The abbot crossed himself and sat heavily. "I thought as much. A clever lad, with much to recommend him, taken, but the Lord Christ leaves me here."

I thought to myself that the Lord Christ had little to do with the novice's death, but held my tongue.

"Was it the pestilence?" the abbot continued.

Brother Gerleys looked to me.

"Nay," I said. "The lad was struck down by a dagger in the back."

Abbot Thurstan was silent for a time, then replied, "I would not wish for any man to die of plague. I have seen the agony in which the afflicted die. But I had hoped that the death was not the work of some other man's hand. When plague first visited this house nearly twenty years past I saw Brother Oswalt try to rise from his bed and flee the infirmary, thinking he could escape his torment if he could leave the abbey. I thought perhaps John, crazed by pain, might have done likewise."

"Had the youth given sign that he was ill?" I asked.

"Nay," Brother Gerleys said.

"The pestilence can slay a man quickly," the abbot said, "but so will a blade."

"I wish you success in discovering the felon," I said.

The abbot looked from his clerk to the novice-master and then to me. "I remember," he said, "when you discovered 'twas a brother of this house who stole Master Wyclif's books. We have no man so skilled at sniffing out felons."

"Has Eynsham no bailiff or constable?"

"A bailiff. But Richard is nearly as old as me. He sees little and hears less. He is competent for the mundane duties of a bailiff, but seeking a murderer will be beyond his competence."

I saw the direction this conversation was taking and sought to deflect its path.

"I am bound for Oxford," I said, "and hope to arrive before nightfall. The days grow short, so I need to be on my way."

"I am sorry to delay your travel." The abbot coughed again. "You have business in Oxford?"

"I intend to make a purchase there, and then return promptly to Bampton. My wife will give birth to our second child soon after Twelfth Night and I do not wish for her to be alone any longer than need be."

"Ah… certainly. But," I saw in his eyes that the elderly

monk's mind was working, "could you not spare us a few days to sort out this calamity? Surely your purchase can wait, and there is a midwife of Eynsham who could be sent to Bampton to attend your wife 'till this matter is settled. I will pay the woman from abbey funds. What is it you wish to obtain in Oxford?"

"A Bible."

"Ah, Lord Gilbert must regard your service highly."

"He is liberal with wages to those whose service he values," I agreed.

"As am I. In our scriptorium there are many brothers who are accomplished with pen and ink. Brother Robert and Brother Bertran are particularly skilled. The abbey has no important commissions just now. If you will set yourself to discovering the murderer among us I will put the scriptorium to work upon a Bible." Abbot Thurstan coughed heavily again. "You will have it by St. John's Day, or soon thereafter."

The youngest son of a minor Lancashire knight, as I am, learns frugality at an early age. I have become modestly prosperous, but not so that I would willingly forgo the saving of thirty shillings. I stood silently before the abbot, as if considering his offer, but I knew already that I would accept.

"If I am unable to discover the murderer, what then?"

"The Lord Christ," the abbot said, "commands only that we strive to do His will. He does not demand that we always succeed. So I ask only for your best effort. If you give the abbey that it will suffice. You will receive your Bible.

"I will command all who live in the abbey, monks and lay brothers, that they are to assist you in whatever way you need." The abbot's frail shoulders were once again wracked with deep coughs.

"Very well. But I must return to Bampton to tell my Kate of this alteration in my plans. When will you send the woman to keep my wife company 'til this matter can be resolved? And will she accept your commission?"

"Agnes is a widow, and since the pestilence too few babes are born in Eynsham to provide her a livelihood. She is unlikely to refuse my offer. I will send her tomorrow."

So it was that Arthur and I returned to Bampton that day, and I spent the evening sitting upon a bench before the hearth with my Kate, considering who might wish to slay a novice and why they would do so.

Chapter 2

My employer, Lord Gilbert Talbot, had departed Bampton three days after Michaelmas, bound for Goodrich Castle. He traveled only with his children. Lady Petronilla had died in the late spring. The pestilence has claimed several others in Bampton and the Weald since then.

I pray each evening that the curse would spare my house and family. And as of November the Lord Christ has seen fit to honor my plea. Others have surely made the same request, but death visited their houses anyway. Is the Lord Christ more pleased with me than with others who have seen spouses and children die? This cannot be, for no man outside a monastery is more saintly than Hubert Shillside, but his wife died in great agony a fortnight before Lammastide.

It is Lord Gilbert's custom to spend each winter at Goodrich, leaving Bampton Castle in September, while roads are yet firm. Although he mourned Lady Petronilla's death, he saw no reason to change his practice. So I, his bailiff in Bampton, was left to see to the manor and castle in his absence. Most of his retainers – knights, squires, pages, valets, and grooms – departed with him, leaving but a few grooms and pages under my authority to maintain the fabric.

I had looked forward to a peaceful winter, with but three concerns: one common to all Englishmen – keeping warm; the others, that my Kate be safely delivered of a healthy babe, and that the pestilence leave Bampton with no more deaths. Perhaps a woodcutter might mistake his toes for a log, or some man slip and fall upon the ice come January, but generally winter is a peaceful time, when men do not seek a surgeon's services, and would, as in any season, prefer to avoid a bailiff's attention.

Arthur is one of Lord Gilbert's grooms, who remains at Bampton Castle when others forsake the place to serve Lord

Gilbert at his other properties. This is so because Arthur was wed, and had a family which he preferred not to uproot.

But Cicily died of the pestilence on midsummer's eve, and his children, all grown and also in Lord Gilbert's service, traveled with their lord to Goodrich. So Arthur did not much object to a journey to Oxford, or any other place, to break the monotony of life in a nearly empty castle.

I had told Arthur to return to Galen House with the horses on Wednesday, about noon. I thought by then Abbot Thurstan would have sent the midwife, and Arthur would have filled his belly with the simple repast provided when Lord Gilbert was absent from Bampton Castle hall.

My Kate is supple, but as her time nears she finds it irksome to bend to pots and pans upon the hearth. I am no cook, but to assist her I can stir a kettle when need be. So it was that I was tending the pottage when I heard a rapping upon our door. Kate rose heavily from her seat upon a bench, approached the door, and returned with a woman nearly as young as herself and two black-garbed men. Abbot Thurstan had kept the first part of his bargain.

The woman was named Agnes Shortnekke. I was troubled that she was not as old as Katherine Pecham, midwife to Bampton. Her unlined face seemed to me to warn of a lack of experience. But it immediately occurred to me that others no doubt considered my own youthful features as evidence of shallow surgical skills. I am as competent with scalpel and needle as any man, so I bit my tongue and made no remark about the midwife's youth. And Katherine Pecham was but two hundred paces distant if the babe decided to present himself early to the world. I had hope that I could discover a murderer well before St. Stephen's Day.

Kate had not planned on guests at our table, but hospitality required that they be invited to join our simple meal. There was little need to scrub the pot when the lay brothers finished their portion of the pottage.

Kate and Agnes discovered many interests in common, and chattered freely while I and the lay brothers waited for Arthur to appear with the horses. This he did when the pale sun stood directly over the end of Church View Street. Arthur is nothing if not reliable.

My Kate stood in the door of Galen House to bid me "God-speed," Mistress Shortnekke behind her peering over her shoulder. I saw Arthur look twice in the direction of Galen House's door. Likely he was as startled as I had been at the midwife's youthful appearance. Well, not youthful, exactly; but not aged, as are most of her profession.

In times past I would have climbed upon the broad back of Bruce, an old dexter Lord Gilbert had provided for my use. The beast had carried my employer into battle at Poitiers many years past, and I had grown fond of the creature, although his gait was lumpy and left my nether portion tender whenever I was required to ride any distance. But the old beast had died two days before Michaelmas. His eyes were rheumy with age, so I know not if the pestilence took him as well as men and women of town and castle. The palfrey I rode now was a more agreeable seat, but I missed my old companion nevertheless.

Arthur, I, and the lay brothers greeted the Eynsham Abbey porter as the monks of the house were leaving the church after nones. Abbot Thurstan shuffled along at their head, followed by Brother Gerleys and a tall monk who I soon learned was Brother Philip, the prior.

The abbot's eyes traveled to our horses as they were being led to the abbey stables, and he looked to the gatehouse and recognized me. He lifted a hand and motioned for me to follow. I nodded to Arthur and we fell in behind the tottering old abbot. The prior did likewise.

"We buried John Whytyng this morning," the abbot said as he led us to his chamber.

"Has his father been told?"

"I sent a lay brother to Wantage this morning. Sir Henry has been a reliable benefactor. He will be much displeased that we were unable to keep his son safe."

There was a thought left unspoken in Abbot Thurstan's words. Eynsham Abbey would not like to lose the favor of a prosperous knight who had been generous with his coin. If I could find who had slain the novice the discovery might go far to assuaging the father's anger, or at least turning his wrath to the felon and away from the abbey. Unless the murderer was a monk of the house. Certainly Abbot Thurstan wished for me to discover the felon, yet he was likely fearful of what I would learn and how the discovery would affect his abbey.

Abbot Thurstan coughed, collapsed into his chair, motioned for me to take another, and Prior Philip sat in a third. Arthur glanced about the chamber and seated himself upon a bench drawn up against a wall.

The abbot sighed deeply, then spoke. "I set much store by John Whytyng. Brother Gerleys spoke often of his brilliance. I thought perhaps some day, when I have gone to meet the Lord Christ, and Brother John had become a respected monk, his fellows of this house might select him for their abbot."

"Brother Gerleys," I said, "told me he was not happy as a novice here, and when he disappeared, thought he had gone to his father."

The abbot sighed again. "I wish Brother Gerleys had spoken to me of this. Of course, he may have done and I paid him no heed. I have the disease of the ears.

"My eyes are clouded, my ears hear little, my joints creak and groan, my fingers ache and will no longer grip a pen. But it is all well. If an old man could see and hear and leap as well as when he was a lad, no man would ever be content to die. The frailty of age brings a man to welcome the release of death from the gaol his body has become. I pray daily that the Lord Christ will soon free me from this prison."

"Perhaps He has work for you yet to do," the prior said. I noticed that he smiled while he spoke.

"I do not question His will," the abbot said, "although I admit it is often a mystery to me."

"To us all," I agreed. "Since I was last in this chamber, have you learned any new thing about the novice's death?"

"Nothing," Prior Philip said, "but this morning, after John

was buried, Brother Gerleys took a boar's head to the edge of the meadow near to where John was found. He said you advised him to do so."

"I did. Birds will soon discover it, and we may learn how long it will take them to do to a pig's head the same harm that was done to the novice."

"You believe that John did not lie in the forest from the time he left the abbey until you found him?"

"I do not know. We may soon learn."

"Was he struck down there?" the abbot asked.

"I think not. He was pierced three times, but I found no blood under him."

"Three times," Abbot Thurstan repeated softly. "Brother Gerleys told me of this. How will you begin your search?"

"I must seek Brother Gerleys and his novices. Perhaps they know of some enemy which John feared, or heard him speak of some danger."

"I'll see you to the novices' chamber," the prior said. "Brother Gerleys insisted that they be about their studies, even though their companion was buried this morn."

It was difficult to take my gaze from the prior's face during this conversation. He was, I thought, the ugliest man I had ever seen. His forehead and chin sloped back above and below a large nose which was afflicted with lumps and pustules. His upper teeth protruded over his lower lip, and his cheeks were red and crusted with cast-off skin. He was a man who, unless he was wealthy and possessed lands and a title, few women would find appealing. No wonder he sought life in a monastery.

We found the novices and their instructor at a silent lesson. The novice-master was teaching his charges the signs they would use to communicate when in the cloister and refectory, where silence reigned. Brother Gerleys faced the door to this chamber, so he saw me, Arthur, and the prior while his pupils had their backs to us. The lads saw his fluttering fingers hesitate and his eyes rise to us. They turned to see what had interrupted their exercise.

The classroom was warm, heated by a small blaze upon a hearth. Benedictines deal gently with novices, perhaps not wishing to deter them from taking their vows. The only other heated room in the abbey would be the calefactory, where monks warm themselves when winter comes.

The novices sprang to their feet when they saw the prior at their door. One lad was quite small, a frail youth with pale hair and skin, his features blotchy with that scourge of youth, pimples. I thought him likely no more than fifteen years old, although his reed-like form may have clouded my judgment. The other lad was much larger, nearly a full-grown man. A few scattered whiskers grew from his chin and upper lip. The novice-master would soon need to instruct this one in the fortnightly use of a razor.

"Master Hugh wishes to speak to you and the lads," Prior Philip said to Brother Gerleys. I did not expect the tone I heard in the prior's voice. He had seemed an amicable sort of man while with Abbot Thurstan, but there was no friendship in his words to Brother Gerleys.

The novice-master bowed silently, and the prior turned and walked from the chamber. Arthur had also noted the prior's hostility, and glanced toward me with an expression which said silently, "What think you of that?"

"Master Hugh," Brother Gerleys said when the prior's footsteps had faded, "here are Osbert Homersley and Henry Fuller, novices of this house."

The youths bowed to me by way of greeting and I motioned them to return to their bench.

Brother Gerleys had seemed to take no offense to the prior's curt greeting and announcement. "How may we serve you?" he said in a level voice.

"I wish to speak to you of John Whytyng. Abbot Thurstan has charged me with the task of discovering his murderer. When did you last see him?" I asked the two novices.

I expected Henry, being the older of the two, to speak, but 'twas Osbert who replied. He spoke in fractured tones, not yet a man, but no longer a child.

"Thursday," the lad said. "He was seated with us in the retrochoir for compline, and returned to our chamber with us. When we rose for lauds his bed was cold."

"What of vigils?" I asked.

"Novices of this house are not required to rise in the night for that office," Brother Gerleys said.

To Osbert I said, "I have heard that John was not well suited for the vows he was soon to take. Did he speak to you of this?"

"Aye. I was not surprised to find him away."

"Had he ever departed your chamber in the night before?"

Neither novice replied, until Brother Gerleys nodded, then Osbert spoke. "Twice, that I know of."

"That you know of? You believe he was often away in the night?"

"Once I heard him rise to visit the reredorter and I saw him return. 'Twas near dawn. Another time I lay awake but Henry slept. John thought we both did, and crept from his bed."

"When did he return?"

"Don't know. Finally I fell to sleep. He was in his bed when the sacrist rang the bell for lauds."

"Did you tell Brother Gerleys of this?"

"He did," the novice-master replied. "I questioned John sharply about these nocturnal prowls."

"What did he say?"

"Claimed that when he could not sleep he would walk the cloister and meditate."

"You believe this?"

Brother Gerleys was silent for some time. The two novices stared at him, open-mouthed, awaiting his answer.

"I wanted to. But now that he has been found slain outside the abbey precincts, I believe it must not be so. No man would stab him in the cloister, I think, then drag him half a mile to the place you found him. And if murder was done in the cloister, how did the felon get himself and a corpse from the abbey in the night?"

"Two men might," I said.

"Oh... aye, perhaps."

34

"What of the explorators?" I asked. "Have you spoken to them? Did they never see John out of his bed?"

"They have never said so. It is their duty to see to the locks and that all of the brothers are abed in the dormitory after compline. Then they seek their own rest. 'Tis not required of them then to prowl the abbey throughout the night."

"Come," I said. "We will seek permission from Abbot Thurstan for me and Arthur to enter the cloister. If he grants it, we will walk the cloister and seek any sign that murder may have been done there."

Abbot Thurstan's lodging, as with most Benedictine houses, is in the west range of the abbey. We found the abbot there in conversation with the prior and another monk I had not before seen. I was introduced. Brother Gerald was the guest-master, and would be responsible for my comfort in the guest parlor while Arthur and I remained at the abbey.

Abbot Thurstan readily granted permission for Arthur and me to visit the cloister any time I thought necessary. I invited Brother Gerleys and his novices to assist us.

"What do we seek?" the novice-master asked.

"John was stabbed three times. He surely bled freely. Look for bloodstains."

"Would not the villains have scrubbed away such defilement?"

"Probably. But they might have overlooked a drop. A similar thing happened six months past and led me to a felon."

The late-afternoon sun left much of the cloister in shadows. If there were bloodstains upon the flags they would have been difficult to see. Osbert and Henry entered into the search with the enthusiasm of youth, but after circling the enclosure twice the five of us accepted defeat. Either there was no murder done in the cloister, or all trace of the felony had been wiped away, or the approaching night obscured evidence of death.

"I am pleased we found nothing," Brother Gerleys said. "Had we done so, 'twould mean that a brother of this house was guilty. I would not want to think it could be so."

"I am told that you took a boar's head to the edge of the wood, near to where John was found," I said to Brother Gerleys as we returned to the novices' chamber.

"Aye."

"We will see it tomorrow, after terce," I said, "to learn if the birds have found it yet."

"'Tis an odd thing," the novice-master then said, "about John. Most did not see, for a man might swoon to look upon a face so ravaged as was John's, but when we covered the lad with a black linen shroud this morning, and took him to his grave, I saw water leaking from his mouth and nose... or what remained of the poor lad's mouth and nose."

His words caught my attention. "Water, you say? Not blood?"

"Nay. 'Twas but a trickle, but 'twas water."

When I turned the novice to discover the wounds in his back I had not noticed water, or any other fluid, draining from his nose or mouth. Of course, I was not seeking such a thing, and after I saw the lacerations in John's back and the slashes in his habit I had eyes only for these signs of death. There may have been water I did not then see, but if so, from whence had it come?

"This water you saw, did it appear while the novice was laid out upon his back, or when he was turned?"

"He was upon his back before the altar. And 'twas but a trickle. We have buried several brothers of this house recently, but I never before saw water issue from a dead man's mouth. You think it due to the manner of his death... being stabbed so many times?"

"Nay. I've seen men slain with dagger and sword, but none was ever found with water coming from his lips."

Brother Gerleys told Osbert and Henry to remain in his chamber until his return, then walked with us to the guest house. The way took us past one of the abbey fishponds, its calm waters reflecting the stars and the sliver of new moon in the fading light. The tranquil scene belied the wickedness which had visited the abbey.

The guest-master showed us to our chamber in the guest house and told us that a lay brother would soon arrive with a meal. The monk spoke true, for the words were but out of his mouth when two men appeared at the door with a bowl of water for washing hands, a roasted capon, maslin loaves, and ale.

Arthur and I ate by the light of a single cresset. Arthur was silent but for the smacking of lips and licking of fingers as he consumed his portion of the fowl and loaves. Nor did I speak. Brother Gerleys' tale of water leaking from John Whytyng's torn lips as he lay upon his bier would not leave my mind. As it happened, the announcement also puzzled Arthur. He drank the last of his ale, pushed his bench back from the table, and unburdened his mind.

"Seen men dead before, but never seen one what leaked."

"And his wounds did not," I replied.

Arthur peered at me quizzically.

"Yesterday," I said, "when we found the lad, do you remember? There was no blood upon his habit, nor upon the soil and leaves beneath him, nor even upon his flesh."

"How could that be?" Arthur asked. "Even was he slain somewhere else and left where the birds found 'im, there would be blood upon 'is habit."

"Unless he was already dead when his assailant plunged a dagger into him. Dead men do not bleed."

"Oh," Arthur said thoughtfully. "Then why stab a dead man three times?"

"Perhaps he was yet alive when the felon pierced him."

"But you said... would he not then bleed?"

"Aye," I said. "Much."

"You speak in riddles," Arthur complained.

"Nay. I show you a riddle. And I have no solution for it."

The guest-master had seen that a blaze was laid upon the guest house hearth to warm us, but this fire now burned low. I placed another log upon the embers and sought my bed.

Whenever I share a sleeping chamber with Arthur the fellow always falls to sleep before me. He snores like an ungreased mill wheel and this makes slumber difficult for any near. So I lay abed, tried to ignore Arthur's rattling and wheezing, and thought of a bloodless corpse from which water drained rather than gore. I finally fell to sleep with the issue unresolved.

Some time in the night I awoke. The fire had burned down to just a few glowing embers. The blanket provided was too thin to ward off the November chill. And Arthur was snoring as loudly as a novice musician tootling upon a sackbut. A possible answer to the riddle of John Whytyng's death came to me there in the darkened chamber, and I lay for the remainder of the night impatient for the dawn to try my speculation and see if I might find evidence that it was so.

Chapter 3

I am accustomed to waking in our chamber at Galen House to Father Thomas de Bowlegh's clerk ringing the Angelus Bell in the tower of the Church of St. Beornwald. So when the sacrist rang Eynsham Abbey's great bell for lauds I was not much startled. Indeed, I welcomed the deep, thunderous peal, for it meant that the notion which had come to me in the night could soon be investigated in the light of day.

Monks do not break their fast, but 'tis common for abbey guests to be offered a loaf. A short time after the monks were called from their beds an elderly lay brother appeared with two loaves and a ewer of ale. Arthur and I consumed the meal – the ale was quite foul – and waited for the misty dawn to become day. While we ate I told him of my supposition, and he nodded understanding while munching upon his loaf.

A day of sunshine in November is a rare thing, and as the sun appeared it seemed that Eynsham would enjoy its fifth in succession. Perhaps the Lord Christ smiled upon my endeavor and wished to provide the illumination necessary for success.

"You think the lad maybe drowned in a fishpond, an' got stabbed after somebody fished 'im out, eh?" Arthur reviewed what I had explained to him between his last bites of maslin loaf.

"This might explain the lack of blood upon his slashed habit. If he drowned, he would not have bled much, as dead men do not do so. If he was first stabbed, then fell into the fishpond, blood from his wounds would have been washed away, and he might yet have been alive when he went into the water, so that his lungs filled as he died."

"But why'd the water come from 'is mouth?"

"Dead men soon begin to bloat, as decay sets upon them. This happens soonest when 'tis warm, but even in cool November putrefaction will soon begin. A corpse begins to swell from the rot within."

"But how'd that cause the lad to leak so?"

"The bloating put pressure upon his lungs, and forced water there out through his throat."

"Ah... so what do you think," Arthur said thoughtfully, "drowned first, then stabbed, or other way 'round?"

"Stabbed first, I think, and he would surely have died of his wounds had he not fallen or been cast into a fishpond."

"Mayhap he went into the water to escape the man who attacked 'im," Arthur said.

"That also," I agreed.

There are two fishponds at Eynsham Abbey, one to the west, the other to the east of abbey precincts. Monks, or more likely lay brothers and abbey villeins, had created these a century past by diverting the flow of a small brook. The ponds are not large, but the abbey is a small house so there are few monks to feed.

Since it was closest to the guest house, we circled the west pond first. I sought some sign of struggle; broken reeds, perhaps, or footprints in the mud where earth and water meet, where no man would be likely to tread. I found nothing.

The east pond is past the monks' dormitory and near to where the brook now flows. Beyond the brook is a wood, which extends to the south and west as far as the place where birds discovered John Whytyng's corpse.

It was on the far side of the east pond, where bare oak and beech limbs cast interlacing shadows to the edge of the pond, that I saw the broken reeds. As I saw them I heard Arthur say, "When did it last rain?"

"What?"

"Rain," he said. "Was it Wednesday last week?"

"Why do you ask?"

"Look there... footprints in the mud. Too dry an' crusty for a man to leave footprints now."

The broken reeds had so caught my attention that I had overlooked the footprints in the mud which Arthur saw. And they were not deep. My gaze followed Arthur's extended arm and I saw that the footprints led to the place on the bank of the pond where I had noticed the broken reeds. I put an arm out to stop Arthur, who was intent upon standing over the footprints for a better view.

"Stay back," I said. "We must not trample upon this place. There may be something to learn from these marks."

Arthur drew back as if a viper had appeared among the reeds. We stood where grass covered the bank. The footprints he had found extended only through a narrow, muddy section of the bank between the grass and the reeds.

I approached the footprints cautiously. It seemed to me at first glance that two people had left the marks. One set was large, nearly as large as my own shoes would leave behind should I step in such a place. The other footprints were small, made by a youth, I thought, or perhaps a woman.

John Whytyng was buried, so there was no way to learn how large the lad's feet might have been. But he was nearly a full-grown man. Surely too large to have left behind the smaller of the footprints. Perhaps these marks were made by a father and son poaching fish from the abbey ponds, and had nothing to do with the death of a novice. I spoke so to Arthur, who nodded a silent assent.

Where the reeds were broken I saw the larger set of footprints slide down the bank toward the water, as if the maker had lost his footing and slipped into the pond. I was near to concluding that my supposition of poachers was the likely explanation for the footprints and broken reeds when I noticed that the larger set of footprints seemed of slightly different sizes, as if before me were the marks of three trespassers on abbey property, not two.

I knelt beside the reed bed and broke off a dried shoot. From this I snapped another length of reed until I had a segment the length of the largest muddy print. I then placed the reed over the other footprints. Just as I had supposed, the larger prints were not of the same size! What I had thought were the footprints of one man and a youth were in fact the marks of two men and a lad. It was the maker of the smaller of the large footprints who had lost his footing and carved a sliding path through the mud of the bank and into the pond.

Three poachers? A father, older son, and child, all seeking fish from the abbey's pond? This seemed likely, and I was about to turn from the place and resume circumnavigation of the pond when I saw the boot.

I did not know the object to be a boot when I first saw it. Light from a watery sun cast a beam through the branches of the trees which bordered the brook and pond, and in the shaft of sunlight I saw something illuminated just below the surface of the water about two paces from the bank. Arthur had watched silently as I measured footprints with the broken reed, and now followed my puzzled gaze. He also saw the submerged object.

"What d'you suppose that is?" he said.

By the time he asked the question I had decided that the object was a shoe. Perhaps the poacher's lad had lost it, sucked from his feet by the mire, when he slipped into the pond.

"'Tis a shoe, I think. Let's find a downed limb in that wood and see if we can drag it to shore."

Eynsham Abbey's tenants had thoroughly gleaned the wood of downed branches for their winter fuel. Nothing thicker than my little finger nor longer than my forearm was to be found. I was not fond of the idea of wading into the cold water to retrieve the shoe. I might have required Arthur to do it, and he would have, without protest, but rather than demand this of him I sent him to the abbey stables for a rake.

"And tell the lay brother who keeps the stable to tie a horseshoe to the rake to weight it, so it will sink and we may use it to fetch the shoe from its place."

I had heard the sacrist ring the smaller bell to call the monks to prime while Arthur and I began to search the east pond. Now, as he returned with the rake, the bell rang for terce.

I took the rake from Arthur and thrust it into the pond. A moment later I drew a boot to the bank – for boot it was, and no shoe. Another thing not common to a fishpond was also entangled with the tines: a small pouch.

The sack was made of black woolen cloth, much like the fabric from which Benedictines stitch their habits. It was closed with a length of hempen cord so thin it might better be called string. This twine was tied tight to close the pouch, and inside the sodden bag I felt some oddly shaped object.

Because the cord was soaked it had swollen and was difficult to loosen. When the knot eventually came free and I was able to open the sack, I drew from it a crude key. Arthur, who had picked up the boot, peered at the key and spoke. He voiced my own question.

"What lock does that key work, you think? An' why is it found here? An' look at this boot. No poacher ever wore such a boot."

I transferred my attention to the boot, and Arthur held it before me as to emphasize his appraisal. He spoke true. The boot was of finest-quality leather, well sewn, and it had not been long in the pond, for it showed no sign of decay. On one side of the boot was a small rip in the leather, which had been carefully stitched closed.

Water had issued from John Whytyng's lips when he lay upon his bier. I had found him shoeless at the fringe of the abbey's wood. Here in the abbey fishpond was a boot, and sign that some man had slipped into the water. Had he drowned here, and been drawn from the pond by those whose footprints were also visible upon the muddy bank?

John Whytyng had been stabbed. Was it here that the attack took place? Did the novice plunge into the pond to escape? Was he so near death from the wounds that he could not save himself, and filled his lungs with water as he tried to breathe?

If this was so, who stood upon this bank and watched Whytyng die? Did the same man, or men, or man and boy, pull him from the pond and set him down where the birds and I found him? Why do so? Surely his corpse would have been quickly found if he remained in the pond, but sooner or later he would be found where he was left, at the fringe of the wood. Why leave him there? Why not hide the corpse where it would not be found, if it was to be moved from the fishpond?

Here were many questions and no answers. I was not even sure that John Whytyng had met his death here among the broken reeds at the edge of the pond.

While these thoughts occupied my mind Arthur studied the boot, then bent to the dried mud to compare it to the prints there. 'Twas a match to the footprints of him who had slipped from bank to pond.

I told Arthur of my thoughts, and the questions this discovery had raised in my mind.

"If the folks what did away with the lad murdered 'im here, an' 'e tried to escape, where did they draw 'im from the water?"

Arthur's point was well taken. 'Twas plain to see the long, sliding path of a foot as it entered the pond, but no place was there any sign that some man had been dragged dead from the water.

"Let's seek some other place where such a thing might have happened," I said.

We walked north no more than five paces when we saw more broken reeds. "Here is the place," I said. "See how the rushes are laying broken toward the bank, rather than toward the water. Something was drawn from the pond here, not toward it."

Grass here covered the bank, so that no footprints were to be seen. But I had no doubt that the large and small footprints left in the mud five paces away would also be found here but for the sod.

One shoe, or boot, looks much like another, unless it is made for some gentleman of great wealth. Nevertheless, I thought it possible that John Whytyng's companions might recognize the sodden boot we had found in the pond because of the tear. If indeed it had belonged to Whytyng. I took the boot from Arthur and he followed as I led the way to the novices' chamber, where I thought they had likely returned after terce.

Brother Gerleys led his charges into the chamber as we approached. The three looked up as Arthur and I followed them through the door, and as one their eyes went to the boot I held out before me. I saw Henry Fuller's mouth drop open and his eyes widen when he saw what was in my hand.

The lad drew in his breath sharply, so that Brother Gerleys and Osbert turned from me to Henry.

"This," I said, "was found in the east fishpond. Do you recognize it?"

Henry's mouth opened and closed like a fish drawn from the pond and tossed upon the bank. He finally found words.

"'Tis John's," he gulped. Osbert nodded agreement.

"How can you be sure?" I asked.

The novice pointed to the boot. "See there, where a tear has been repaired. I watched John stitch the rip not a fortnight past. We'd been set to work cutting rushes to replace those covering the floor of the refectory. John swung his scythe and the point went through his boot. Angry about it, he was. His father'd bought them for him before he came to us, just after St. John's Day."

"Abbot Thurstan allowed him to keep them," Brother Gerleys said.

Osbert pointed to his feet. "Henry and I wear shoes... nothing so fine as John's boots."

Brother Gerleys also looked to his own feet, and I saw below his habit and trousers a pair of well-worn shoes which would do little to warm his feet in the months to come. John Whytyng's father must be a man of influence for his son to be permitted to keep such fine boots.

"John was stabbed," Brother Gerleys said. "How came his boot to be in the fishpond, and where is the other?"

"You told me yesterday that water issued from John Whytyng's mouth," I said. Brother Gerleys nodded. "'Tis my belief that he was pierced while standing upon the bank of the pond. There are footprints in the mud which reveal that three souls, one small and perhaps but a child, were there at one time some days past, before the mud dried.

"One of these plunged a dagger into the novice's back three times. I believe he fell into the water, or leaped there to escape his assailant, and in the water he died."

45

"His other boot, then, is somewhere in the pond?" Brother Gerleys asked.

"No doubt."

I handed the boot to the novice-master, then withdrew the crude bag and key from my own pouch.

"This also came from the pond when I used a rake to draw the boot to shore. Was it John's?"

Brother Gerleys and the novices studied the pouch and key and shook their heads.

"What novice would need a key?" Brother Gerleys said. "Monks own nothing and so have no need of keys to lock away possessions; nor novices, either."

"What locks are found in the abbey?" I asked.

The novice-master absent-mindedly scratched his chin, where several days' stubble was flowering into what would become a beard if a razor was not soon applied.

"Explorators have keys to the church and cloister, of course. Brother Gerald has a key to the guest house. And Abbot Thurstan and Prior Philip have keys."

"Are there no other locks?" I asked. "What of the gatehouse?"

"Oh, aye. Nearly forgot. Stephen Porter will have a key, although I think the gatehouse is seldom locked. Has not been so since I've been here. The explorators lock the church each night, so no man can enter and make off with the silver candlesticks and other altar pieces. Only the door to the night stairs has no lock, so brothers may enter for vigils."

"You were about to begin lessons," I said. "We will detain you no longer."

I nodded to Arthur to follow and we left the novices and walked through the empty refectory, thence past the kitchen garden to our lodging in the guest house.

"What now?" Arthur asked.

"I would like to find the lock this key will open."

We went first to the gatehouse, where Stephen, a lay brother, greeted us pleasantly. I showed him the crude key, and he pursed his lips, then turned to a small chest upon a shelf in

46

his chamber and drew from it an ancient key. One glance showed that this key in no way resembled the key we had fished from the pond. Nevertheless I asked to try the mysterious key in the gatehouse lock. It did not turn.

"Odd sort of key," the porter observed as I twisted the key unsuccessfully in the lock. This was so. Rather than iron, the key was made of pewter. It was therefore soft, so that it bent somewhat when I tried to turn it in the gatehouse lock. Whatever lock this key was made to undo must open readily, for the key was too pliable to work an old, rusted lock.

No novice should possess a key, but this key was not made by some skillful smith. What it was made for I could not tell, nor could I be sure that the pouch it was found in belonged to John Whytyng.

We went next to the west entrance to the church, entered the nave, and found a lock hanging from a hasp used to fasten closed the doors in the night. I pushed the lock closed, then tried the key and was again unsuccessful, although as I twisted the key it seemed to me that this well-kept lock nearly yielded to the pressure. The explorators would wonder how the lock came to be closed when they made their rounds this night.

I led Arthur through the dim nave, past the choir, to the north porch. There another lock hung upon another hasp, ready to be fastened when night came. I pushed the lock closed, inserted the key, and turned it. The well-oiled lock opened readily.

"I think," Arthur said, "that when John Whytyng rose in the night 'twas not to meditate in the cloister."

"If this was indeed his key," I said.

"Whose else? But how did he lose it in the pond?"

"I've thought on that," I replied. "I believe one of the strokes of the dagger must have cut the cord which bound the pouch to him. Perhaps he concealed the pouch under his habit, so that the other novices could not see it. When he went into the pond the key and pouch fell free."

"Oh," Arthur said thoughtfully. "But where would a novice get such a thing?"

47

"Made it. See how crude it is."

"Of what, an' how?"

"'Tis near time for dinner. We will seek answers to those questions later."

Our dinner came from the abbot's kitchen, and since 'twas not a fast day we enjoyed roasted pork, with wheaten loaves and a pottage of dried cherries from the abbey orchard.

The abbey kitchen, or the abbot's kitchen, would be the most likely place for a novice to find some pewter object which might be fashioned into a key. Basins and kettles made of such stuff are common. I thought that perhaps some pot might have gone missing recently.

The abbot's cook insisted that all of his vessels were accounted for, but the abbey kitchener had, since Michaelmas, been missing a large pewter spoon. If the utensil was large enough a key the size of the one in my pouch might have been hammered and chiseled from it. I asked, and the kitchener placed both of his hands together to indicate the size of the missing ladle. Large enough for the key within my pouch.

But how could a novice make a key which would fit the lock to the church's north porch? Keys are similar, 'tis true, but the failure of the pewter key to open either the gatehouse lock or the lock to the west doors of the nave was evidence that even small differences may make a great mismatch. Perhaps John made several keys from the stolen spoon, 'till he happened upon one which succeeded.

Or perhaps the key and its pouch had nothing to do with John Whytyng and his death. If so, finding the key alongside the novice's boot was a great coincidence. Bailiffs do not believe in coincidences.

"I been thinkin' about them footprints," Arthur said. "There was three novices, now but two, an' three sets of footprints where we found the boot. Henry is a strapping lad, but Osbert is puny. Mayhap all three was on the bank of the fishpond together, Henry's bein' the big footprints an' Osbert's the little."

48

"I think not," I replied. Arthur's expression was somewhere between crestfallen and doubtful. "I wondered that very thing. Have you seen a pup grow to become a hound?" I did not wait for Arthur's reply. "Their paws are often full-grown while the dog is but half-grown. So it is with Osbert. Next time you see him, examine his shoes. They are as large as Henry's though he weighs hardly half as much."

"So who made them other footprints? Village folk poachin' the abbey fish, likely?"

"It may be so. But as I think on it, I have doubts. Would a man slay another for a few fish? If John unwittingly approached poachers he would not have thought to be silent, not expecting to meet any such folk there in the night – although he may have intended to meet someone there, whereas the poachers would surely have been alert to discovery. They'd have seen or heard the novice approach, and retreated to the wood to avoid being found out."

"If the novice did plan to meet someone there by the fishpond," Arthur said, "mayhap when 'e got there the folk what was there wasn't who 'e expected."

Here was a new thought, and one worthy of investigation, although how I would go about it was unclear. John Whytyng had a key which would open the door to the north porch of the abbey church. This entrance to the church was beyond the abbey wall, and so allowed access to the village. Whether he had made the key or acquired it from another I could not know, and it probably did not matter. That the key was John's I was certain, because of where it was found. Had the novice used it before, to slip away from the abbey in the night? It must be so, for some man, or men, expected him to be at the fishpond. Unless John had actually surprised poachers in the act of casting a net.

Chapter 4

Near to the east pond was a substantial house of three bays, its daub whitewashed, its roof well thatched, its barns well kept, its toft filled with hens.

I sought Brother Gerleys and asked whose house adjoined the abbey to the east.

"Simon... Simon atte Pond he is called. Eynsham Abbey's reeve."

"It seems the house of a prosperous man. And nearby, across the road, is another grand house. Who lives there?"

"The reeve has five yardlands of the abbey, and village folk in hallmote have chosen him reeve for many years. Across the way is the house of Sir Richard Cyne, lord of his manor at Eynsham."

If a man is chosen reeve by his neighbors for many years, it is generally because he allows no man to shirk the labor which is his obligation, but is fair when responsibilities for fields and forests and ditches and fences are assigned. No one wishes to be appointed more labor than he believes is his due; nor does he want his neighbor to escape his share of manor obligations. A reeve, like a bailiff, finds it easy to anger many folk and difficult to please most.

The reeve's dwelling lay but a hundred paces to the east of the abbey church. Hens retreated deeper into the toft as Arthur and I approached the house. When I rapped upon the substantial oaken door it opened almost immediately and a youth of perhaps twelve years peered through the opening. My first thought upon seeing the lad was that here is a boy about the proper age to make the smallest set of footprints I had seen a few hours earlier, less than a hundred paces from where I now stood.

I glanced to his feet and saw that, like those of the novice Osbert, they had outgrown his slender form and were nearly as large as my own or Arthur's. Whatever youth had stood upon the verge of the fishpond four or five days past, here was not the lad who did so.

"I seek Simon atte Pond," I said. "Is he at home?"

"Nay, sir. Master is dealing with them what's ditching out Swinford Road."

I knew Swinford Road well, having traveled it to Oxford many times, and once, also in company with Arthur, fleeing an attack as we galloped our beasts to Eynsham and the abbey, seeking sanctuary from men who sought to do us harm.

"Master," the lad had called the reeve. This is not uncommon. Since the great pestilence many who have escaped death now have tenancy of many yardlands and wealth enough to employ servants. Indeed, some knights and squires resent the prosperity of such men, who may not add "Sir" to their names even though they carry a heavy purse.

We found the reeve and six of the abbey's tenants at work but three hundred paces east of the village. At first I could not identify the reeve, for all seven men plied spades where I could see that water had gathered in the past, and was beginning to create a swamp which impinged upon the adjacent field. These laborers had yet several hundred paces of ditch to clear before the water which might accumulate in the place could flow freely to a small brook.

One of the diggers looked up from his work, saw us approach, spoke a word, and as one the others rested upon their spades to watch us draw near. The fellows had likely been at this labor since shortly after dawn, and so were pleased for any diversion which would grant a moment of ease.

Arthur and I had approached within a few paces of the ditchers when one man lifted his spade to a shoulder and spoke.

"I give you good day. How may I serve you?"

"I seek Simon atte Pond, reeve of Eynsham."

"You found 'im."

The autumn day was cool, but the reeve and those who worked with him had discarded their cotehardies and worked dressed only in kirtles and loose chauces. Yet even so lightly clad, the reeve passed the sleeve of his kirtle across his forehead to wipe away sweat as he spoke. I was prepared to like the fellow. Any reeve who will labor with the men he oversees is likely to be worthy of trust.

"Perhaps you will not mind ceasing your labor for a moment," I said. "Abbot Thurstan has employed me to seek a murderer. I am Hugh de Singleton, bailiff to Lord Gilbert Talbot at Bampton."

The reeve bowed and tugged a forelock, a thing he likely was taught when young, although now his rank was near to my own and his worth perhaps as great.

"Heard about the lad," he said. News of death, especially one so attended with mystery and wickedness as that of John Whytyng, spreads through a small village as rapidly as the pestilence.

"What have you heard?"

"'E was found yesterday, most of 'is face peeled away by birds. Stabbed in the back, some do say."

"What do others say?"

"Just stabbed."

"Did you know the novice?"

"Nay. I have little to do with the monks."

"Did others of the village know the lad? Did any speak of him?"

The reeve was strangely silent for a moment. "Some knew of 'im, I think. Monks keep to themselves. Lay brothers are about the village often enough, but not so much the monks or novices."

"Then how did some of the village know of John Whytyng, if monks and novices keep to themselves?"

"Don't know that many folk did know of 'im. I said I thought some in the village knew of 'im. That's all."

"Your home is adjacent to the abbey fishpond."

"Aye. That's how folk do call me."

"You are closer to the pond than any monk. Do you ever see folk, or hear them in the night, taking fish from the abbey ponds?"

"What's that to do with the novice bein' slain?"

"Perhaps nothing."

"That would be the bailiff's worry, or the abbot's; not mine."

"I am told that Eynsham's bailiff is a venerable man and may, perhaps, be less alert than a younger man for miscreants in the village."

"That's as may be, but poachin' the abbey's fish is the bailiff's concern, or the abbot's; not mine."

"You have not answered my question," I said. "Do you awaken in the night and hear men prowling about the pond in the dark?"

"Folks who'd be takin' the abbey's fish would be silent while about it."

"But a net thrown into the water would make a splash."

The reeve was silent for a moment, long enough for me to wonder if my first assessment of his character was in error. Perhaps he knew of villagers who dined upon the abbey's fish, and had done so himself, and so intended to keep silence about the offense.

"Folk be slayin' pigs now. Most have no need to risk takin' abbey fish," the reeve finally said.

"But when winter is past," I said, "perhaps by Whitsuntide, when pork is gone, then you hear men at the pond?"

"Aye," he admitted. "But not now."

"When was the last time you heard men in the night and thought it likely they broke curfew to take abbey fish?"

The reeve scratched at his beard as he considered the question. "Not since Lammastide... a fortnight after."

"But you neither heard nor saw any man near the pond at night last week?"

"Last week? Nay."

The laborers had rested upon their spades during this conversation, listening intently, for any such talk of village gossip will excite attention. And perhaps among the ditchers was a man who had helped himself to an abbey pike at some time in the past.

Arthur and I left the reeve and his workers to their labor and retraced our steps along Swinford Road to the village. When we were out of earshot of the reeve Arthur spoke.

"Never heard of a reeve what didn't know everyone else's business. An' what's a reeve doin' with them as is ditchin'? That's a hayward's work, seems to me."

"Perhaps," I said, thinking out loud, "the pestilence carried off the hayward, and the reeve has taken upon himself some of the bailiff's duty, the bailiff being old and incompetent. Men will not say to a bailiff the same words they would to a reeve... even a bailiff who is but a reeve."

"Hmmm. Mayhap."

We were passing a field where wheat stubble, left standing after harvest, was being cut to mix with hay for winter fodder. Arthur's attention was drawn to the women who were busy with scythes at this task, one of whom was a comely lass. She stood from her work to watch us pass, but at a sharp word from an older woman – her mother, perhaps – turned away and bent to her labor. Most matrons would prefer that their daughters not catch the eye of passing strangers.

The lass, or some other in the wheatfield, had caught another eye as well. A few paces beyond the west edge of the field, and on the opposite side of the road, was a large house, well thatched, surrounded by many barns and outbuildings; the residence of Eynsham's lord, Sir Richard Cyne. A man stood at an upper window, which was open to the chill November breeze. Why it would be so was plain. The fellow stared over our heads toward the women cutting wheat stubble.

Arthur saw me turn to look to my right and followed my gaze. As he did so the man at the window noticed us passing and withdrew. A moment later an arm appeared and drew the window closed. Arthur chuckled.

"Wanted a better look at yon lass than he'd 'ave through the ripples of window glass, eh?"

I agreed that this might be so.

The sun lay low in the southwest, and it would soon be

night. I had learned what I could this day, although this was little enough. A mighty castle may, however, be brought down by the incessant pounding of a trebuchet.

We passed the west entrance to the abbey church, entered the door to the west range of the cloister, and found the door to the abbot's lodging open. Nones had ended but a short while past. I saw the abbot, head in hands, seated at his desk and bent over an open book. I thought at first that he was deep in study and contemplation, but when I politely coughed to announce our presence at his door, the old monk started as if pricked.

Abbot Thurstan looked up from his book, blinked away the effects of his slumber, and recognized who it was who darkened his door.

"Ah, Master Hugh. What news?" He pointed to a chair and bench. "Be seated... be seated, and tell me what you have learned this day."

I did. I had learned little enough, so the recitation did not take long. The day's events had raised as many questions as answers. I tried some of the questions on the abbot.

"Who are the abbey explorators?"

"Prior Philip and Brother Eustace see to locking the abbey doors at night," he replied.

"How old is Sir Richard Cyne?"

"Sir Richard?" The old abbot stammered at this abrupt change of subject, then continued. "Not so old as me... few men are. Has two grown sons. Wife died when plague came twenty years past. Lost a daughter then, also."

I glanced toward Arthur and he smiled knowingly in return. 'Twas a stout young man we had seen standing at the upper window of Sir Richard's house. One of the sons, surely, but knowledge of this would do us no good in discovering the felon who murdered John Whytyng.

Monks have no supper when days grow short, but visitors in the guest house are fed from the abbot's kitchen. So when Arthur and I entered our lodging the lay brother assigned to attend us told us that he would soon return with our meal.

'Twas but a simple pease pottage, but flavored with a few bits of pork, and with a maslin loaf the supper was most satisfactory. I could not say the same for the abbey's ale. The monk in charge of brewing the abbey's ale was ill chosen. Perhaps this is by Abbot Thurstan's design. A man seldom finds himself in trouble for drinking too little ale, and no monk of Eynsham Abbey was likely to imbibe too much of the foul stuff Arthur and I found in the ewer.

Night comes quickly in the days past Martinmas. The feeble light of a cresset gave illumination to our guest chamber. Was I at home in Bampton, I would light another cresset and read from one of my books, perhaps the gospel of St. John. Next year I might read from my own Bible. But I was not in Galen House, I had no book, the night was chill, and so I was about to surrender to the darkness and seek my bed when it occurred to me that on such a night, when darkness came early to Eynsham, was John Whytyng slain. If poachers were to blame, might they not seek the abbey fishpond again? No man knew of what Arthur and I had found beside the fishpond but for Brother Gerleys, Abbot Thurstan, and the novices.

I told Arthur of my plan. "That reeve," he replied, "said folk was most likely to take fish from abbey ponds come Whitsuntide, but days is long then. A man would need to wait 'till near the middle of the night, else he'd be seen. Not so after Martinmas."

The abbey church bell had just rung for compline when Arthur and I left the guest house. We walked silently, hesitantly, past the southern end of the dormitory. I did not much fear discovery. The monks would all be in their choir stalls. Our progress was slow because we had only the light of stars to guide us, the moon not yet being risen. If some men were seeking the abbey's fish I wanted to be upon them before they could hear us approach.

I found the pond, saw the stars reflected in its mirror-like surface, and together Arthur and I followed the bank until we were near the place where we had found the novice's boot.

I whispered to Arthur that we should seat ourselves against

the base of a beech tree which grew nearby at the verge of the wood. It seemed to me that if poachers wished to take abbey fish at this season they would do so soon after compline, while the monks slept, and before they awoke for vigils. What man would willingly forsake a warm bed in this season if he could complete his mischief and return to his home before the coldest part of the night?

I was required twice to put an elbow into Arthur's ribs before the new moon rose over the wood behind us. The man's snoring would frighten off a host of poachers. If Abbot Thurstan would build a hut at the edge of the pond, and hire Arthur to sleep there, he would never lose another fish.

We remained in shadow, but the pond was now faintly illuminated. If I were a poacher I would have come and gone by this time. Arthur agreed. "A man would have to be witless to cast a net into the pond now," he whispered. I agreed, told him we would return to the guest house, and stood from my seat at the base of the old beech tree. This was not so easily accomplished as when I was a youth. Muscles had grown stiff with cold and inactivity. Arthur also stood slowly, then stretched. I heard a joint pop somewhere in his back. If his snoring did not chase poachers away, his stretching might.

We returned to the guest house more rapidly than we had left it. The cresset in our chamber had gone out, but there was enough moonlight through a south window that I found my bed without stubbing a toe.

Since monks do not break their fast, neither Abbot Thurstan nor his kitchener remembered to provide us with a loaf when the new day dawned. Very well. Some ancient Greek whose words I remember from my studies at Baliol College wrote that a man thinks most clearly when his stomach is empty. When he is well fed he becomes somnolent and neither his body nor his wit performs well. If this is so, I knew many scholars while at Oxford who might profitably have restricted their diet.

The lay brother provided us with ewer, basin, water, and towel, and after washing, Arthur said, "What now?"

I had asked myself the same question before I fell to sleep the night before, and was prepared with an answer.

"John Whytyng was likely slain where we found his boot and pouch yesterday. We know that the key found in the pouch fits the lock used to secure the north porch to the church, and was perhaps made from a missing ladle. We may assume, I think, that the novice used the key to leave the abbey in the night. Whether or not he had done so many times, or but once, we do not know. Nor do we know if he made the key himself or had some other man make it."

"Might be useful to know that," Arthur said.

"Aye. We must keep the question in mind. But this morning I intend to walk a path between the pond and the place where we found Whytyng's corpse. There may be some sign of how the novice was carried from the one place to the other, and Brother Gerleys said there is a boar's head somewhere near where John was found. I would like to know if birds have found it yet, and if so, what damage they have done to it."

I had hoped, even expected, to find some track in the fallen leaves at the edge of the forest where a low stone wall divided woodland from meadow, which might show how the novice had been dragged from the pond to where Arthur, I, and the birds had found him. I found no such marks. Perhaps the last of autumn's falling leaves covered the trail, or two men – one with small feet – had carried the corpse. Or perhaps the murderer had dragged the novice through the fallow field most of the way, where there are no leaves to disturb. I walked part of the way through this meadow, seeking some sign that grass had been disturbed, but if it had once been crushed down, it had sprung back up and grazing sheep had obliterated any sign.

To my sinister side, as I walked the meadow, I saw birds perched upon an oak where woodland and meadow met near the stone wall. Occasionally two or three would descend to the ground where there was likely a boar's head for them to feast upon.

I thought it unlikely that a murderer would haul a corpse through an open meadow, where even on a moonless night a man with good vision might see the deed. So after visiting the place where the novice's corpse had lain I returned to the abbey, skirting the wall at the verge of the woodland. After forty or so paces I came near the birds and found what had attracted them. The hog's eyes were gone, but most of the flesh was not yet devoured.

Arthur looked upon the boar's head with distaste. Most of the time he is eager to see pork before him, but not in such a fashion as this.

"How long, you think, before them birds do to this pig's head what they did to the novice?"

I had asked myself the same question. "Three or four days, I think."

"Then whoso murdered the lad did not leave 'im in the pond, but put 'im over against the wood soon as 'e was dead."

"Aye," I agreed. "So it seems, and 'twould make no sense, I think, to do otherwise."

"But why leave 'im where someone was sure to find 'im?"

"The lad was last seen last Thursday. That was a moonless night."

Arthur's expression told me that he did not follow my thought.

"If his murderer dragged him across yon meadow, there would likely have been enough starlight for the killer to see where it was he was going."

"Ah," Arthur said, "I see. When 'e got to the wood all was dark, even with the leaves gone from the trees an' only naked branches to shut out the starlight. The felon could not see where 'e was takin' the corpse, an' was likely stumblin' about in the shadows, so 'e left the novice there, where the wood became so dark 'e could see 'is way no further.

"Too bad them sheep can't tell what they seen." Arthur nodded toward the flock.

I was still not convinced that John Whytyng's killer would have risked exposure by dragging a dead body through an open field even with no moon to give him away. I thought it more likely

59

that the felon would have kept to the edge of the woodland, near the wall, where his shadow in the starlight would have been black against the trees. I said this to Arthur, and bid him watch for broken branches or twigs while we walked slowly back to the fishpond. Halfway there I saw the fur.

A thick patch of brambles lay on both sides of the overgrown wall, between meadow and woodland. Villagers and birds had long since plucked the berries, and I paid the naked thorns little attention until I saw a tuft of fur caught upon a bramble.

At first even the glimpse of fur did not seize my thoughts. It is not unusual, I think, for a rabbit to lose a bit of fur when seeking refuge from a hawk in a briar patch. But rabbits are mostly grey, and the fur which I plucked from the thorns was a silken brown. Rabbits are small creatures. The bit of brown fur I held was fixed to a thorn higher above the ground than my knee.

Arthur saw me studying my fingers. "Caught on one o' them thorns, eh?" he chuckled. "Doubt as any man would drag another through there."

"Not through, perhaps," I said. "But in the dark he might blunder near before he knew where he was going."

"What 'ave you found?" he asked.

I held the patch of fur out for Arthur's examination. He at first thought as I had. "Rabbit got himself caught, I 'spect."

"I found the fur here," I said, and touched the knee-high thorn which had captured it.

"So?" Arthur said.

"A large rabbit, to leave a bit of his hide so far from the ground," I replied.

"Rabbits jump," he said.

"Aye. But few of them are chestnut brown in color."

Arthur studied the fur again. "Aye, that's so. What beast you think got entangled 'ere?"

"Mayhap a beast," I said. "A hound or fox chasing a rabbit might have left this remnant of his passing, or a deer... or a man wearing a fur coat."

"What would a knight or franklin be doin' in a patch of brambles? A man what owns a fur coat would likely send servants to pluck berries."

I own a fur coat, which Lord Gilbert Talbot gave me as an inducement to enter his service as Bampton's bailiff. I have often plucked berries and have no servant to command. But 'tis true, I have not sought berries while wearing my fur coat.

"There are other men," I replied, "who may wear fur coats, or coats lined in fur."

"Be against the law did they do so," Arthur said.

"Abbots and priors may wear fur coats."

"An' not only abbots an' priors, I hear," Arthur said.

'Tis surely true that most Benedictines own more than the two habits and two cowls permitted them in the Rule of St. Benedict. In their defense they remind folk that the esteemed St. Benedict, the founder of their order, lived in Italy, where cold winds blow less frequently and vigorously than in England.

How long would a tuft of fur remain impaled upon a thorn? A few days? A fortnight? Half a year? It seemed to me that if a monk or knight sought berries he would do so when the fruit came ripe – well before such a man would don a fur-lined garment to fend off the cold. The thought caused me to wish that my own fur coat was upon my shoulders rather than within my chest at Galen House.

I placed the scrap of fur in my pouch, stepped carefully to avoid the brambles which had spread to the meadow, and turned toward the abbey. Arthur followed.

Chapter 5

$\mathfrak{W}$e were nearly to the guest house when I saw two women pass through the abbey gate. Our path to the guest house brought us close to these visitors. Close enough that I could identify them as the comely lass and her older companion who the day before had been cutting straw in the wheatfield. Just inside the gate, in the outer court, is the abbey laundry. The women entered this building as Arthur and I watched.

The lay brother assigned to serve us met us at the door to the guest house and announced when he saw us that our dinner was ready. He had been watching the women enter the laundry. I nodded toward the disappearing females and asked the man who they were.

"Juliana an' Maude."

"The abbey employs them to do its laundry?"

"Aye... well, not exactly. Simon atte Pond is commissioned for the work. His servants do it, 'course."

"And these two are among his servants?"

"Servant an' daughter, which, to Simon an' his wife Alyce, is much the same thing."

"Which is which?"

"Juliana Chator is servant. She's the old 'un with the sharp tongue. Maude's the reeve's daughter, wearin' the fine cotehardie. Abbey's no place for such a lass."

"Why so?"

"An ugly old harridan like Juliana's not likely to cause a monk to lose sleep of a night if he remembers her face when he takes to his bed, but Maude... how does a man, even one who's taken vows, forget such a lass?"

His point was well taken.

'Twas a fast day. Our dinner was a pike in balloc broth, a pottage of raisins, and a wheaten loaf with honey. The abbot, and perhaps the prior, would dine upon similar fare, but no doubt in the refectory the monks consumed but a bowl of pottage and a maslin loaf, washed down with a pint of the abbey's foul ale. No flesh of a four-legged animal is to be consumed in the refectory. So said St. Benedict in the Rule. But abbots dine in their own chamber, so do not heed the ordinance, and monks alternate taking meals in the misericord, where meat is not proscribed. So perhaps some few monks consumed pike this day.

As I ate, it occurred to me that, among the monks of Eynsham Abbey, there must be more than a few who hoped that their brothers would choose them to replace Abbot Thurstan when he died, if for no other reason than the reward of dining from the abbot's kitchen. Prior Philip was likely the foremost of these pretenders.

Consuming the pike caused my mind to return to the fishpond. Simon atte Pond told me that he had heard no poachers near the abbey fishponds since shortly after Lammastide. No doubt such miscreants would keep silence, but casting even a small net into a pond will be heard for some distance on a still night. I wondered if the reeve, no longer a young man, might not hear sounds in the night as well as a youth.

I explained my thought to Arthur, then sent him to the reeve's house to question atte Pond's younger servants. Perhaps one of them heard what their master could not. I intended to visit Brother Gerleys.

Not all monks are skilled with a pen or brush. I found the novice-master bent over Osbert and Henry, instructing them in the use of a goose quill. I asked the monk if we might speak privily, and with a final admonishment to Henry to dip his pen less deeply into the ink pot, he followed me from the chamber.

I bid Brother Gerleys follow me to the kitchen garden, where no man would be this season, even onions and cabbages having been long since harvested. We might speak without violating the Rule where no other man would hear.

Perhaps the monk thought I had some information about the identity of a murderer that I wished to share with him but keep from the novices. I turned to face Brother Gerleys when we reached the center of the garden, but before I could speak, he did so.

"What have you discovered? I have heard that you and your man crossed the meadow beyond the fishponds and visited the place where you found John. Did the murderer leave any clue?"

I had seen no man observe us from either the abbey or the road as Arthur and I investigated the meadow, the wood, the boar's head, and the bramble patch. But someone did, and told others. Unless I was more careful in my actions, the felon I sought was likely to learn of my discoveries soon after I made them, and mayhap use the knowledge to escape capture.

Perhaps it is thus in all abbeys and priories. Days are the same but for the change of seasons, so any event worthy of gossip, even though the Rule forbids idle chatter, is likely to excite much whispered discourse.

I might have mentioned the tuft of brown fur to Brother Gerleys but decided against it. If I did so, even if I pledged Brother Gerleys to silence, I feared that news of the find would soon fill the abbey. If some monk who possessed a fur-lined habit or coat heard of it I would find it difficult to identify the fellow, for he would surely endure the cold rather than wear the garment and so make of himself a suspect to murder. And word of such a discovery might soon escape the cloister, so that if a wealthy villager slew John Whytyng the man would be forewarned to lock his fur coat away in a chest until I gave up pursuit.

Knowing a thing that other men do not know seldom leads to failure. Even better is to know a thing that other men do not suspect that you know. I left the tuft of fur in my pouch.

"I found the boar's head," I said. "Birds have begun to feast upon it, but it will be several days before it will match John Whytyng when I found him."

"He died the night he disappeared, then?"

"So it seems."

I withdrew the pewter key from my pouch and handed it to the novice-master. "I have found the lock this key opens," I said. "The door to the north porch of the abbey church."

"How would John have come by this?" the monk said.

"The monk's kitchener told me that a pewter ladle went missing about Michaelmas."

"Ah," Brother Gerleys sighed. "John was assigned to the kitchen then."

"Was he pleased with the assignment?"

"Nay. Said his father had servants for such work."

"Do not lay brothers perform the menial tasks of the kitchen?" I asked.

"They do... but Abbot Thurstan assigns all novices to such work for a few weeks to learn if they are humble or haughty."

"The abbot learned then of John's pride, but did not dismiss him?"

"The lad's father sent forty shillings with him, which I believe Abbot Thurstan was loath to return."

"You said that the lad was quick to learn."

"He was. Abbot Thurstan spoke of sending him to Oxford, to Gloucester College, when he had proven himself."

"Did Osbert and Henry know of the abbot's plans? Would they wish to study at Gloucester College also?"

"Osbert might. But to be frank, Henry is too dull for such study, and he knows this... although his hand is better than Osbert's. He will find a useful life in the scriptorium, I think."

"Did Osbert or Henry resent John's wit?"

Brother Gerleys chewed upon his lower lip, then replied, "I know what you're thinking. Osbert and Henry often suffered sharp rebukes from John when he disagreed with them, but neither would slay him... my life upon it."

"Think back to their most recent dispute. What was it about? And when?"

"Ah," Brother Gerleys sighed again. "A fortnight past, I believe. 'Twas about a lass."

"Novices speaking of a maid? You allowed this?"

"Nay. I came upon them as the quarrel ended."

"A lass, you said. Was this a maid known to the three?"

"Aye... Maude atte Pond. The reeve's daughter."

"What did John say of her?"

"Don't know. I came upon them as Henry was telling John 'twas not meet to speak so of the lass."

"But you did not hear what John said which troubled Henry?"

"Nay."

"What did John reply?"

"Laughed, and said as how Henry was not likely ever to learn how to please a lass. Then he saw me appear and fell silent, as did Henry and Osbert."

"Osbert is shrewd, you say, and Henry is dull?"

"Aye."

"When John had dispute with either, did they rebut him or allow his challenges to pass unanswered?"

"Henry soon learned that any reply he might make to John would be turned against him. But Osbert could occasionally parry an attack and respond with a thrust of his own."

"You condoned such bickering?"

"Of course not. 'Tis my work... 'twas my work, to teach John Whytyng humility and to teach patience to Osbert and Henry. Both virtues are needful in a monk."

"Did you succeed?"

Brother Gerleys chewed again upon his lower lip before speaking. "Osbert and Henry are apt students. I was unable to persuade John that there were others who might know more than he did. John is... was like the cock who believes the sun rises to hear him crow."

"What of the monks of the abbey? Had John belittled any of them as he did Osbert and Henry?"

"I think not. Novices have little to do with those who have taken vows, but for Prior Philip and Abbot Thurstan. And even John Whytyng would have held his tongue in the presence of abbot or prior."

I thought it might be illuminating to discover from Osbert and Henry what it was that John Whytyng had said about the reeve's daughter. Our conversation in the kitchen garden having ended, I told Brother Gerleys my intention and walked with him back to the novices' chamber, where Osbert and Henry bent over ink pots and parchment, which had been scraped clean of writing for reuse. A brief glance over Henry's shoulders confirmed Brother Gerleys' observation that he might become a skilled copyist. He was, I assumed, the older of the two, but age could not completely account for the difference in the quality of the two novices' work.

"Put down your pens," Brother Gerleys said. "Master Hugh wishes to discuss a matter with you."

The novices did as commanded and peered up at me expectantly. I drew up a bench and sat across the table from them.

"Brother Gerleys has told me that a fortnight past you and John Whytyng were heard in dispute about Maude atte Pond. What did John say of the lass which you took amiss?"

Osbert's expression did not change, but Henry's face reddened as if he'd been dunked head first into a vat of madder. Neither youth spoke.

"Come, lads," the novice-master commanded. "Answer Master Hugh."

The novices cast glances toward each other, each hoping the other would speak. Neither did. Henry's visage continued to glow.

Brother Gerleys grew impatient. "Speak," he said sharply, "or you will spend the night flat upon your faces before the altar, repenting your disobedience."

I believe Henry would have accepted the penalty and kept silent, but Osbert, after a few moments contemplating how cold the church tiles might be, spoke.

"'Twas unseemly to speak of a lass as John did," he said.

When he fell silent, I prodded him to continue. "Why so?"

"John often spoke of comely maids he knew, in Wantage, before he came here," Osbert said.

"How did such talk lead to Maude atte Pond? Had he met the lass?"

"She and one of her father's servants are hired to wash our clothes," Osbert said. "After John saw her once he contrived to be nearby on Monday mornings when she came to the laundry."

"He made conversation with Maude?" I asked. To Brother Gerleys I said, "You permitted this?"

"I did not know of it," the monk said through thin lips. Turning to the novices, he said, "Why did you not speak of this improper behavior?"

Osbert and Henry were again silent. "They stick together," Brother Gerleys grumbled, "even when 'tis to protect one who has belittled them."

"How long past did John begin to seek the lass?"

"He's not been here long. 'Twas before Lammastide, I think," Osbert said.

"What, then, did he say of the lass which was 'unseemly'?" I asked.

Henry sat red-faced, staring at his fingers. Osbert answered.

"John teased us that we'd never kissed a maid, nor ever would. I said there were other things important, especially if a man wished to look upon the Lord Christ when he passed from this life."

"What did John reply?"

"Said as how I'd change my view of what was worth a man's notice if I ever kissed a lass. I asked how he could know such a thing, and he began to boast of the maids he'd kissed."

"And one of these was Maude atte Pond?"

"Aye," Osbert replied. "Said her kisses were the sweetest he'd ever known."

"But... but how could such a thing be?" Brother Gerleys spluttered.

"The key," I reminded him.

"Ah."

"And 'twas as John was explaining the delights of Maude atte Pond's kiss that Brother Gerleys came upon you and heard Henry say to John that he should not speak so freely of a lass?"

Osbert silently nodded agreement to my conclusion. Henry remained stolid, speechless, and flushed.

"Did you never ask John how he knew Maude atte Pond's kisses were honeyed?"

"Once," Osbert said. "He would not say... just smiled."

"He left the abbey in the night to meet the lass," Brother Gerleys said. "Was that what he was about when he was slain?"

The small footprints in the mud where we had found John Whytyng's boot and pouch came to my mind. Were these the marks of a maid, rather than a lad? It seemed possible. Had Maude's father learned of previous trysts beside the fishpond and followed her? Had he been so angry at finding the lass with a novice from the abbey that he plunged a dagger into the youth three times? As I sat across from Osbert and Henry I began to think my investigation of John Whytyng's murder nearly complete.

Arthur's bulky shape darkened the door behind the novices as these thoughts passed through my mind. He was not smiling, and when he saw that his arrival had caught my eye he shrugged and rolled his eyes. I was unsure of his message, but was convinced it betokened no good thing.

Chapter 6

I had learned what I could from Osbert and Henry of John Whytyng and comely maids, so excused myself, nodded from Arthur to the door, and led the groom from the novices' chamber. We had walked but three or four paces from the door when we heard Brother Gerleys begin to speak of misdeeds and contrition and chastisement. Osbert and Henry, I thought, would not much enjoy the next few days, even though 'twas John Whytyng who had transgressed the Rule. Aye, for not informing Brother Gerleys, Osbert and Henry had also flouted the Rule and would suffer for it. Perhaps a night upon the cold tiles before the church altar was yet in their near future.

"Nobody in the reeve's house heard anyone out in the night after curfew," Arthur said. "You'd think they was all deaf. Even the reeve said he'd heard poachers back in the summer."

"Men, and women too, are more likely to sleep with the shutters open in the summer," I said in their defense. "With the shutters closed against an autumn chill a man might not hear poachers throw a net into a pond."

"Aye. But might also be that Simon atte Pond's servants don't much care if folks they know take a fish or two from abbey ponds. What them novices 'ave to say?"

I told Arthur of John Whytyng's carnal boasting. He was silent for a moment, then thought, as I had done, of Maude atte Pond and the smallest footprints we had discovered.

"Think someone came upon the lovers there by the pond? Another suitor, mayhap?"

Here was a new thought. I had considered the reeve to be a likely felon, protecting his daughter's honor. Which was more than the lass did, was it she who left the small footprints beside the pond. A lass like Maude would attract many lads. But why would some other suitor be prowling about the abbey fishponds at midnight so as to come upon John and Maude in the dark?

"Possibly," I said, "but I hold with the maid's father. He may have heard his daughter leave his house, followed, and come upon an embrace which would surely have infuriated him."

"Oh, aye. A lass might do well was she kept by a bishop, but she'd 'ave little was she tied to a monk... 'less he was abbot." Arthur grinned sarcastically as he spoke.

"It would be good to speak to Maude atte Pond," I said. "If 'twas she who left the small footprints at the pond, she will know who struck down the novice."

"Might not want to say, was it her father."

We approached the reeve's fine house from the rear, from the direction Maude would have chosen if it was she whose footprints mingled with John Whytyng's aside the pond. Smoke rose from the toft, and when we drew near we saw that the fumes came from a small shed. White smoke wreathed the hut, filtering out through chinks in the daub and the thin thatching of the roof. A youth stood near the door of this shed, and as I watched he opened the door and tossed a small log into the structure. 'Twas the lad who had yesterday answered the reeve's door, and his task this afternoon was to see to the smoking of hams and bacon from the reeve's freshly butchered hogs.

The youth saw us approach and tugged a forelock. He watched warily as we circled the house, then turned back to keep an eye on the smoke which billowed from every crevice of the shed.

My knock upon the reeve's door was not soon answered. When the door did open a woman of formidable proportions stood in the opening. She wore a cotehardie of fine russet wool, a heavy silver cross hung about her neck, and her pompous gaze left no doubt that here was the mistress of the house. I had the momentary impression that no matter how prosperous her husband might become, his success would be inadequate in this woman's eyes. 'Tis no great achievement for a young woman to be fair to look upon. But a woman who remains comely when her daughter is of marriageable age has achieved a rare thing. The reeve's wife had failed this test.

The woman did not speak, but stood gazing imperiously at me. The ensuing silence was not broken until the matron looked over my shoulder, saw Arthur, and spoke.

"You was here before... talkin' to the servants." She made the statement sound like an accusation. "What do you want now?"

Although the question was directed to Arthur, I replied. "I am Hugh de Singleton, bailiff to Lord Gilbert Talbot on his manor at Bampton. Abbot Thurstan has charged me with discovering who murdered a novice of his house a few days past."

"What has that to do with us, or our servants?"

"Perhaps nothing. My man has spoken to your servants. I wish to speak to your daughter."

"Which one? Why?"

"Her name is Maude, and as she visits the abbey each week, with another, doing the monks' laundry, I would like to know if she has seen anything out of the ordinary in recent visits, or heard some whispered conversation."

I wished to know other things as well, but thought it not the moment to mention this. Mistress atte Pond turned to the interior of the house and bawled out Maude's name. The woman was clearly accustomed to obedience, for three heartbeats later, no more, the lass scurried into view from a side chamber. The maid approached with her eyes downcast, and, it seemed to me, nearly flinched as she came near her mother.

"These men wish to speak to you about your work for the abbey," the woman said, then folded her substantial arms and awaited my questions and her daughter's replies. The interview was not going according to plan.

"I would like for Maude to show us the path she customarily follows when she walks to the abbey laundry and returns," I said.

If the mother had any wit she would have recognized the subterfuge, but I needed to get the maid away from her mother, and this ploy was the first thought which came to my mind.

I led Maude from her front door to the abbey gatehouse, with Arthur following. From the gatehouse we circled past the guest house and the monks' dormitory, then approached the east fishpond. All this time I said nothing but to tell the lass to follow. I glanced at Maude as we passed the laundry house and saw a tear fall from her eye. Perhaps she perceived where I led her, and why.

I stopped at the place where Arthur and I had found boot and pouch. As there had been no rain, the dry, hardened footprints were yet visible. I told the maid to place her foot beside one of the smaller prints, which she did without protest. Here, I thought, was a lass who had been taught to obey, and from the way Maude shrank from her mother when she came near her I could guess how the lessons were administered.

Maude's shoe matched the small footprints in the mud. Arthur glanced toward me and nodded knowingly.

"How many times after Lammastide did you meet the novice John Whytyng here?" I asked.

Maude did not soon reply, but cast her eyes about as if seeking upon the dried mud some explanation for the match made by her shoe when placed alongside the smaller footprints. I thought she was about to deny the accusation, and indeed, other than the similar footprints and John Whytyng's boasting, I had little evidence for the charge.

"Thrice," Maude finally whispered. "Must you tell my mother of this?"

"Not if I have the truth of matters from you. Where else," I said on impulse, "did you meet the lad?"

She raised her eyes to her father's holding some two hundred paces distant, and said, "The barn, when it rained."

"Last week, when you met the novice here by the pond, your father followed, did he not?"

"Oh, nay, sir."

Arthur and I exchanged frowns, and Arthur said, "Told you she'd say that."

"John Whytyng was slain that night, while he was here with you. If 'twas not your father who did murder, who was it?"

"Don't know," Maude said softly, and tears began to flow copiously down her cheeks.

"You were here when he was struck down, were you not?"

"Over there," she pointed to the nearby wood, "John told me to hide myself in the shadows," Maude sniffled.

"Why? Did you hear some man approach?"

"Aye. I came to this place first, an' John came soon after. A moment later we heard someone coming near. John whispered that he must have been followed, that I must conceal myself among the trees, and he would remain, so that whoso followed him would find him alone."

The maid's tears flowed freely as her thoughts returned to the night John Whytyng was slain.

"Did you see who approached?"

"Nay. 'Twas too dark. There was no moon."

"Did they speak? Were you close enough to hear?"

"I hid behind yon beech tree," Maude said, and pointed to a tree twenty paces distant. If John Whytyng and whoso followed him spoke softly, the lass would have heard little.

"I heard John greet a man," she continued, "and there was a reply." The maid swallowed and choked upon her tears, then resumed her discourse. "I heard only whispering. 'Twas as if John and the other feared that some other man might hear their words."

"You think the other fellow knew that you were in the shadows?"

"Nay. He did not seek for me after..." The maid's sobbing again overwhelmed her words. "After he murdered poor John."

"If the fellow had known you were hidden in the wood he might have slain you as well," I said. "If the felon was not your father."

"If 'twas dark and moonless," Arthur said, "how do you know 'twas not your father who stabbed the novice?"

"'Twas not his voice I heard," Maude replied.

"But you said they spoke softly, so you could not hear their words," I said.

"They became angry," she said, "and began to speak so I could hear."

"What was said?"

74

"John said, 'I will never do so.'"

"What did the other man say in reply?"

Maude was again wracked with sobs, but eventually gained control of her voice. "'You leave me no choice,' the other said. Then, 'Do not turn from me when I speak to you.'"

"And this was when the man spoke loudly enough that you knew 'twas not your father?"

"Aye."

"What then?"

"Nothing more was said. All was silent for a long time. I thought perhaps John had returned to the abbey. I was about to leave my hiding place when I heard a thump, then a cry, and then more blows. A moment later came a splashing from the pond, then all became silent again."

"What did you then do?"

"I dared not move from my place. I knew someone had gone into the water, but not who. I was too affrighted to leave the shadows for half of an hour. But when I heard no man move or speak I took courage and approached the pond."

"Did you see anything there?"

"Aye," she sobbed. "A man floated in the pond. I feared it might be John, and was about to draw up my cotehardie and wade out to the man when I heard footsteps and whispered conversation. I fled back to the shadow of the wood."

Maude seemed to find courage as she related the tale. Her sobs interrupted less frequently.

"Two men came and drew a corpse from the pond?" I asked.

Maude nodded. "I could see little, but heard some of their whispers. One man said, 'Where shall we take him?' The other said, 'It need not be far.'"

"Did you know then 'twas John Whytyng who was slain?"

"Aye," Maude said. "Even though the men spoke softly, I knew that neither was John... so the corpse in the pond must be him."

"You told no one of this," I said, "'till now?"

"I could not. I wanted to. To do so would place me together with a novice in the dark of night."

"Why did you do such a thing?" I asked.

"John wished to leave the abbey and return to his father. Said he was not suited for a monk's life."

"What did he intend? Did he speak of it?"

"He had no prospect of lands," Maude said. "He thought to travel to Oxford and become a scholar... study law or some such thing."

"And call for you when he had completed his studies?"

"Aye," Maude whispered. "So we planned."

Whether or not John Whytyng would have kept this bargain no man can know. Maude is a comely lass, but there are other fair maids. Some inhabit Oxford, although one the less since I married Kate and took her from the town. A few pretty maids may have the prospect of lands, which increases their beauty manyfold. I did not know if Maude was likely to inherit property or not. Her mother had mentioned a sister. If the lass had brothers or not I did not then know. I soon discovered that she did not, and her lack of brothers might have done more to ensure John's return than her pretty face ever could.

I now knew what had happened the night John Whytyng was slain, if Maude atte Pond spoke true. I did not know why it happened, or who was involved. But knowing what is an excellent first step toward knowing why and then who. Or who and then why.

Arthur and I escorted Maude back to her home. It would have been quicker to approach the reeve's house from the rear, but I did not want her mother to see us arrive in the toft from that direction. I knew it was likely that someone in the abbey had looked out across the fishpond and seen Arthur and me prowl the meadow and wood the day before, and might now see us circling the abbey buildings with Maude. That could not be helped.

So we walked around the abbey and approached Maude's home from the street. This route took us past Sir Richard's manor house, from which upper window I had seen a man watching women cutting chaff. I glanced to the window as we passed and saw the same fellow gazing from it. He was finely garbed, so I bowed my head in greeting and the man did likewise.

Maude saw the movement from the corner of her eye and turned to see the cause. I saw her glance to the window, then quickly look away without acknowledging the man standing there. I thought I saw her shudder.

The youth at the window was not handsome, as John Whytyng was reported to be before the birds found him, and was stout, but I could see nothing about his appearance or demeanor which might cause a maid to tremble.

"Is that Sir Richard?" I asked.

"Oh, nay, sir. Sir Richard is older than my father. That is his son, Sir Thomas, home for a time."

"He lives elsewhere?"

"Aye. Near to Swindon, I am told, where he serves Sir Andrew Myhalle."

I thought Sir Thomas had looked down with some appreciation upon Maude as we passed, and wondered if he might somehow have discovered her secret meeting with John Whytyng, his appreciation of Maude's beauty causing the knight to follow her unseen. Of course, that a man would look approvingly upon the reeve's daughter should not make him suspect to murder, else all of the male population of the realm might be charged.

I glanced back over my shoulder at Sir Thomas as we approached the reeve's house and saw him yet watching. Did the young knight know of the mutual attraction between Maude and John Whytyng? How could he? He lived elsewhere, and John Whytyng was quite new to Eynsham Abbey. And what if he did? Perhaps I am too suspicious, but 'tis what bailiffs are paid for.

We left Maude before her door, then returned to the abbey guest house. Night was near, the air was chill, clouds obscured the setting sun, and I wished for my fur coat. The guest-master had laid a fire upon the guest house hearth, anticipating our return, and although the blaze had burned low, it warmed the chamber. More logs were ready at hand, and Arthur soon had the fire renewed, so that when the lay brother brought our supper we consumed the pottage with warm fingers wrapped about our bowls.

I slept through the ringing of the church bell for vigils, so when the thunderous pounding erupted upon the guest house door I was deep aslumber. Arthur and I stumbled to our feet in the darkened chamber and nearly collided as we both made for the door. A few embers faintly illuminated the hearth, else we surely would have become entangled.

I opened the guest house door and saw before me a monk. In the dark I could not recognize the man, but he breathlessly introduced himself.

"I am Brother Guibert, infirmarer. Brother Gerleys has told me that you are a surgeon."

"Aye, I am."

"Come, then... don your cotehardie and come quickly. Abbot Thurstan has fallen."

I did as the monk asked, as did Arthur, who followed me into the night as I followed the infirmarer. The moon illuminated our path to the west range and the abbot's lodging. Monks crowded the corridor outside the abbot's chamber, but melted aside as Brother Guibert and I appeared. The infirmarer led me into the chamber, and by the light of several cressets I saw the motionless form of Abbot Thurstan upon his bed. Prior Philip, Brother Gerleys, and two other monks hovered over the supine abbot, but parted when the infirmarer and I entered.

I spoke to Brother Gerleys, of the monks present the one I knew best, but 'twas the prior who answered when I asked of the abbot's injury.

"We were returning from vigils," he said. "He stumbled at the top of the stairs leading from the south transept to the cloister. I reached out to steady him, but he fell from my grasp. We carried him here, to his bed. He has been insensible since, and breathes but does not move."

I brought a cresset near to the white fringe of hair about the abbot's skull and found the cause of his stillness. A few drops of blood had dried upon a lump growing above the abbot's right ear. His tumble had no doubt ended against the stones of steps or wall or floor.

"Bring cold water," I said, "and a cloth."

Cold water in November is easy to come by. A basin quickly appeared, and a towel. I soaked the linen in water and applied it to the abbot's injury. I thought I saw his eyelids flicker as I did so, but the cresset provided little light, so I may have been mistaken.

I regularly refreshed the wet cloth, and twice asked for the basin to be refilled, before Abbot Thurstan opened his eyes and looked up at the somber faces gazing down upon him. He tried to lift himself to an elbow, the better to see those who encircled his bed. I was ready to restrain him, but 'twas not necessary. The effort was beyond his strength, and he sank back upon his pillow.

The abbot's body was weak, but his mind seemed clear, even after the blow he had received. He recognized me. "Master Hugh," he whispered. "What has happened? Where am I?"

"You fell, returning from vigils," Prior Philip answered. "Upon the cloister stairs. You are in your own chamber, in your bed."

The abbot did not speak for some time, and closed his eyes as if in sleep again. But this was not so, I think. He spoke again.

"What injury have I?"

"You have a great lump aside your head," I said, "where you ended your fall against the flags."

"Ah, yes... I remember now tumbling down the stairs. But if I struck my head, why do I feel pain in my leg?"

The abbot's question filled me with sudden dread. "Where," I asked, "is this pain you feel? Is it above your knee, or below?"

"Above," he wheezed, and lifted his hand to touch a place upon his hip. "Just there," he said.

I feared that the old abbot had suffered a broken hip, but could not know for a certainty without a close examination, which would lay his wizened body open to the gaze of all those in the chamber. No dying man should endure such an indignity, and if the abbot's hip was indeed broken, he was likely on his way to meet the Lord Christ, as he had wished to do for many years.

The infirmarer understood the import of Abbot Thurstan's words and gestures. "His hip," he said softly in my ear.

"Aye," I replied. "I fear so. I cannot know without an examination." Then, louder, I said to all in the chamber, "Abbot Thurstan complains of pain in his hip. With his permission I will see what injury is there. This will require that I partially remove his habit. He would likely wish the chamber cleared, but perhaps for Brother Guibert."

I turned to the abbot. "You heard? Do you wish this examination?"

"Aye... but all must leave – even Brother Guibert," he whispered.

Prior Philip opened his mouth as if to object, but remained silent and, with the others, shuffled from the chamber. He was the last to leave, and, I noticed, left the chamber door open when he departed. I crossed the room and pushed the door closed.

Chapter 7

"T is not the knob on my head which troubles you, is it?" the abbot said. "I could not hear your words, or Brother Guibert's, but I saw you exchange sour glances when I complained of my hip."

"It may be but a bruise which pains you," I replied.

"It may also be that my hip is broken. Is this not so?"

"It may be," I admitted.

"Then best be about your task and tell me if I am to linger longer in this world, or soon be released to the next."

I did as he commanded, and it took but little poking and prodding, Abbot Thurstan wincing in pain when I did so, to convince me that his hip was indeed fractured. I told him this.

"Then I will soon pass to the next world. How long, you think? A week? A fortnight?"

"Perhaps as long as that," I said. I have heard of broken hips which mended, but do not know if this is so, or but myth.

"Brother Infirmarer will have herbs which will dull the pain," I said.

"The Lord Christ does provide for all our needs," the abbot said. Then, as I was about to open the door to admit those who had been dismissed, he spoke again.

"Nay. Not yet. I have more to say to you, which must be heard by no other man. Not yet.

"My flesh will soon be food for worms, but my wit is returning, even though I have a sore head. There are things which you and no other must know.

"Prior Philip has urged me to discharge you. He said my promise to you of a Bible is too great a price, and you have made no progress in discovering a murderer. He has asked to be assigned the task, and promises me that he will find whoso has slain John Whytyng, and at no expense to the abbey."

This speech seemed to tire the abbot. He had lifted his head

81

from the pillow to speak, but it fell back when he grew silent and I saw his eyes close.

"This night," he continued, "'tis true... I stumbled at the top of the stairs. But then, when I placed a hand upon the wall to steady myself, Brother Prior reached for my hand, drew it from the wall, and with his other hand pushed upon my shoulder. I heard him tell you that he had tried to check my fall, but as I look back upon it, he did the opposite. Of course, he will claim that I am demented, that the blow to my skull has unhinged me. 'Tis not so. Prior Philip wishes us both away from Eynsham Abbey. As for me, he will have his wish. He has long desired to replace me as abbot. Do not allow him to drive you off also."

"How can I prevent it? If I cannot find who murdered the novice before your death, the prior will be left in charge of the abbey, and he may tell any man to leave the place."

"I have thought on that," the abbot said, his voice becoming weak. "I will leave written instructions with my clerk that you are to remain in the abbey, commissioned to find a felon, until you are successful, or you give up the quest."

"Will Prior Philip accept such a command?"

"He will. He wishes to be chosen abbot in my place, and will know that his brother monks hold me in some esteem. To show disrespect to my final request would cost him the support of many brothers. There are already those who would wish Brother Gerleys to replace me, and Brother Prior knows this. No, he will not chase you away before your work is completed."

Rain had not fallen for more than a week, but as the abbot fell silent I looked to the chamber window and saw there in the dim light of dawn a few beads of water upon the glass. My mood was dark, and the gloomy morning did nothing to improve it. I wondered what Prior Philip might do to rid the abbey of my presence if he was willing to pitch a frail old man down a flight of stairs. Perhaps Abbot Thurstan imagined the prior's guilt, and he had genuinely tried to arrest the abbot's fall. But 'twould be safest to assume the abbot's allegation accurate, and look to my own safety.

I opened the chamber door and found the corridor crowded with monks and lay brothers. Some had been in muted conversation, but became silent as I passed through the opening.

"Well?" Prior Philip asked. "What news?"

"His hip is surely broken," I said, and saw the monks near me, whose faces were faintly visible, take on an even more somber aspect. Several crossed themselves.

"How long?" Brother Guibert asked.

"Not long, I fear. He is a feeble old man, and he does not wish to live."

"A week, then?" Prior Philip said.

"Perhaps. Mayhap a fortnight."

From within the abbot's chamber we in the corridor heard him speak. "Send Brother Theodore," he said clearly. "All others must depart. Brother Theodore will relate my wishes at chapter this morn. 'Tis nearly time for lauds. Begone, and pray for my soul."

A monk made his way through the press of black habits and passed through the chamber door. Prior Philip made to follow this monk, but had gone only a few steps into the room when I heard Abbot Thurstan say, "Nay... I'll have only my clerk attend me." I knew what he intended to do.

There was a window in the corridor, and in the soft light of early dawn I searched faces until I found Brother Guibert, who had been jostled from his place near the door by other monks eager for a word about their abbot.

"What herbs have you," I asked the infirmarer, "which we may use to dull Abbot Thurstan's pain?"

"I have a pouch of hemp seeds," he replied.

"Crush some, and bring a thimbleful together with a cup of ale." Then, remembering the quality of the abbey's ale, I added, "Or wine."

The monk nodded and departed. "You heard Abbot Thurstan," the prior said sternly. "Leave this place and assemble in the choir. We will pray there for his soul."

I thought to myself that if the good abbot had not faith and deeds enough to recommend his soul to the Lord Christ, no prayers from monks would do so. Such thoughts are surely heretical. I keep them to myself. I have a wife and child – soon two – to care for, which I could not do if hanging from a gibbet.

Brother Guibert's infirmary is in a separate structure, away from cloister and dormitory, so it was some time before he returned with the crushed hemp seeds and, I was pleased to see, a cup of wine. I pushed open the abbot's chamber door, and heard him abruptly stop speaking to Brother Theodore. The abbot labored to turn in his bed and see who had interrupted his dictation, saw it was me, and bade me enter. Brother Guibert followed, while Arthur, a silent observer to all of this, remained in the corridor.

"Brother Guibert has a potion for you," I said. "'Twill ease your pain."

"If it will also dull my wit I do not want it," the abbot said in a surprisingly strong voice. "I do not wish to end my days in a daze," he said, then chuckled through his pain.

"'Tis the crushed seed of hemp," Brother Guibert said. "Only a thimbleful. Not enough to afflict your mind."

I was silent in the face of Abbot Thurstan's jest. Could I be so light-hearted as he if I knew that I would stand before the Lord Christ before St. Catherine's Day? He had spent his life in prayer and worship, preparing for this time. For what, I thought, am I preparing? What can be more important to a man's life than preparing well for its end? What, then? Should all men be monks and all women nuns? That would be a sure way to end all men's lives, for there would be no children to follow after.

"Here," the infirmarer said, and placed an arm under the abbot's head. "Drink it down."

Brother Guibert's words interrupted my thoughts, which was good, as they were not productive in the matter Abbot Thurstan had assigned me to find a murderer. But then, perhaps that is how we must live to prepare well for death. We do what the Lord Christ has assigned us to do, as well as we may.

Brother Guibert and I left Abbot Thurstan with Brother Theodore. The infirmarer turned to join his brothers in the church, while Arthur and I returned to the guest house. A cold mist wetted us as we passed from the abbot's lodging in the west range to the guest house. I hoped that we would find a loaf and ale awaiting us. We did not, but when the lay brother assigned to us realized that we had returned he soon appeared and we broke our fast.

While we consumed maslin loaves I told Arthur of the abbot's accusation against Prior Philip.

"Don't surprise me none," Arthur said. "That prior's not a man to be content with second place."

While I finished my loaf I thought of what Maude atte Pond had said of John Whytyng's last words. "I will never do so," he had said. What was it he would not do? Who had authority enough that they could make a demand of the novice? Did his reluctance cause his death?

What might a man of the town want John to do, or what might a monk or lay brother wish of the novice? Whatever it was, he would not do it, and for this unwillingness he was apparently slain.

Maude was near the age when the banns might soon be read for her and some swain. Sir Thomas Cyne was certainly taken with the lass, and likely several others. She would not bring much land to a knight like Sir Thomas, but a pretty face may supplant half a yardland or so, and some land was better than none at all.

It would not do to ask the reeve what men had shown interest in his daughter. I must discover possible suitors in some other way. I thought that Brother Gerleys might be of some help. Not that he would know of village gossip, but he might direct me to one who would.

Arthur followed me to the novices' chamber. We found the place empty, which was not surprising. The chapter, meeting after lauds, would be long this morning, the brothers having many questions about the future leadership of the house.

We waited nearly an hour before voices in the corridor indicated the arrival of Brother Gerleys and his charges. "Little enough punishment for such a sin," the novice-master said to Henry as he entered the chamber. He saw me awaiting him and was silent.

"I wish to speak to you privily," I said.

Brother Gerleys turned to his novices and instructed them to seek the kitchener and ask what service they could be to him this morn.

The lads obeyed and soon their footsteps could no longer be heard. The monk closed the door to his chamber, pointed to the table and benches in the center of the room, and said, "Be seated. What is it you wish of me?"

"Did Abbot Thurstan's clerk read out a message from the abbot at chapter this morning?"

"Aye, he did."

"Did the message cause controversy in chapter?"

"Some. Prior Philip and his cohort would see you away from the abbey."

"The prior has opposition in this matter?"

"Aye. There are those who believe John Whytyng's death requires a more thorough explanation than Prior Philip would deliver."

"Are you among these?"

"Aye."

"Abbot Thurstan said privily to me that there are among the brothers many who wish to see you elevated to the abbacy above Prior Philip."

"'Tis not a post I seek."

"And the prior does? Likely your reluctance explains the regard your brother monks have for you. But that is abbey business, and none of mine. If I wanted to know the gossip of the town, to whom would I go?"

"Ah... that would be Adam Skillyng, keeper of the ale house."

"His ale loosens men's tongues?"

"Just so. The man serves good ale, so his patrons drink too much of it."

"Unlike the abbey's ale." I could not resist the comparison.

"Aye," he laughed. "Holy Scripture says we all must take up our cross and follow the Lord Christ, and Brother Gervase, who brews the abbey ale, sees to it that we swallow splinters when we consume his ale."

The ale house, for inn or tavern it could not be rightly called, was a little more than one hundred paces from the abbey gatehouse. The establishment was but a house with an enlarged bay, where villagers whose wives could not or would not brew the household ale might meet and drink. The place was empty when Arthur and I entered, and dark. On such a day little light penetrated the old, yellowed skins which covered the windows.

The proprietor heard the hinges of his door squeal when we entered the place and immediately appeared. I asked for two cups of ale, and placed two farthings upon a well-worn table. This payment was evidently sufficient, for the toothless fellow swept the coins into a palm, left the room, and reappeared with two large leather tankards.

Brother Gerleys spoke true. Adam Skillyng's ale was better than most, and not watered. Whether this was due to Skillyng's honesty or the village taster's vigilance, who could say? Arthur smacked his lips in appreciation after his first swallow, and the man beamed in appreciation of the compliment.

"Travelers?" he asked.

"Nay," I replied, and placed two more farthings upon the table. "Abbot Thurstan has commissioned me to find a felon. Have you heard of the murder of an abbey novice?"

"Aye," the man said, and crossed himself.

"We are lodged in the abbey guest house… but the abbey ale is so noisome that when we learned of this place we came seeking better."

"Ah. In times past many monks did also, but the prior forbids it now."

The farthings remained upon the table, and I saw Skillyng glance at them. "More ale?" he finally said.

"Nay. Your ale is pleasant, but I seek information of you." As

I said this I pushed the coins toward the fellow. "The reeve's lass, Maude, is a comely maiden. Has she many suitors?"

"Hah," Skillyng grinned. "Has Oxford many scholars?"

"That many?" I said.

"Well, nay. But more than a few."

"She will bring little land to a husband... only a reeve's daughter."

"Simon has no sons. Got Maude an' her sister, what's younger. An' since the pestilence come second time he's taken up more of the abbey's lands. Has servants, does Simon."

"How much of the abbey's manor is in his tenancy?"

"Five an' a half yardlands. Has subtenants for three yardlands."

"Whoso weds Maude will gain more than a comely wife, then."

"Aye, an' there be plenty of lads eager to win 'er."

"Who?" I pushed the coins closer to the man and he scooped them into stubby fingers.

"Sir Thomas, for one."

"Sir Richard's son? Him who is in service to a knight of Swindon?"

"Aye. But he's returned for a time. To press 'is suit, folk do say. Ralph's not pleased, I'd wager."

"Ralph?"

"Aye. Ralph Bigge. Father sent 'im to serve Sir Richard when 'e was but a page. Lived here in Eynsham, in service to Sir Richard as page an' squire, for near fifteen years."

"And he has an eye for Maude also?"

"So 'tis said. 'Course, her father'd favor Sir Thomas."

"Why so?"

"Ralph has no lands, an now we're at peace with France, no prospect of takin' prisoners for ransom, an' little chance to win honor in battle so to be knighted. Sir Thomas has no lands, but he's a knight."

"Sir Richard has two sons?"

"Aye. Sir Geoffrey's older. 'Bout a year. Sir Richard's wife died soon after Sir Thomas was born. Truth to tell, Sir Geoffrey's got a wanderin' eye, folk say. Wouldn't surprise me none did he chase after Maude on the sly, like."

"Sir Geoffrey is wed?"

"Aye. To Hawisa. Got a son, an' another babe on the way."

"Sir Thomas and Ralph seek the favor of a lass beneath their station. Are there no men of her station who are suitors?"

"Oh, aye. Osbern Mallory, 'tis said, has approached her father about paying court. A widower, is Osbern. Has lands of Osney Abbey in Cumnor, beyond Swinford. Wealthy fellow, but no title. An' Maude may be of the commons, but Simon's got a heavy purse. Inherited 'is brother's shop in Oxford when 'e died."

"Who of these suitors does the reeve prefer?"

"Sir Thomas, 'tis said."

"And Maude? What is her opinion?"

"Ralph is a handsome fellow, an' so is Osbern. Folk do say she prefers them. Sir Thomas bein' stout an' not so pleasin' to look upon."

"But the reeve cares little for a son-in-law's appearance," I said. "If his daughter wed the son of the lord of a manor his position would be much enhanced."

"Aye. Sure enough."

I thanked the man for his time, and he replied with a toothless grin. Well he might. He had earned a penny for but two cups of ale.

"Lots of fellows who'd be displeased to know a novice of the abbey was payin' court to Maude," Arthur said as we left the ale house.

"Aye. It will be well to speak to them. But first I will visit Abbot Thurstan and see how he fares."

Chapter 8

He did not fare well.

I found Brother Guibert attending his abbot, both men silent, waiting. I thought Abbot Thurstan to be asleep, so spoke to the infirmarer.

"Does he complain of pain?"

It was the abbot who replied. "He does not," the old monk said softly.

"The hemp seeds," Brother Guibert said, "seem effective. He has slept some this morning."

"Has he taken any more of the seeds since before dawn?"

"Nay."

"It is near to noon. Perhaps he should have another potion, and again after compline, so he may sleep the better."

The infirmarer rose from his bench and silently left the chamber. I took his place upon the bench, to sit with Abbot Thurstan until Brother Guibert returned.

"For many years," the abbot said softly, "I have desired death. But now that it is near, I fear it."

"All men do," I said, "if they be truthful. 'Tis a great mystery, but all will be plain when you see the Lord Christ and gaze upon His blessed face."

"Aye. But I fear many years will pass before I am able to do so."

I knew then what Abbot Thurstan feared.

"My sins are many," he continued, "and I have not confessed them in chapter as I ought, as I require of those under me. My pride will send me to purgatory for many years. And now 'tis too late to confess... What penance can I do from my bed?"

"Your faith is strong?" I asked.

"Oh, aye. But I am a weak man in many ways. My sins will not soon be purged."

"Did not the Lord Christ already do so?" I said. "Upon His cross, where He died for men's sins?"

"Aye, He did so... but my sins..."

All men's sins loom large before them, I think, when death draws near. 'Twould be well for our souls if we were more attentive to our sins when we are hale and hearty.

"My punishment will be great," the abbot said after a time of silence.

"Why? Was not the Lord Christ's death enough to gain a man's salvation?"

"Nay. A man must suffer for his unrighteousness."

"I remember, when a student at Baliol College, discussing this matter. One read from the first epistle of St. John, where the apostle wrote, 'If we confess our sins, He is faithful and just to forgive us our sins, and to cleanse us from all unrighteousness.' Another read from St. Paul's letter to the Colossians: 'Now He has reconciled in the body of His flesh through death, to present you holy, and blameless, and irreproachable in His sight – if indeed you continue in the faith.'"

The abbot said nothing for a moment, and closed his eyes as if he sought sleep. Then, with eyes yet closed, he spoke. "Was Master Wyclif one of these?"

"Nay. But he was present."

"I thought as much. His views are becoming known. How is it you recall these verses so well?"

"When I heard them it seemed to me that they contradicted the teaching I had always heard. Next day I sought a Bible, and found the scriptures true as they were read. I took pen and parchment and copied them, and having read these passages often, I now remember them well.

"Do these scriptures not bring you comfort?" I continued. "Do you confess your sins?"

"Daily," Abbot Thurstan replied.

"Then believe the apostle when he wrote that you are cleansed from all unrighteousness. Why must you be cleansed of sin in purgatory when the Lord Christ has taken away all unrighteousness?"

"I retained you to seek a murderer. Now you teach me the Scriptures. I have studied and read them all of my life."

"I do not mean any impertinence."

"Can a man be impertinent who only repeats Holy Writ?"

The abbot then fell silent. His eyes opened and he stared at the boss of the vaulted ceiling of his chamber. I spoke again. I should perhaps have remained silent.

"If the Lord Christ has already made you holy, and blameless, and irreproachable in His sight, why would He condemn you to a purgatory... to require you be purged of that which you do not have?"

The abbot continued staring silently at his chamber ceiling for a time. "Bishop Bokyngham would think you a heretic for such thoughts," he finally said.

"I will be careful to hold my tongue in his presence," I said.

"What would happen to this abbey, to churches and chapels and cathedrals, if men did not offer coin so that priests and monks pray for their souls?"

Here was a question for which I had no ready answer. But I spoke my uncertainty. "Can Holy Church only continue if it requires men to pay for salvation which the Lord Christ has already provided upon the cross? I cannot believe it so."

"You speak like a theologian, and a troublesome one, rather than a surgeon and bailiff."

"Must only priests and monks know what the Lord Christ has said in Holy Scripture?"

Brother Guibert appeared in the chamber door, a silver cup in his hands. He peered at me strangely as he approached the abbot's bed, then lifted his superior's shoulders so he might drink the mixture of wine and crushed hemp seeds. The infirmarer apologized for the delay of his return. He had, he said, to crush more hemp seeds to make the potion.

Abbot Thurstan sipped from the offered cup. As I watched I saw a shadow pass through the chamber door. 'Twas Brother

Theodore. He saw what Brother Guibert was about and waited near the door until the cup was empty, then approached the bed.

"The archdeacon has arrived," he said.

Abbot Thurstan passed a hand across his forehead and grimaced. "I had forgot that he was coming. Make apology for me, and tell him I must receive him here. Tell Brother Gerald to make place for his party in the guest house. Archdeacon Stephen will sleep in my visitors' chamber, as always." Then, under his breath, to himself, the abbot said, "What a time for him to show himself."

Considering the thoughts I had recently shared with the abbot, I had no desire to meet an archdeacon. I bid the abbot "Farewell," and departed the chamber. Brother Guibert did likewise, and Brother Theodore followed.

Our footsteps echoed upon the planks of the corridor, but could not muffle the sound of a stentorian voice which came from the stairs to the lower level of the west range.

Brother Theodore hurried ahead and stumbled down the stairs. The infirmarer and I followed at a more cautious pace. One abbey resident had already fallen down a stairwell.

Prior Philip and the guest-master were in conversation with several men I had not before seen about the abbey; the archdeacon, I assumed, with his party. Conversation this discourse could not rightly be called, for the prior was mostly silent. A large man, dressed in a fine white cassock spattered with mud about the hem, spoke. All others listened.

Prior Philip nodded assent as the archdeacon instructed him. Brother Theodore eventually gained notice, and as Arthur and I departed the cloister I heard him tell the newcomers of the abbot's injury.

'Twas nearly time for our dinner, so we returned to the guest house and awaited the lay brother who would bring our meal from the abbot's kitchen. The fellow was much delayed. No doubt the archdeacon's arrival had thrown the kitchener and his staff out of joint.

When our dinner finally appeared 'twas but two bowls of pease pottage and maslin loaves. Saturday is a fast day, to be sure, but we were given no fish. I suspect that the meal planned for Abbot Thurstan and his guests fed the archdeacon rather than Arthur and me, and we consumed the plain fare served to the monks in the refectory.

"What's an archdeacon doin' at the abbey?" Arthur said as we finished our pottage.

"The Bishop of Lincoln will have sent him, to see that all is proper and in accord with the Rule."

"What rule?"

"The Rule of St. Benedict."

"Oh... that prior didn't seem much pleased to see 'im."

"Likely not. The purpose of an archdeacon's visit is to ferret out what is wrong in an abbey, not to discover that all is as it should be."

"Ah," Arthur said thoughtfully. "If the archdeacon reports no wrongdoin' the bishop will believe he's incompetent... an' so he'll always find some evil to report. No wonder his visit is unwelcome."

"Aye. But that is for the monks and clerics to sort out," I said. "As for us, we'll see to that boar's head that Brother Gerleys placed near the wood, then visit a suitor or two. Perhaps we should begin with Sir Thomas."

"Spends much time gazin' at Maude from windows, does Sir Thomas," Arthur grinned. "Might be put off if he knew a lad more handsome than 'im was attendin' Maude of a midnight. 'Course, whether or not John Whytyng was handsome we must take the word of them what knew 'im. His looks wasn't so pleasin' when we found 'im."

I expected much of the flesh to be gone from the boar's head and was not disappointed. Three days had passed since Brother Gerleys had left the head at the edge of the wood, and in another day, or two at the most, the thing would have as much flesh peeled from it as John Whytyng's face when we found him. Of course, the thick, bristly skin of a boar might prove a tougher meal for the birds than the soft flesh of a novice. Birds had flapped noisily from the place when we approached, and sat above us, patiently waiting for us to depart.

This we soon did. There was little more to be learned from a decaying boar's head. As we passed the brambles where I had found the tuft of fur, Arthur spoke.

"If that fur you found has to do with the novice's death, it'll be one of them knights that did for 'im, I'm thinkin'."

I agreed, and asked how he had reached that conclusion.

"How many monks 'ave a fur coat... maybe the abbot? He's too frail to follow a man in the night and plunge a dagger into 'im three times. An' that yeoman of Cumnor..."

"Osbern Mallory," I prompted him.

"Aye, Mallory. Such as 'im can't wear fur at all."

"They can, but only of the meaner sort: rabbit, cat, or fox."

"Oh. Suppose that tuft is fox?"

"Mayhap. But I agree with you. 'Tis my belief that either Sir Thomas or Ralph is our quarry. Or Perhaps even Sir Geoffrey."

"Him what's married?"

"Has a wandering eye, so said Adam."

"An' where an eye wanders," Arthur said, "other parts of a fellow is likely to follow."

Sir Richard Cyne, I decided as we approached his house, was a prosperous man. His manor house had been recently whitewashed, was well thatched, and had what I believe was a nearly new bay rising above the older part of the structure. This, I learned, was a new hall. The loss of laborers and rents since the great death seemed not to have afflicted Sir Richard so badly as others of his station. Or he was much in debt and living on borrowed shillings.

The manor house door was stout. I rapped firmly upon it several times before a servant pulled it open on well-greased hinges, and my knuckles can attest to the substantial nature of its construction.

The servant noted my fine cotehardie, fashionable cap and liripipe, and possibly identified Arthur's livery. He tugged a forelock.

"Good day, sirs," he said. "How may I serve you?"

"I am Hugh de Singleton, bailiff to Lord Gilbert Talbot, here to speak to Sir Thomas."

"Ah, I must then disappoint you. Sir Thomas has gone off a-riding."

"When will he return? Did he say?"

"Nay. I heard him say to Sir Richard that he was off to Cumnor an' would return anon."

I thanked the fellow, told him I would return later, and exchanged glances with Arthur.

"Cumnor," Arthur said when the door closed behind us. "That's where that yeoman suitor's from. Is it far?"

"Beyond Swinford a few miles. You'll remember Swinford."

"Hah. Not likely to forget. Wonder if that fellow I knocked into the river's got the water out of his ears yet. We gonna chase after Sir Thomas?"

"'Chase' is not the proper term. We will seek him on the road to Cumnor."

"An' likely find 'im somewhere near to Osbern Mallory's holdings, or I'll miss my guess."

A lay brother saddled our palfreys, and less than an hour after standing before the manor house we approached Swinford. The day was chill, although the misting rain had ceased, and the Thames was cold and dark. We had to spur our beasts to convince them 'twas in their interest to enter the water and splash to the eastern side.

Like many other villages, plague had done much harm to Cumnor. Several houses stood collapsing and empty. I saw dwellings which gave evidence of care and occupation, but many were derelict. Before a well-kept house a fine horse stood tethered.

The beast shifted skittishly as we approached, and when we drew near I understood why. Angry voices raised in argument sounded from the open door of the house. As I watched, a tiny lass of no more than six or seven years scurried out of the door into the street. She did not halt her flight until she reached the verge on the other side, where she turned, quivering, and sucked upon a grimy fist.

The argument may have begun with shouted words, but it advanced to blows. Two men toppled through the door as Arthur and I dismounted. They rolled toward the tethered horse, which bucked and squealed in fright, then broke free and galloped off toward Swinford, throwing clots of mud from its hooves.

Arthur's beast and my own danced about nervously as Sir Thomas's horse – I was sure of the owner – charged past. Arthur and I held tight to the palfreys and watched the brawl before us. The combatants seemed evenly matched. They alternated between rolling in an angry embrace in the mud and standing, calling curses upon each other, before coming again to blows.

I had first thought Sir Thomas fat. Such was the appearance he gave when standing at his window. I soon learned that there was a heavily muscled man under that bulging belly. His thick arms and legs hid much strength below their plump outlines.

His opponent was not so solidly assembled as Sir Thomas, but was taller, and possessed of a lean strength developed from years of following a plow and doing the thousand other tasks necessary to wring sustenance from England's soil. He was the sort of man who, with a few thousand companions, had sent flights of arrows down upon the French at Poitiers.

I thought that the brawl would soon end, and had no interest in putting myself, or Arthur, between two powerful, angry men. I was wrong. They fought on, standing to catch a breath only momentarily before sallying back to the fray.

Arthur and I tied the palfreys to a convenient shrub while thus entertained. I could see in Arthur's eyes that he would willingly join the combat if he knew which man most deserved aid. This eventually became apparent.

After flinging themselves about in the mud again the fighters stood and I saw Sir Thomas draw his dagger. His opponent raised his hands and backed away when he saw the blade. A fair fight was no longer so. Osbern Mallory was in retreat toward his house. Perhaps in the house he had a dagger, but he did not at the moment. And even had he possessed then a weapon he would not likely be so skilled in its use as a knight.

Sir Thomas advanced upon the yeoman as he hacked away. The knight was not content to win the skirmish, I thought, but intended a more permanent triumph.

I felt Arthur stiffen beside me, turned and saw his face twist into a scowl. The dagger in Sir Thomas's hand offended his sense of fairness. He had been enjoying the combat of equally matched foes, but that pleasure was now ended.

Sir Thomas lunged for Mallory, his dagger describing great sweeping arcs as, with each slashing stroke, the knight's blade came closer to the yeoman. Unless Mallory turned quickly and ran, one of Sir Thomas's thrusts would, sooner or later, find its mark.

"Halt," I yelled. "Cease this combat."

I might as well have called for two drakes to stop fighting over a duck. My shout had no effect. Sir Thomas continued to advance upon his foe without so much as turning his head to see whence the bellowed command had come. I reached for my dagger and saw from the corner of my eye that Arthur had drawn his as well. Before I could take a step Arthur started for the combatants, intent on evening the unbalanced conflict.

We were too late. Sir Thomas lunged and again swept his dagger before him. The weapon slashed through the sleeve of Mallory's cotehardie. The blade found another mark also. I saw the yeoman look to his forearm, and at the same instant a red stain appeared upon the edges of his gashed garment. Mallory put a hand to his arm, and blood flowed between his fingers. The man's arm was sorely wounded.

Sir Thomas must have thought the same. He glanced down at his dagger as if he found it incredible that the weapon could have done such an injury. I thought he might press his advantage against his wounded adversary, but not so. The blood oozing between Mallory's fingers seemed to cancel Sir Thomas's wrath. With a last look at his dagger he thrust it into its sheath. He then turned and glared at me. 'Twas then I saw blood dripping from his nose and upper lip. Sometime during the altercation Osbern Mallory had delivered a telling blow.

"Saw you with Maude atte Pond," the knight snarled. "You'll learn 'tis best to keep to your own business."

Sir Thomas turned and strode off toward Swinford, hoping, no doubt, to find his horse before he reached the ford.

I turned from the departing knight to the wounded yeoman. Mallory was fixed to the place where he had stood when he was cut, as if unable to comprehend the injury done to him. I hurried to the fellow to learn how deep was his wound.

When I came near, Mallory looked up from his dripping arm and spoke. "You saw... this cut may be the death of me. See to it the sheriff knows."

"A man may survive such a wound," I said.

"Who are you?"

"I am Hugh de Singleton, bailiff to Lord Gilbert Talbot, and also a surgeon. I can sew you together again."

I took one elbow, and Arthur the other, and together we helped Mallory through the open door of his house and set him upon a bench. He stumbled upon the threshold and I feared that he was already grown weak from loss of blood. Much gore had puddled his toft where he stood immobile after being wounded, and a trail of large drops followed from the place to his doorway.

With my dagger I completed the work which Sir Thomas had begun and opened Mallory's ripped sleeve until I could see his wound clearly. The cut was as long as my hand, and when I spread the edges it bled copiously again. But I saw in so doing that the gash was not deep. It had laid open flesh, but not to the bone.

"The cut is not severe," I said. Then, to Arthur, "Make haste to the abbey and fetch my pouch of instruments. And bring a flask of wine. Explain to the cellarer that it is needed to wash this man's wound."

"What did you do to bring such fury to Sir Thomas?" I asked when Arthur had left us.

"Nothing, yet. 'Tis what he fears I may do which caused his choler." The man spoke strongly even though wounded.

"What could a yeoman do to so anger a knight?" I thought I knew the answer, but wished to hear it from Mallory.

"Nothing of your concern... but I do thank you for driving the fellow off."

"Sir Thomas seems to hold a grudge."

"Aye," Mallory managed to smile through his pain and thickening lips. Sir Thomas had landed a fist or two, as well as a dagger stroke. "That he does."

While he spoke I lifted the lid of a chest and found there a kirtle. I used it to press against Mallory's cut and staunch the blood which yet flowed, if more slowly, from the wound.

"No doubt the grudge has to do with Maude atte Pond," I said.

Mallory looked as if Sir Thomas had caught him upon the ear with one of those large fists. His mouth worked open and closed several times before he replied.

"'Ow'd you know that?"

"Eynsham gossip has it that you've an interest in the maid, as does Sir Thomas... and others."

As I spoke, the child, evidently reassured that angry adults no longer contended with one another, appeared in the doorway and stared open-mouthed at her bloodied father.

"And others," Mallory agreed. "I've near as much land of Osney Abbey as Maude's father has of Eynsham Abbey, an' more than Sir Thomas, but no title, so 'er father refuses me permission to pay her court."

"You have asked him?"

"Twice. Always, 'Nay.' Wants Maude to rise above 'er station. Be a lady."

"Does Sir Thomas know that Maude's father has forbidden your suit?"

"Don't know. Guess not, else 'e'd not have come here today."

"His purpose was to dissuade you from seeking the lass's favor?"

"Dissuade? Hah. His purpose was to threaten."

"Which you did not take well? Simon atte Pond forbade your suit, you say. Who did he favor? Who did Maude favor?"

"Dunno. Couldn't find a way to speak to Maude but once, an'

atte Pond wouldn't tell me even did he prefer Sir Thomas over that squire."

"You spoke to Maude? When? How so?"

"Michaelmas. Went to Eynsham with some others to watch the horn dancers. I'd seen Maude before, in past years. Knew her father. But she'd grown up, like, an' me bein' alone since me wife died, I spoke to the maid."

"Did you offer to pay her court?"

"Aye."

"How did she respond?"

"Said she must ask her father. My hopes was high, for I'd known Simon for many years. But when I spoke to him later that day he refused. Surprised me. I'd make a good husband for a reeve's lass.

"Odd thing about Maude that day, though. Some of the monks come from the abbey to watch the horn dancers. Maude spent more time watchin' them than the dancers. Probably never seen much of monks."

"You said her father refused you twice?"

"Aye. Maude's not an easy lass to forget. Went to Eynsham a fortnight later to see could I change Simon's mind. He'd hear none of it. 'Twas then 'e told me of Sir Thomas an' Ralph. Can't blame a man for wantin' to see a daughter well settled, I s'pose. But, despite having no 'Sir' before me name, no man would do better by Maude than me."

"You said that while watching the horn dancers she gave attention to the monks?"

"Aye."

"Could you tell if 'twas any monk in particular?"

"Nay. Why'd she do so? Them monks was all standin' together, anyway, so if there was one she was watchin' more than the others no man could tell. Why do you ask?"

"A novice of the abbey was slain four days past."

"Heard about that. What's that to do with Maude?"

"Perhaps nothing. But the lad had boasted to his fellows of his prowess with maids, and Maude enters the abbey each week to do the monks' laundry. He might have made her acquaintance at such times."

Mallory was quick of wit. "So you've come to see if I might have slain the novice, seein' 'im as competition for my own suit. But I've got no suit. Not unless Simon atte Pond relents, which I don't see 'im doin'."

"Perhaps Sir Thomas thought he might," I said, "or finds his own suit faltering, and believes you the cause."

"He'd be mistaken. I've given up on the lass. Tried to tell that to Sir Thomas, but 'e didn't come here to talk, or listen."

The conversation seemed to tire Mallory. I bid him say no more, held the bloody kirtle firm against the gash, and awaited Arthur's return.

I did not wait much longer. Palfreys are not speedy beasts, but Arthur must have put his heels to the creature's ribs, for 'twas not long before I heard the hoofbeats of a galloping horse. The animal halted before Mallory's dwelling, and a moment later Arthur plunged through the open door, my instruments sack in one hand and a flagon of wine in the other.

"Pity to waste that," Mallory said with a grimace as I poured wine into his laceration. I sopped up the excess with a corner of the blood-stained kirtle, then threaded a length of silk through a needle.

I closed the yeoman's wound with twelve stitches, urged him to avoid labor with that arm for a fortnight, and told him that I would return about St. Nicholas's Day to remove the sutures.

"How much do I owe you for this?" He pointed to his arm.

"Two pence."

"A bargain," Mallory replied. "Most work I can deal with myself... but not such as this."

The yeoman cautiously stood, prodded the stitches tentatively with a finger, then spoke to the child who had watched us suspiciously from a far corner of the house. "Get the little box for me... there's a good lass."

The girl went to her father's bed, ducked and crawled under it, and reappeared with a small casket. Mallory took the box from her and produced my fee. I explained to the man that he should leave his wound uncovered, and that I would apply no salve. I follow the practice of Henri de Mondeville, who in dealing with battle wounds discovered that cuts left dry and unbandaged healed most readily.

We bid Osbern Mallory "Good day," retrieved the horses from the shrub, and set off for Swinford. I thought it likely we would come upon Sir Thomas, unless he had found his horse and ridden ahead of us back to Eynsham. I said so to Arthur.

"He was near to Swinford when I come back from Eynsham with your instruments," Arthur replied. "Still afoot. Saw nothing of his beast along the road."

We came upon the knight at the ford. He stood contemplating the cold current, evidently trying to decide whether or not a quick return to Eynsham was worth wading through frigid water which would reach above his waist. He heard our approach, turned, and scowled.

The fellow was no doubt of two minds regarding our arrival. On the one hand Arthur and I had interfered with his attack on Osbern Mallory. On the other, our arrival meant that, were we amenable, he might climb behind one of us and cross the icy stream dry-shod.

I was not amenable. Not until I asked some questions of the knight and received acceptable answers. If he chose not to reply, he could continue to seek his beast, or soak in the Thames.

Sir Thomas's martial ardor had cooled. Perhaps he had put a toe into the river. He frowned as I dismounted, but made no move to carry out his earlier threat that mischance might follow if I did not mind my own business. Perhaps he had reconsidered, and now thought that my business should include his transfer from one side of the Thames to the other.

I had two questions for Sir Thomas, and depending upon his answer to the first, the second might be irrelevant.

"Your beast has left you on the wrong side of the river," I said with a smile. My expression was not due to a felicitous meeting, but rather I smiled at Sir Thomas because I knew the effect a grin on my face would have on the thwarted knight. This may have been a sin. May the Lord Christ forgive me.

Sir Thomas desired our aid in crossing the river, but it pained him to ask. His conceit caused him to bite his lip and remain silent. I placed a foot in a stirrup and readied myself to remount the palfrey. Sir Thomas saw his chance for gaining the opposite bank dry-shod about to vanish and swallowed his pride.

"My horse has disappeared," he said. "I'd be in your debt if you'd carry me across the water. I'll not trouble you further... 'tis but a short walk on to Eynsham."

"Are you left-handed?" I asked.

"Aye."

Sir Thomas scowled again. This was an expression he performed well – due, I suspect, to much practice. But he is to be forgiven. My question had nothing to do with his need.

"Just curious. One other matter, then we will cross the river and you may be on your way. Do you own a fur coat?"

"A fur coat? Do you jest at my misfortune? Aye," he snapped, "I have a coat lined in fur. Glad I am I did not wear it today, to have it spoilt in the mud and in the water."

"It will soon be cold enough you will find it needful," I said.

"Aye," he muttered. "I will have it from my chest anon. What has that to do with crossing this stream?"

"Nothing. Here, take my hand and climb up behind me."

Sir Thomas placed a foot in the stirrup after I had withdrawn my own, and ignoring my offer of a hand in assistance grasped the saddle and swung himself upon the palfrey's haunches with a grace that belied his bulk. A few moments later we were across the Thames and again upon solid ground.

Sir Thomas muttered, "Much thanks for this aid," dropped to the road, and set off for Eynsham. Arthur and I followed and soon passed him. When we were well beyond the knight Arthur spoke. "Owns a fur-lined coat, does Sir Thomas."

"Aye," I said. "But he's left-handed. I suspected so when I watched him battle with Osbern Mallory. The blows he aimed at

Mallory came mostly from his left fist, and he held his dagger in that hand as well."

"Is that important?"

"Cast your mind back to the wounds which took John Whytyng's life."

"Stabbed in the back. What's that to do with Sir Thomas bein' left-handed?"

"The novice was pierced three times. Two of the wounds were upon the right side of his back, below his right shoulder-blade. Only one stroke caught him to the left of his spine, likely because he turned to face his assailant before he fled in the only direction he could go."

"Into the fishpond."

"Aye."

"So if his murderer was left-handed the wounds would have been on t'other side," Arthur said.

"Aye," I agreed. "And most knights own a fur coat, or at least a cloak with a fur lining, so that Sir Thomas possesses one, which is yet in his chest, tells us little."

"If it is in his chest," Arthur said.

A few moments later we traveled around a bend in the road but a half-mile from Eynsham, and came upon Sir Thomas's horse. The beast had evidently decided that danger had passed, and was contentedly cropping what remained of the grass at the verge of the road. The animal lifted his head to watch us approach, determined that we presented no threat, and returned to his occupation.

"Should we return 'im to Sir Thomas?" Arthur asked.

"He's not far behind," I said, "and the walk will do him good... provide him time to consider his sins."

Chapter 9

Simon atte Pond and his lads were again at ditching. This task seemed nearly concluded, which was good, as the November day was nearly done. Only a dozen or so paces remained before the low place would be drained. The reeve looked up from his work, nodded, and his three laborers tugged forelocks as we passed. I wondered how the reeve would greet Sir Thomas when he approached. The knight would have found and mounted his horse before he reached the place.

A hundred paces beyond the ditchers an arm of woodland extended to the north edge of the road. I drew my palfrey to a halt and told Arthur to do likewise. We led our beasts into the darkness of the trees, tied them, and I explained the reason while we returned to the road.

We hid ourselves behind the largest oak, which was barely large enough to conceal Arthur alone, and watched for Sir Thomas to appear around the bend of the road. We did not wait long.

I was too far from the reeve to hear any greeting or conversation, but men may speak with body and face as well as words. Sir Thomas halted before the reeve and the men exchanged a few words. The knight then dismounted and led his horse toward our place of concealment. Atte Pond followed.

They had walked perhaps thirty paces from the ditchers when Sir Thomas halted and the two resumed their conversation out of the hearing of the others.

This discourse was at first unaccompanied by any gestures and seemed right amicable. But after a few minutes I saw Sir Thomas respond to the reeve with a shake of his head. Then he spoke a few words, and the reeve replied with a long speech which he punctuated with several waves of his arms.

To this display Sir Thomas again responded with a shake of his head, then replied with an oration as long as the reeve's. Atte Pond looked away several times as Sir Thomas spoke, as if other matters interested him more than the knight's words, and once he looked to the road at his feet and idly toed a pebble he found there.

When Sir Thomas ended his remarks it was the reeve's turn to shake his head. He then turned abruptly to return to his laborers, but Sir Thomas reached for his arm to detain him.

Atte Pond took this gesture badly. He yanked his arm free and slapped at Sir Thomas's offending fingers with his free hand. But if the knight had intended the restraint to halt the reeve's return to join his workers, he succeeded. Atte Pond stepped back to Sir Thomas and I could see the men face each other, their complexions grown livid, from little more than a hand's breadth apart. I expected next to see blows exchanged.

This did not happen. No reeve wishes to be charged with assaulting a knight, especially, I suppose, if the lad may become his son-in-law. And Sir Thomas had but to peer over atte Pond's shoulder to see the ditchers, picks and spades in hand, to understand that if he unsheathed his dagger he would soon be overwhelmed. Prudence overcame rashness.

"Them fellas ain't pleased with each other," Arthur whispered. "Wonder what's got 'em so upset?"

I wondered the same, and did not reply, as I had no answer. Was Sir Thomas unhappy with the reeve's ditching? That seemed unlikely, for neither man had looked to the work, either where it was currently being done, or where it was complete. And the work was upon abbey land, not that of Sir Thomas's father.

The only other reason the two might have conversation, it seemed to me, was concerning Maude's future. Why would that cause such a heated disagreement? Did the men disagree upon dowry and dower?

A moment later Sir Thomas turned from his antagonist, climbed to his saddle, and without looking back at the reeve spurred the beast cruelly. I took Arthur's arm and drew him deeper into the darkening wood. Sir Thomas's wrath might blind him to men partly hidden among the trees, but I desired to be more sure of our concealment.

We waited until I was sure that Sir Thomas was well away, then led the palfreys to the road and mounted. 'Twas but a short way to Eynsham and the abbey.

"Must be true what folk do say," Arthur said, "that money don't buy happiness. Them chaps is rich, but they sure ain't happy."

"Rich? A reeve and the younger son of a minor knight?"

"Any man what's got more coin in 'is purse than me is rich," Arthur said.

"Are you happy?" I asked.

The groom was silent for a few moments. "Content," he replied. "Was happy, 'till plague took my Cicily. Don't worry, as some cotters do, about what I'll eat come the morrow."

"Do you suppose," I asked, "that there are some poor cotters who are happy?"

"Mayhap, but I doubt so. Pennies in a man's pouch don't promise happiness, but an empty purse won't buy anythin'... includin' happiness. Havin' a few coins to spare may not make a man joyful," Arthur said thoughtfully, "but they might make sorrow easier to bear."

We passed the manor house as Arthur concluded this thought. At that moment Sir Thomas appeared between the house and stables, saw us, and stared open-mouthed. We had gone ahead of the knight after leaving the ford, but now were behind him in entering the village. He would surely wonder why, and might guess that we had seen or heard his dispute with Simon atte Pond.

We gave the palfreys to a lay brother and sought the guest house as the day faded from grey to black. I assumed that our supper would be another bowl of pease pottage, so was not much disappointed when the meal appeared. The loaves which accompanied the pottage, though, were wheaten, and of best quality. And the ale seemed some better than the abbey's usual fare. Perhaps the arrival of an archdeacon had influence.

Next morning Arthur and I joined Eynsham villagers in the church nave for prime and the mass. Abbot Thurstan, of course, took no part in this, being unable to rise from his bed. Prior Philip and the archdeacon led the service.

Sir Thomas, his lip swollen and an eye turning purple, entered the church as the archdeacon's clerk rang the bell. Sir Thomas was in company with three others: an older man, fat and bald, whom I took to be his father, Sir Richard, and a man and woman of near his own age, whom I assumed were his older brother, Sir Geoffrey, and wife.

There was little remarkable about the mass. I had endured many like it. The archdeacon's sermon was forgettable. I don't remember what it was about. Indeed, several women of the village found it so wearying that they gossiped among themselves while the archdeacon droned on. These women stood immediately behind Arthur and me, and at first I found their prattle annoying, but soon gave my attention to them rather than the archdeacon.

"Come back intendin' to wed an' take 'er off," one woman whispered. "But Sir Richard don't approve."

"Her bein' a reeve's daughter, 'tis no wonder," another said.

"Got no prospects in Essex, I'd guess, else he'd not return for but a reeve's daughter."

"You see 'is eye? All black it is."

"Aye. Wonder who done that?"

"Wouldn't surprise me none if 'twas 'is brother."

"Ha. More likely Sir Geoffrey'll have 'is own blackened eye after Hawisa deals with 'im does 'e not keep from Maude."

"Wouldn't be a bad thing was Sir Thomas to wed the lass an' take her from Eynsham. A maid that pert causes too much trouble."

"Not 'er fault."

"Nay... s'pose not. She don't behave unseemly. Alyce sees to that."

The women chuckled at that remark, then one said in a voice so low I could barely make out the words, "Maude told my Agnes that she'd soon be off to Wantage."

"Wantage? Sir Thomas returned from Chelmsford. What suitor's from Wantage? Ralph?"

"Nay. Ralph's of Banbury."

"Would Simon put her out to service in Wantage?"

"Don't think so. Alyce wouldn't hear of it. Works the lass from dawn to dusk, does Alyce. An' Simon puts 'er and Juliana to work at the monks' laundry."

"The prior's of Wantage... so I heard."

My thoughts had begun to wander from the gossip behind me, but this remark caught my attention. John Whytyng came from Wantage. Would the prior have known the novice or his family before the lad came to the abbey? And if so, what might that have to do with Whytyng's murder? Probably nothing. But I had few other notions that morning about paths I might follow in seeking a killer. Perhaps a brief journey to Wantage was in order.

Dinner this day was splendid. The abbot's kitchen had roasted a boar in honor of the archdeacon's visit, and there was plenty of pork to share with humble residents of the guest house.

When our meal was done I told Arthur to see the palfreys readied at the stables, then crossed the kitchen garden, passed through the refectory to the west range, and rapped upon the closed door of the abbot's chamber. Brother Guibert opened the heavy door, frowning at whoso intruded upon the abbot's rest, but when he saw 'twas me his visage softened and he bid me enter.

Abbot Thurstan lay as I had seen him last, his face pale, wispy white hairs scattered upon the pillow. He coughed, then turned his head to see who had entered his chamber, and would have lifted it from the pillow but had not the strength.

"His breathing is weak and shallow," the infirmarer said.

I bent close to the abbot to listen as his chest rose and fell beneath the blanket, and discovered the truth of Brother Guibert's words. Abbot Thurstan knew this also.

"Not much longer now, I think," the abbot said in a whisper, which was all the volume he seemed able to manage. "Your words yesterday have given me much to consider. I thank you. I am content, as I was not before, to pass to the next world. The Lord Christ will not turn away anyone who is so minded as I am to go to Him."

"He will take no more of the pounded hemp seeds," the infirmarer said.

"Does your hip not pain you?" I asked.

"Aye," he murmured. "But it dulls my wits. I wish to go to the Lord Christ with a prayer upon my lips, not asleep, as the unwise virgins."

"I must leave the abbey for a few days," I said.

Abbot Thurstan's eyebrows raised, and I explained. "John Whytyng was of Wantage. I have just today learned that Prior Philip is also of that place. I intend to visit the town and learn if there be any connection between the two, or their families."

"Surely you cannot think that Prior Philip had any part in the novice's death," the abbot said.

"I confess that I do not know what to think of this death. So I must seek what knowledge I may, even if it seems a foolish waste to do so. What family is Prior Philip's?"

"Thorpe. His father was Sir John, brother to Sir William, once Chief Justice of the King's Bench."

"A man of influence," I replied. "Does Prior Philip's uncle yet live?"

"Nay. And not so much influence if he did. Sir William was imprisoned many years past for accepting bribes."

The abbot's words seemed to tire him. He closed his eyes, and for a moment, 'till I saw his chest rise slightly, I thought he might have died before me from the exertion of his speech.

The wind increased while I stood before the abbot, and rain began to rattle the chamber windows. The sound nearly obscured the abbot's next words.

I saw his eyes blink open, and heard him say, "Prior Philip's brother is Sir John Thorpe. He inherited the manor, so Philip came to us. Doesn't speak of his brother... don't believe they got along well. Philip is an able man, but can be peevish."

And impatient, I reflected, as I considered that it was likely the prior's desire to succeed Abbot Thurstan which led to the old monk's injury.

I had no desire to travel to Wantage in a cold November downpour, so found Arthur and told him to return to the stables and inform the lay brother in charge that our plans were changed. We would travel on the morrow. Arthur seemed glad of the alteration.

I awoke in the night and was pleased to no longer hear pelting rain upon the guest house window. The sky had cleared in the night. The dawn was bright but cold. We would not be wet traveling this day, but neither would we be warm.

A lay brother appeared with a maslin loaf and ale with which we broke our fast. The abbey stable had our palfreys ready, as Arthur had requested, and we were away to Cumnor and beyond, to Wantage, before the day was an hour old.

A skim of ice crusted puddles in the road and ditches, and I wished again for my fur coat. The sun soon rose above the trees and warmed us some while we traveled. At Cumnor I called upon Osbern Mallory to inspect his wound. There was some redness about the cut, but it oozed no pus. Some believe this an ill sign; that a thick pus issuing from a wound is best, and a thin, watery pus, or none at all, is a dangerous sign. But I hold with de Mondeville, whose book, *Surgery*, I own, that no pus at all from a cut is best.

The road to Wantage passes through East Hanney, where a year past Arthur and I had discovered a stolen maiden and a plot to seize a cache of ancient silver coins. Sir Simon Trillowe, who was involved in the plot, and whose designs for Kate Caxton I had thwarted, lived in the village upon his father's manor. I preferred to avoid the fellow, so as we drew near the place I wrapped my liripipe about my neck and face as if to ward off the chill. No one paid us any attention as we passed through the village.

Wantage is but two miles beyond East Hanney. We entered the town before noon, found an inn, left the palfreys at the stable, and sought a meal.

Arthur and I shared a roasted capon and maslin loaf, spoke little, and listened to the local gossip. We learned a great deal, but nothing of either John Whytyng or Prior Philip. I decided to seek the novice's father first, and asked the innkeeper where I might find him.

The fellow gazed suspiciously at me. Strangers are generally mistrusted, and especially so when they ask of a local villager. Folk wonder why a stranger should be curious about their doings.

Arthur remained at our table, licking grease from his fingers and downing the last of an ewer of ale. The innkeeper glanced over my shoulder at Arthur, then back to me, before he spoke. He apparently saw no threat in one slender, bearded man and another who was intent upon licking the last of a capon from his fingers. He told me where I could find Sir Henry, for so John Whytyng's father was named.

Sir Henry Whytyng's lands lay to the west of Wantage, half a mile, no more, from the inn. The innkeeper described the place well: a village of six houses, a church in Sir Henry's gift, and a two-story manor house, whitewashed and well thatched.

There was no need to knock upon the manor house door, for it opened as I approached, no more than three or four paces from it. A tall blond-haired man stepped across the threshold, saw me and Arthur, and seemed to stop in mid-stride. The man was too old to be John Whytyng's brother. Here, I thought, was the dead novice's father.

John Whytyng was a tall lad, as was the man who stood before me, and fair-haired. Whether or not his features resembled his father I could not know. The birds had seen to that.

"Good day," the startled fellow said. "How may I serve you?"

"I am Hugh de Singleton, bailiff to Lord Gilbert Talbot at his manor of Bampton, and here is Arthur, groom to Lord Gilbert."

This introduction produced only a blank expression upon the fellow's face. I continued. "I seek Sir Henry Whytyng."

"I am he. What does Lord Gilbert's bailiff want of me?"

"I come from Abbot Thurstan, of Eynsham Abbey, on abbey business."

"Ah, your visit must have to do with John. Well, then, come in... come in."

We followed the knight into a chamber warmed by a fire, and as we did so Sir Henry called out, "Bring wine… and three cups," to an invisible servant.

"What news have you? And how does the abbot?" Sir Henry asked as he swept his hand toward several chairs in an invitation to be seated.

"He is unwell. Abed with a broken hip. He fell upon a stairway some days past."

"Ah, this is indeed ill news. Will he live?"

"'Tis not likely."

"And he sent you to tell me of this? I am much obliged that you have done so."

"Nay. Another matter brings us to Wantage."

Sir Henry's eyebrows rose, but before I could explain, a servant appeared with an ewer and three cups. We drank in silence for a few minutes, then Sir Henry spoke.

"What other matter, then? Something about John?"

"Abbot Thurstan sent a lay brother to tell you of the death of your son," I replied.

"Aye." I saw the knight's shoulders slump and it seemed he shrank in size before me.

"The pestilence has returned to Wantage as well," he said. "Five have died since Michaelmas."

Pestilence? Is that what the messenger had told the man? Did Abbot Thurstan so instruct him? I must tread carefully here, but I was not of a mind to allow such mendacity to continue unchallenged. There were things I needed to learn in Wantage, but could not do so if this falsehood was not overturned.

"John did not die of the pestilence," I said.

Sir Henry frowned, set his cup upon a table, and spoke. "But the lay brother said the plague had returned to Eynsham."

"Aye, so it has, and other places also. Did he say that the sickness had taken John's life?"

Sir Henry was silent for a moment, casting his mind back to a conversation which was surely burned into his memory.

"In this very room he told me that my son was dead. I asked

him the cause, and he replied that the pestilence had returned to the abbey."

"Did he say nothing else?"

"Of John's death? Nay."

"The man did not lie, but he intended you to believe an untrue thing, which is that John died of the plague."

"He did not? What, then?"

"He was murdered... stabbed three times."

Sir Henry's eyebrows furrowed into a scowl and his lips became thin. "Who did this? Is the felon known?"

"Nay. Abbot Thurstan has asked me to discover the murderer."

I wondered if the abbot was the source of Sir Henry's misinformation, or if the lay brother had himself invented the deception. I resolved to ask the abbot when I returned to Eynsham, if he yet lived.

"I am told that Prior Philip is also of Wantage," I said.

I saw the frown on Sir Henry's face become a sneer as his upper lip curled slightly. "Aye," he said. "His brother lives here yet. But what of my son? Have you any in mind who may have slain John?"

"Several," I replied.

"Several? That means you do not know. Had he made enemies in Eynsham?"

"A few. Did you know he intended to leave the abbey?"

"Nay. Did he say so?"

"He did. He had in mind to study law at Oxford, so he told another."

"Then he thought to leave the abbey because he had made enemies there, you think?"

"Mayhap. And there was at least one other reason. I will tell you at some later time, when this puzzle is solved."

The knight was not pleased with this reply. He took his cup from the table and drained the last of his wine. Before he could demand more of me I asked again of Prior Philip.

"Do you know Prior Philip well?"

"Hah, you might say so."

"I have heard that his older brother possesses the family manor."

"Aye. Near to Grove. You'd pass the place comin' from Eynsham. 'Tis north of Wantage a short way."

"I have heard also that the prior and his brother are not on amicable terms."

"What has this to do with my son's murder? You said that Abbot Thurstan had retained you to find the felon."

"Perhaps nothing. Probably nothing. But I will not know until I know. I trust I make myself obscure."

"Perfectly."

"About the prior," I continued.

"'Tis true enough, Sir John and Prior Philip don't get on… never have done, even when lads. Of course, there's nothing much odd about that. Philip Thorpe never got along with anyone, as I can remember."

"Why so?"

"Was his looks, I always thought."

"He is not a handsome man," I agreed.

"Aye. Never was, lad an' man. Knew it, an' so thought folks demeaned him because of it. Made him sour. Got worse when the warts began to speckle his face. Always seemed to be alone, but none could abide his presence… an' not because of his looks."

I began to feel sorry for the prior, but then remembered the stairs and Abbot Thurstan's accusation against him, and the sentiment passed.

"Always disliked me," Whytyng continued. "Shouldn't have taken the matter so personally. She wouldn't have had him even was I not a suitor. She'd have chosen some other, not Philip."

I was uncertain of whom the knight spoke, but thought that if I held my tongue he would explain the matter.

"Margaret scorned his suit an' took up with me. Next I heard Philip was off to Eynsham as a novice. Wasn't long 'till we heard he was made sub-prior, and a few years later, prior."

"How long was Philip at Eynsham before he became prior?"

The knight scratched his chin. "Six years... maybe seven. No more."

Philip could have been no more than twenty-six years old when he assumed the office of prior. Such positions have often been filled by younger men since the pestilence struck England, but even so, to be chosen prior and be not yet thirty years old was a considerable achievement, likely made possible by the transfer of a substantial purse to the abbey treasury while his father was yet alive.

There was silence while I considered these things, then Sir Henry spoke again. "My Margaret's been gone seven years now. Died when the pestilence first returned. Mostly children died hereabouts then, but Margaret died an' John lived. He was but eleven years old. Cried himself to sleep many nights... so did I."

"I am sorry for your loss."

"Many suffered the same, or worse."

The knight glanced out of his window at the darkening sky. "Where do you lodge?" he asked.

"At the inn."

"Bah... vermin-infested place. You have not brought welcome news, but truth should be rewarded. You shall lodge with me this night. Do you return to Eynsham on the morrow?"

"Aye. But first I'd like to speak to Prior Philip's brother. I've no thought as to what I might learn, but 'twould be a pity to ride all this way and not do so. And for your invitation I give you much thanks."

I was indeed grateful for Sir Henry's offer. There may be in England an inn not infested with fleas and lice, but I have never spent a night in such a place. And the Boar's Head, for such was the inn's name, did not seem upon entering the inn to be unlike other such establishments scattered about the realm.

"Your beasts are at the inn stable? Send your man for them."

I looked to Arthur, who had remained silent during this conversation. He stood from his bench, tugged a forelock in Sir Henry's direction, and turned for the door.

"Best be off, then, to return before dark," he said.

"Your words have been a second bolt to me," Sir Henry said when Arthur was away. "First to learn that John was dead, and now to discover that he was slain… and wished to leave the abbey, also."

As he completed the statement I heard a door open and close and then heavy footsteps upon the flags of an adjacent chamber. Sir Henry looked to the door and called out, "Will, come here."

A tall, blond, handsome young man answered the summons. The fellow was in appearance a more youthful image of Sir Henry. Here, I thought, was John Whytyng's older brother, and if John resembled Will, 'twas no wonder he attracted maids. The image of the novice's bird-ravaged face came to mind, but I cast the thought aside and stood to greet the newcomer.

Sir Henry introduced us and told his son what news I had brought. I explained again that Abbot Thurstan had commissioned me to discover John's killer, and promised that I would be diligent in the effort.

By the time I had made this pledge we heard Arthur return from the inn, riding upon his palfrey and leading mine. "That'll be your man," Sir Henry said. Then, to Will, "See to their beasts."

Sir Henry's cook had prepared a supper of muntelate for his master. I, the knight, his son and daughter-in-law, Arthur, and two of Sir Henry's grooms cleaned the pot.

One of the grooms then showed us, with the feeble light of a cresset, to an upper chamber where a straw-filled pallet had been laid upon the floor beside a bed. "'Twas John's chamber," the man said. Arthur, knowing his place, went to the pallet while the groom set his cresset upon a stand. This room had no fireplace, so Arthur and I were eager to crawl under blankets.

I lay awake, certain that Arthur would soon fall to sleep and shake the rafters with his snoring. He did not, but after a time of silence he spoke.

"Wonder how much Prior Philip dislikes Sir Henry?" he said. "Enough to slay 'is son as revenge for losin' the maid… what was 'er name?"

"Margaret."

"Aye, Margaret."

"Men have done murder for less," I said. "And I've had similar thoughts these past hours."

"Would a prior own a fur coat?" Arthur asked.

"The Rule forbids such, I think, but Benedictines, especially those of authority, pay little attention to that," I replied.

"Sir Henry said Prior Philip an' 'is brother don't get along. Think you'll learn much from the fellow?"

"Probably not, but what I do not learn may tell me something."

"How so? I don't understand."

"Neither do I," I said. "Let us await tomorrow and see if any of this muddle becomes more clear."

Chapter 10

I fell to sleep considering why Prior Philip would slay John Whytyng and how he might have arranged to do so. These thoughts came to me because of my dislike for the fellow. I had no sympathy for a man who would pitch his aged superior down a flight of stairs so to advance his own station. From that moment I was satisfied that the prior must be the felon who had slain John Whytyng. As prior he had opportunity, for he could go where he wished in the abbey or its grounds, whenever he wished. And now I had discovered a reason for his doing murder: to avenge himself upon Sir Henry by slaying his son. It only remained for me to prove this presumption. So I thought.

A single small window of oiled skin under the thatched eave faintly illuminated the chamber as dawn drove away the dark. The cresset had been extinguished in the night, its oil likely consumed, so even that small flame gave no aid to the half-light of early morn.

Sir Henry provided wheaten loaves, cheese, and ale with which we broke our fast. A groom made ready our palfreys, and before the second hour we bid Sir Henry "Good day," and set off for Sir John Thorpe and the manor to the north of Wantage upon which Prior Philip was reared.

Sir John's tenants were about the work of November. Some, men and women both, could be seen prowling a wood a hundred paces from the road, gathering fallen branches for winter fuel. Their collections were small. 'Twas likely the wood had been gleaned already, perhaps several times since Michaelmas.

We passed a marsh, where the road lay low and muddy, and saw folk cutting reeds to dry for thatching. A few glanced from their work to watch us pass, but most were more intent upon providing for a dry home than observing two strangers.

The tiny village surrounding Sir John Thorpe's manor house surely had a name, but I did not ask it, and to this day do not know what place it is called. Sir John's house was much like Sir Henry Whytyng's: two stories, whitewashed recently, and new-thatched against the coming winter.

A small commons of a hundred or so paces in length by thirty wide separated the manor house from a small stone church. A dozen houses surrounded the commons, three derelict for want of inhabitants – due, no doubt, to the great pestilence. A lass drew a bucket of water from the village well at the edge of the commons, peered at us mistrustfully, and scurried off toward her home.

Sir John Thorpe had conveniently provided a hitching rail before his house. We left the palfreys there and Arthur followed as I approached the door. At this house there was no prompt answer to my knock, and I was required to belabor the door several times before a scowling servant finally pulled it open. I greeted the fellow pleasantly, which did nothing to alter his visage, and asked of Sir John.

"Who wants 'im?" the servant asked in a most unfriendly tone. I wondered what pleasant occupation I had interrupted.

"I am Hugh de Singleton, bailiff to Lord Gilbert Talbot at Bampton." From the tone of the groom's voice I thought 'twould be no bad thing to introduce myself and my employer as well. The effect was salutary.

"'E's at stable. Got a mare what's ailin'. Come inside. I'll fetch 'im."

The groom disappeared into a rear chamber and a moment later I heard a door latch thrown and the squeal of hinges. A heartbeat later I heard another squeal, followed by a string of curses indicating a vocabulary such as I had not heard since a student at Baliol College when I sometimes frequented inns upon Fish Street.

I looked to Arthur and he replied with pursed lips and raised eyebrows. The tirade gradually subsided. From the few words I could hear plainly I concluded that a beast had kicked a man, and the bellowed oaths were the fellow's response.

The yelping subsided, but also seemed to draw near. The

squeaking door was shoved farther open, and I heard a man sit heavily upon a bench in the adjacent chamber. Curiosity propelled me to the door, and I peered around the jamb.

A man sat upon a bench clutching his arm while a woman and the groom who had greeted us at the door hovered solicitously about. Another groom stood in a doorway leading to a rear toft and stables beyond.

"Miserable beast," the injured man exclaimed. "Broke my arm, sure enough. Ought to slit her throat and make food for the hounds of her."

"But she was your favorite," the woman said. "She'd not have kicked out but for the pain."

At that moment the injured man raised his face to the door and saw me. I knew this must be Prior Philip's brother, for his countenance was a duplicate of the prior's, but for the warts, for which the fellow should give thanks each day.

The woman attending him I took to be his wife. She was of pleasing features; more evidence, if any is needed, of the improvement which land and wealth can impart to an ill-formed face.

"Who are you?" the man growled through clenched teeth, and clutched his arm tighter. This caused him to grimace anew.

The groom spoke before I could. "Asked to see you. Comes from Lord Gilbert Talbot."

This was not precisely true, but I saw no need in the circumstances to correct the fellow.

"What does Lord Gilbert want of me? I owe service to Sir Richard Fayling, not Lord Gilbert."

I left the door, walked to Sir John, and said, "I am Lord Gilbert's bailiff at Bampton, but I do not come on his business. I am also a surgeon, trained in Paris. Will you have me examine your arm?"

"A surgeon, you say? You are well-met. Aye... 'tis surely broken. The beast lashed out at me when I walked behind her. Caught me square and sent me into next stall. Constriction of the bowels. She'll have to be put away."

The man spoke more sensibly than when under the first influence of shock and pain.

"You are Sir John Thorpe?" I asked as I began to prod his injured limb.

"Aye," he said, and winced as my fingers found the break. Flesh about the injury was already purple and swollen.

Arthur had followed me into this second chamber. I turned and told him to seek the men cutting rushes at the verge of the marsh, and bring a bundle of sturdy reeds to me.

"I will need some linen. An old kirtle ripped to strips will do."

Sir John looked to his wife, for so the woman was, and she bustled off to the stairs. A moment later I heard her in the chamber above us, and soon after I heard the lid of a chest slam shut.

The break was just above Sir John's right elbow. I would be required to immobilize his arm from wrist to shoulder. His wife returned with two kirtles and I showed her how to tear them into usable strips. She had no sooner begun the work than Arthur plunged through the chamber door with an armful of reeds – enough that I could have set the broken arms of half of Oxford. Arthur is not a man to do things by halves.

With my dagger I cut a dozen reeds to proper length, then used the linen strips to bind these about Sir John's arm. I had no herbs to give the knight to reduce his pain, so each time I tied another linen strip about the man's arm he gasped. I was careful, before I began the business, to be sure that the broken bones met properly. This work also caused Sir John much pain, but the prodding and poking was necessary to ensure that the break knitted properly.

When the reeds were bound securely about the break I wrapped the remaining linen strips about Sir John's arm, from wrist to shoulder, in such a fashion that his elbow was bent across his belly. Finally I took a section of untorn kirtle, drew it under the knight's forearm, and tied it behind his neck. This caused the injured limb to rest across his sizeable paunch, immobile.

"I thank you," Sir John said when I had finished. "But you did not come here to mend my broken arm. If you are not about Lord Gilbert's business, what has brought you here?"

"You are the brother to Philip, prior of Eynsham Abbey?" I asked.

"Aye."

"I am told that before he took a vocation, he had an interest in a maid named Margaret."

Sir John shrugged, winced from the effect of the gesture upon his injured arm, then replied.

"He did. So did most lads hereabout. Why does Lord Gilbert's bailiff concern himself with such a matter? You do not come on Lord Gilbert's business, you said."

"Aye. Murder has been done at Eynsham Abbey, and Abbot Thurstan has charged me with discovering the felon."

"What has that to do with Philip? Was he the one slain? I've heard nothing of this."

"Nay. Your brother is well."

"More's the pity," Sir John's wife said under her breath. The knight heard, and glanced toward her, but did not display anger or even disagree with the comment.

"Then why have you come? If Philip is not killed, then he must be suspect. Why else would you be here?"

"Your brother is no more suspect than any man of Eynsham," I said. "I traveled here to speak to Sir Henry Whytyng. 'Tis his son, John, who was slain."

"The novice?"

"Aye. You knew him?"

"Not well. His mother was Margaret, of whom you spoke."

"When the lass rejected Philip's suit, did he then choose the monastery, or had he considered a vocation before?"

"Never heard him speak of it 'till after Margaret wed Sir Henry. Margaret wasn't the only maid to turn from his suit."

"There was Emmaline Maunder," the woman said. "She'd have had him."

"A butcher's daughter?" Sir John said.

"He's a butcher's looks," she said sharply.

"Aye, I grant you his looks."

"He chose life as a monk, then, because no lass would have him?" I said.

"No lass with prospects. He'd no land, so wanted to find a maid with no brother, or a widow."

"But none would have him?"

"None were so desperate as to consider him," the woman said. "There are worse things than being a spinster. Being wed to Philip would be one of them."

Again I saw no objection in Sir John's face.

"Wasn't only his looks," the woman continued. "Folks as knew Philip couldn't abide his notions."

"Sir Henry said that Philip could be irascible," I said.

"Hah. Wasn't just that. He would tell folk that..."

"Enough!" Sir John said sharply. His abrupt interjection caused his wife to immediately fall silent. He had seemingly agreed with her earlier comments critical of his brother, but now a scowl furrowed his brow. What more than churlishness and an uncomely face had made Philip repugnant? Were those two not enough? What was it he would tell folk which Sir John did not want me to know? Whatever this matter was, I was not likely to discover it from Sir John. His face was hard, his lips thin, and his wife silent, staring now at the floor in reaction to his command.

"For all his faults, Philip is my brother," the knight said. "I'll hear no more of this."

These words were directed to his wife, but the knight then turned to me. "You'll have learned from Sir Henry that Philip and I have a troubled past. That's well known. 'Tis more of his doing than my own. Philip has a troubled past with most who've known him long. But if you believe he'd do murder of John Whytyng to avenge himself of Sir Henry, you are much mistaken. That is what you think, is it not? Why else come here to learn of him?"

I made no reply. None was required.

"I thank you for dealing with this," Sir John said, looking to his injured arm. "How much is owed?"

"Four pence," I replied, "The reeds must remain until Candlemas. You must resist the urge to remove them sooner, else the break may not knit properly."

Sir John nodded to his wife, and she left the chamber. I heard her open and close a chest in the next room, and a moment later she reappeared with four silver pennies which she dropped into my palm. The journey to Wantage had not been a complete waste, although I had learned little enough about the murder of a novice.

Arthur had stood silently against a wall while Sir John, his wife, and I had made conversation. He had watched and listened, and I knew that when on the road to Eynsham he would deliver his opinion of the matter.

We bid Sir John "Good day", mounted the palfreys, and set out for Eynsham. The day was yet young, and I had hope that we might arrive at the abbey before dark if we kept our beasts to a good pace.

I was sure that Arthur was full to bursting with opinions, so held my tongue and awaited his views. We were but a few paces past the village church when he began to unburden himself.

"Odd how we come to Cumnor just in time for you to patch up that Mallory fella after he got himself carved up, an' now we call on Sir John just when his horse kicks 'im. A coincidence, that is."

"Bailiffs," I replied, and not for the first time, "do not believe in coincidence. There is a pattern here. Who has made it I cannot tell. Perhaps the Lord Christ."

"Givin' you hints, like, an' waitin' for you to puzzle 'em out?"

"Aye, perhaps, have I the wit, and if you provide me with good counsel."

"Me?"

"Aye. What do you think of our visit to Sir John Thorpe?"

"Shut 'is wife up sudden enough, didn't 'e?"

"He did."

"Wonder what else she was about to say? What was it Prior Philip told folks that Sir John didn't want you to hear?"

"Whatever it was," I replied, "it surely reflected poorly upon the prior, else Sir John would not have silenced her so."

"Couldn't 'ave had to do with the novice's murder," Arthur said thoughtfully. "They didn't know of it 'till you told 'em."

"So therefore what the woman was about to say was of no value to me in finding a murderer?"

"Aye," Arthur agreed. "Likely."

Once again I wrapped my liripipe about my neck and up to my nose as we passed through East Hanney. In the distance I saw Sir John Trillowe's manor, but no man was visible about the place and we passed without incident.

Chapter 11

We entered the abbey precincts before dark, hungry and saddle sore, and led our beasts to the abbey stables. Two lay brothers greeted us there. One saw to our palfreys but the other hastened away as if upon some pressing duty.

Arthur and I set out for the guest house, hoping for a substantial supper to quiet our growling stomachs. There are no inns on the way between Wantage and Eynsham. We were between stables and kitchen when four men appeared from beyond the abbot's lodging. They were not monks nor lay brothers, and I had not before seen them about the abbey or village. I paid them no heed. Not until they broke into a run and did not slow until they had placed themselves across our path. One of these stepped toward me, a hand upon the hilt of his dagger. He was not smiling. Neither was I. This seemed a most unwelcome reception for weary travelers.

"You are Hugh de Singleton?" their leader asked.

"I am. Who are you?"

"Fulk Wilcoxon. You are to come with me."

"Can it not wait 'till I've had my supper? Where am I to go?"

"M'lord Archdeacon demands your presence. Now."

To be called before an archdeacon could mean no good thing. Rather like a tenant being called before a bailiff.

"The archdeacon awaits you in the abbot's chamber. Come."

The archdeacon's servant turned toward the abbot's chamber and I followed. Arthur did also, but another of the archdeacon's men said, "Not you," and blocked the way.

Arthur's bland expression became a frown, and he glared at the men who barred his path. The archdeacon had not chosen his servants for their pious or scholarly attributes. They were each as brawny as Arthur. I have known Arthur for many years. I understand his thoughts. He was surely considering what chance he and I together might have of overpowering the four men and making an escape, for he understood as well as I that a peremptory summons to appear before an archdeacon could portend much inconvenience.

I caught Arthur's eye and shook my head. I saw him bite his tongue but he made no move to interfere with the archdeacon's minions. This was for the best. We surely would have been overpowered, and matters might then have not concluded so well as they did.

The four servants surrounded me, as if fearing that I might bolt for the abbey gatehouse – a thought which did cross my mind. We left a perplexed Arthur standing near the abbey kitchen, and a few moments later I entered the abbot's chamber. My four companions stopped at the chamber door.

Abbot Thurstan lay upon his bed, yet alive. But not for long. There was little movement of the blankets as his chest rose and fell in the shallow breaths of a man nearing death.

Three other men occupied the chamber. The archdeacon stood in the center of the room with his arms folded across his chest. I noticed that his formerly mud-spattered cassock was clean. Odd, the things one perceives when the mind should be concentrated upon other matters.

Brother Guibert stood at the foot of Abbot Thurstan's bed. I supposed that he was present because of the abbot's precarious grip on life. There was also a black-robed priest in the chamber. He had been sitting upon a bench when I entered but stood and stepped close to the archdeacon when I passed through the doorway.

From the time the archdeacon's servants accosted me, until I stood before the prelate, I assumed the summons had to do with the abbot's warning that Prior Philip wished me gone from the abbey. I had spent the moments before entering the abbot's chamber considering how I would defend my investigation. I wanted to discover a murderer, to see justice done, and to possess my own Bible.

When in the past I had questioned folk about felonies, I had found it productive to stand while the person I interrogated was seated. The archdeacon was familiar with this ploy. He pointed to a bench drawn to the center of the chamber and said, "Sit." Had I known what was to come I might have ignored the command.

As I sat I looked to Abbot Thurstan. His brow was furrowed, and when he saw me glance in his direction he shook his head upon the pillow. No other in the chamber saw this, as infirmarer, priest, and archdeacon were intent upon me. I could not interpret the abbot's silent message, but its import became clear soon enough.

I sat, but the archdeacon neither moved nor spoke. Here was another stratagem I had used to discomfit men I had questioned. The practice is remarkably effective.

"You stand accused of heresy," the archdeacon finally said. Actually, I was seated, but here was no time to point out the error. Heresy? Was this how Prior Philip intended to be rid of me? If a bishop's court found me guilty the scheme would be effective, for I might hang.

"What heresy?" I replied. "Who says so?"

The archdeacon looked to Brother Guibert and said, "Tell again what you heard this fellow say to Abbot Thurstan."

Then I remembered that the infirmarer had entered the chamber as I was explaining to Abbot Thurstan why he need not fear purgatory.

"I was bringing wine with soothing herbs to M'lord Abbot when I heard this fellow say there is no purgatory, for we are holy and righteous and need not be purged of our sins."

The archdeacon, his arms yet crossed, turned from Brother Guibert to me. His expression mingled haughtiness and anger, a combination which is often to be found upon the face of an archdeacon. Or on the face of a bailiff, for that matter.

"What have you to say of this charge?" the archdeacon demanded, in a tone which assured all present that no defense was conceivable. As he spoke I saw from the corner of my eye a fifth man enter the room. 'Twas Prior Philip. A trace of a smile curled his lips but did little to improve his appearance.

I decided to stand. I thought for a moment that the archdeacon might push me back upon the bench. Indeed, he took a step toward me, but if that was his intent he thought better of it. He could easily have done so. Heresy is serious enough; to forcibly resist the Bishop of Lincoln's representative would considerably deepen the pit I was in.

Standing, I was the tallest man in the chamber and could look down my nose at the archdeacon. "M'lord Abbot is near death," I said. "This he knows. I recited verses from the Bible that some time past I committed to memory, which I thought might console him as the time approaches for him to meet the Lord Christ."

"The devil knows and can quote Scripture," the archdeacon said. "So we are told in Holy Writ. What are these verses you spoke to comfort Abbot Thurstan?"

I quoted from the apostle's letter to the Colossians: "'Now He has reconciled in the body of His flesh through death, to present you holy, and blameless, and irreproachable in His sight – if indeed you continue in the faith.' These words of St. Paul I thought would ease the abbot's mind. If our Lord Christ presents a man holy and blameless he will have little to fear of purgatory."

"Bah… you presume to lecture me about Holy Writ? 'Tis for Holy Mother Church to say what is true of purgatory, not some bailiff who pretends to be a scholar."

"I offered no interpretation of the scripture," I replied. "I but spoke what the apostle wrote. Abbot Thurstan may decide its import for himself."

The archdeacon looked to Brother Guibert. "Is this so?" he asked.

"He said to Brother Abbot that he should believe the apostle when he writes that Christian men are cleansed from all unrighteousness. 'Why must you be purged of sin in purgatory,' he said, 'when the Lord Christ has taken away all unrighteousness?'"

"Anything else?" the archdeacon said.

"Aye. I remember it well," Brother Guibert said. "'Twas so repugnant to Holy Mother Church. 'If the Lord Christ has made you holy and blameless,' he said, 'why would He condemn you to purgatory?'"

131

Prior Philip and the archdeacon exchanged triumphant glances. "'Tis enough," the archdeacon said. "I will take this heretical fellow with me on the morrow when I return to Lincoln. Put him in the abbey cell for the night."

Perhaps I should have fled. I could have easily outrun the others in the chamber. But where would I have gone? If I sought refuge in Bampton the archdeacon's servants would be at Galen House's door within a day.

Prior Philip and Brother Guibert each took an elbow and I was led from the abbot's chamber. I did not know where the abbey cell was to be found, but learned soon enough. My gaolers led me to the infirmary, where Brother Guibert opened a door and thrust me through it.

This door had, I think, seen little use, for its hinges squealed loudly as it was slammed shut behind me. I heard a bar fall into place a moment later.

I found myself in a small closet which, I believe, was originally intended as a chamber for the storage of the infirmarer's supplies, but now served to incarcerate monks who had violated one or another of the ordinances. The walls of this cell were of stone, there was no window, and shelves, unused, were fastened to one wall. The only light came through a small opening in the door, about the size of my palm. If I lay down flat, which I did not wish to do as the straw upon the floor was moldy, I could touch one end of the cell with my toes while my head rubbed against the other.

I have been imprisoned before. My employer, Lord Gilbert Talbot, had learned of it and promptly demanded my release. But he was now far away, at Goodrich Castle. Could Arthur tell him of my plight before the bishop's court at Lincoln could act? And would Lord Gilbert confront the bishop on my behalf? 'Tis one thing to obstruct a corrupt justice of the peace. 'Tis another to oppose a bishop.

I resigned myself to this temporary abode and cast my thoughts forward to the morrow. Surely I would not be required to walk to Lincoln? Perhaps my palfrey could gallop fast enough that I could escape the archdeacon and his servants. But not likely.

My stomach had been empty and growling for several hours. I hoped that a loaf and a cup of ale might soon appear through the small opening in the door. Also not likely.

The faint illumination of my prison soon faded. The infirmary had but one window, so even on a bright day little light would enter this cell. I heard the infirmarer going about his business, having returned from vespers, and called out that I was hungry and thirsty. He made no reply, which I thought inhospitable of him.

Shortly after, the infirmary became silent. I was cold, hungry, and abandoned. Was I really a heretic? If so, perhaps I deserved this chastisement. But what, then, of the apostle's words? Could something which seemed so plain be so liable to error that I could misconstrue its meaning?

These thoughts were interrupted by the sound of the infirmary door opening and closing. A moment later the light of a cresset flickered outside my cell and the small opening in the door darkened as a shadow passed before it.

"Here," Brother Guibert said. "Take this."

A loaf appeared in the opening, and after I took it a small cup of ale also materialized. The infirmarer was not devoid of pity.

I could not stand all the night, so after consuming my supper I sat in the filthy straw and tried to sleep. Is there a more helpless feeling than to be locked in a cell? I have been twice in such a place. Sleep eluded me. I thought rather of escape but no plan came to me. I hoped that Arthur knew of my plight and would have the wit to act where I could not. I could not know of what work was at that moment being done for my release, but soon learned of it.

After I was taken from the abbot's chamber Abbot Thurstan had called for his clerk. He sent Brother Theodore to fetch Brother Gerleys, and when the novice-master appeared, the abbot told him of what had happened. Both men knew where

I had been taken, and what might befall me in Lincoln. This they resolved must not happen, and devised a plan to set me free.

Arthur, meanwhile, had gone to the guest house, where the lay brother who attended us brought him a bowl of pottage. There he waited for me, assuming that when my interview with the archdeacon was finished I would appear. He became increasingly fretful as dusk approached, the bell rang to call the monks to vespers, yet I did not return.

Well after compline, when the abbey was dark and quiet and Arthur sat upon his pallet, vexed in spirit, he heard the door to our guest house chamber open. He thought 'twas me, but it was Brother Gerleys whose face he saw in the glow of the cresset the novice-master carried.

I was drowsing when the sound of the bar being lifted startled me to wakefulness. Many thoughts flung themselves through my mind in that instant. Indeed, for a moment I could not recall where I was or why I was there. But the squealing hinges as the closet door was opened brought me to my senses. I thought it must be that the archdeacon intended an early start for Lincoln and had sent his servants to fetch me. I had no idea of how long I might have slept or what hour of the night it might be.

The infirmary was dark and the cell was darker. "Master Hugh?" the monk whispered, knowing that I was within but invisible to him. Brother Gerleys had extinguished his cresset so as to avoid being seen in the night.

"I am here," I said.

"'Tis Brother Gerleys and Arthur, come to free you of this place and take you to a better. Come."

I left the cell and heard Arthur close the door and bar it behind me. There would be consternation in the morning when the cell was found secure but empty, I thought.

"Follow me," Brother Gerleys said softly.

This was not an easy thing to do. I was not familiar with this part of the abbey, and there was little light to see by, a sliver of moon just then beginning to rise above the village to the east.

I stumbled along in the dark, Brother Gerleys before me, Arthur behind, and he also unsure of his path. We soon came to the cloister, where I was more sure of myself, and then the novices' chamber, which I knew well.

Like most Benedictine houses, the novices' chamber at Eynsham Abbey is heated. A few embers upon the hearth helped to illuminate the chamber, and in the gloom I saw Brother Gerleys put a finger to his lips, urging silence as we crept quietly through the doorway.

I heard Osbert and Henry breathing deeply in sleep. Brother Gerleys led the way past their cots to a far corner of the chamber. I saw him bend to the floor and stand with an object in his hands which I could not identify. It was, I soon discovered, a ladder. He propped this against the stones of the chamber wall and silently ascended to the ceiling. I saw his shadowy form approach the ceiling – no vaulting here – and watched as he pushed against the planks which roofed the novices' chamber. A section of the ceiling yielded to Brother Gerleys, and in a moment I saw a dark cavity appear, black against the grey of the chamber ceiling.

Brother Gerleys descended the ladder and whispered, "There has been little time to prepare the space for you, but above our heads is a place where you may be hid 'till the archdeacon is away."

"You are placing yourself at risk," I replied.

"At Abbot Thurstan's request."

"When the archdeacon finds the infirmarer's cell empty will he not search for me in such places?"

"The ladder will be hid before morn, and the opening is concealed when the boards are replaced, which you must do when you ascend the ladder. The upper loft is quite dark, but you will find a pallet where you may sleep. A dormer with a skin window allows light in the day."

"When I am discovered missing come dawn, and the archdeacon and Prior Philip do not find me at the abbey, they will send men to Bampton, assuming I have fled to the safety of Bampton Castle. They will question my wife sharply, and she will worry. Arthur, you must travel to Bampton at first light and tell Kate what has happened. She and Bessie and Agnes must flee to the castle. When I am not discovered at Galen House the archdeacon might seize Kate and demand my appearance in return for her release. He is not likely to try to pluck her from the castle and so raise Lord Gilbert's ire, I think."

This conversation was conducted in low whispers, yet was perhaps loud enough to disturb either Osbert or Henry, for we heard one of the novices turn upon his cot and draw his blanket up about him.

We three stood frozen and silent for some time, then Arthur whispered in my ear, "Shall I return to the abbey, or remain with mistress Kate?"

"Stay in Bampton until the archdeacon's men have come and gone. 'Tis sure they will seek me there. They may not be far behind you when you travel tomorrow. When they leave Bampton return to the abbey. You must be my eyes and ears while I am shut up here, if we are to find a felon.

"Return now to the guest house. Leave the abbey at first light, before the archdeacon discovers me missing, else he may detain you, thinking you can lead him to me."

Arthur padded silently across the flags and disappeared through the door of the novices' chamber.

"Up you go," Brother Gerleys whispered, and grasped the ladder to steady it for my ascent. I obeyed, crawled through the black hole into my lair, and felt about in the dark for the boards which had been fastened together, forming a trapdoor, to conceal the opening. When I found them I was careful to replace the panel silently, then in utter darkness found the pallet Brother Gerleys had provided and sought rest. 'Twas a great improvement over the stinking straw of the infirmarer's cell. But I was a prisoner yet.

Chapter 12

The skin of the dormer window glowed faintly when I awoke, and provided enough light that I could inspect my surroundings. The attic was mostly bare. I saw an unlit cresset, and a chamber pot which Brother Gerleys had thoughtfully provided and then forgotten to mention. And there was the pallet.

I lay awake, watching the small enclosure grow brighter, and soon heard voices below me. The novices had awakened. Although monks do not break their fast, novices in Benedictine houses are permitted a loaf, and as I lay listening, trying to hear the youthful conversation, I heard their chamber door open.

I thought it likely that a lay brother assigned to the kitchen had brought loaves, but not so. The sound of latch and squeaking hinges was followed by excited voices, one of which I readily identified. 'Twas Prior Philip.

The prior was so overwrought that I could at first make nothing of his outburst. But I knew what it must portend.

"Gone!" the prior seethed. "Cell door closed, door barred. Only a devil could escape. A heretic in league with the devil."

"All know you were his friend," Prior Philip continued, speaking, I assumed, to Brother Gerleys, who must have accompanied him to the novices' chamber. "Has he come to you to flee the bishop's justice?"

"Master Hugh? Here? Look about you. Where could he be? There is a small chest against yon wall, but surely too small to hide a man. Where else in the chamber might he be? You and the archdeacon's men may search where you will."

"You've not seen the fellow this night, then?"

"Nay. If he escaped the infirmarer's cell you'll not find him here."

I heard Prior Philip snort in disgust. "If you see him, or learn of where he might be, tell me straightaway."

The chamber door slammed shut, then but a few heartbeats later opened again. Another conversation, more muted, followed. The novices' loaves had arrived. Silence followed while the novices ate, then I heard Brother Gerleys assign tasks for the day. Henry was to attend the monks in the scriptorium, making ink, lining parchments, and perhaps trying his hand at copying some insignificant manuscript. Osbert was to seek the kitchener, a pleasant duty on such a chill day, to stir a pot over a fire or do some other menial chore to help prepare the monks' dinner.

Shortly after the novices set off for their work I heard the ladder scrape against the stone wall below my feet. Where, I wondered, had the novice-master hidden the thing, that it was not visible to Prior Philip, yet so ready to hand when needed?

I watched the trap door and saw it rise. I assisted Brother Gerleys in lifting it and shoved it aside. His face appeared in the opening.

"Come down," he said. "I've saved back a part of a loaf for you."

The ladder did not reach to the ceiling. It was barely as long as I am tall, so descending from the attic meant hanging from the planks upon one's elbows and feeling about with a toe for the top rung of the ladder.

When my feet were safely upon the flags I watched as Brother Gerleys took the ladder and fitted it under the table, where it slid into hidden supports. The novice-master saw my surprise and explained.

"Don't know who built this. Brother Matthias, who was novice-master before me, said his predecessor told him the ladder was there before he came to the office. Probably made during some time of unrest, when 'twas thought good to have a hiding place. If a tall man reaches from the attic he can grasp the top rung of the ladder and pull it up after him."

There was a matter troubling me, and I spoke of it to Brother Gerleys. "You have imperiled your soul for me," I said.

Brother Gerleys looked at me quizzically. "How so?" he said.

"You lied to Prior Philip, your superior, when he asked of me."

"Not so," he chuckled. "When Brother Prior asked if you had come to me I said only that he should look about and see if there was anyplace in the chamber where you might be hid. I did not say that you were not here."

"You intended to deceive him."

"Aye, and did so."

"He asked if you had seen me last night," I said.

"So he did. Well... 'twas dark last night and a man could see little. I saw the shape of a man. Could have been you, I suppose. And when I told him that he'd not find you here, that was no lie either, for he will not, if we are careful.

"And even if I did lie to save you from the archdeacon, there is precedent for it in Holy Bible."

My expression upon hearing this must have been of skepticism, because Brother Gerleys explained himself.

"Have you not read in Exodus of the Hebrew midwives? Surely you know the tale, you being a scholar."

I did, but before I could answer, the novice-master reminded me of it.

"Pharaoh told the midwives to kill the male babes born to Hebrew slave women. Only the lasses were to live. The midwives disobeyed, and when the king learned of their disobedience he demanded of them why they had violated his command.

"They replied that the Hebrew women gave birth so rapidly that their services were not needed. 'Twas a lie, of course, but told to deflect evil and injustice. The Lord God did not punish the midwives for telling this fable, but rather rewarded them, so Holy Writ does say.

"Prior Philip and the archdeacon intend an injustice, and I have chosen to obstruct their designs. I know what you said to Abbot Thurstan."

"You do not think me a heretic for such thoughts?"

"Don't know. May be, may not be. I am uncertain of the matter. Surely if what you said to Abbot Thurstan is true, there

139

will be much hardship for this house and others and the chapels where priests pray for men's souls. Who will give us lands and shillings to pray for their souls if there is no purgatory from which they seek release? But should a man die for thinking such a thing? I cannot believe it should be so."

"I must be more careful in the future," I said, "about quoting objectionable scriptures."

"Most men can find something offensive in Holy Writ," Brother Gerleys said, "when the words conflict with their opinions. Will you cease now the search for John Whytyng's murderer?"

"I told Arthur to return as soon as he is sure that Kate and Bessie are secure in Bampton Castle, and the archdeacon's men have gone. I need to find a way to tell Abbot Thurstan that I am safe and will continue to seek the felon. No one else must know. Other monks must believe that I have fled and that Arthur has inherited the duty to find a killer."

"Prior Philip will object. He did not want you, a bailiff, to prowl about the abbey. He will surely oppose a groom doing so."

"We must pray that Abbot Thurstan lives long enough that the felon can be discovered."

Brother Gerleys withdrew the ladder from its hiding place and told me to climb to the attic again while he sought Abbot Thurstan to tell him of my escape from the archdeacon. When he returned he had much news.

The novice-master called out to me to move the trap door aside so that we might speak softly and yet hear each other. I did so, and looked down from my perch upon his tonsured head.

"M'lord Abbot is near death, I think. His breathing is shallow and sounds like a joiner passing a rasp across a plank. I told him you were safe hid, but he would not have me tell him where you are. Said he feared he might divulge the place in a fit of delirium.

"He is determined to stay alive until you have found John's killer. He knows that Prior Philip will dismiss Arthur if he gains control of abbey affairs. The archdeacon departed for Lincoln soon after dawn, informing Abbot Thurstan that he would advise Bishop Bokyngham that the abbey is badly governed. M'lord Abbot will care little for that. The bishop cannot remove an abbot whom the Lord Christ has already called to His bosom.

"Arthur also departed at dawn, and 'tis well he did so. Prior Philip has sent four lay brothers to Bampton, as you suspected he would, to seek you. Arthur is no more than an hour ahead of them.

"The almoner, Brother Jocelyn, is a friend. When he collects unconsumed food in the refectory after dinner he will leave a portion in a corner of the cloister before he sends the leavings to the porter to give to the poor. I will gather what he leaves and bring it to you."

I did not wish to be the cause of a poor man going hungry, but if I was not to starve saw no better way for the provision of a meal. I thanked Brother Gerleys for his work, and asked a question.

"Does Prior Philip own a fur-lined coat?"

Brother Gerleys rubbed his neck, which was likely growing sore from peering up at me. "Aye. M'lord Abbot does, and Prior Philip's not a man to cherish the cold so as to discipline his body and mind. Why do you ask?"

"I'll tell you anon, if it proves important."

"You traveled to Wantage. John Whytyng's father lives near there, as does Prior Philip's brother. Now you ask of the prior's coat. Do you suspect Brother Prior in this death?"

Brother Gerleys is no fool. "I suspect all men," I replied.

"Even me?"

"Not much. But 'tis best to assume all men capable of murder, and then dismiss those who could not, or would not, do such a felony."

"How will you continue your search while hidden away in the attic?"

"I must think on this. Perhaps, by the time Arthur returns, I will have devised some way to proceed."

Brother Gerleys promised to return with my dinner when he could. I slid the trap door into place and reclined upon the pallet to consider my plight, and how I would overcome it to discover John Whytyng's killer. When Brother Gerleys appeared with my meal I had no plan, but as the skin of the dormer window darkened, a procedure took form in my mind. But it could not be accomplished from the attic above the novices' chamber.

Osbert and Henry returned while the dormer skin yet glowed with fading light. I was careful to move about cautiously so as not to elicit a creak from the planks of my refuge. I would have liked to light the cresset, but Brother Gerleys, while thoughtful enough to provide the lamp, had not supplied flint and steel with which to strike a flame. This was just as well. The sound of flint against steel might be heard by lads with keen ears, and when the novices' chamber grew dark any crack between the attic planks might allow a gleam of light where none should be, which would give away my presence.

If the novices knew I was hidden above them, would they give me up to Prior Philip? Who could know? They had surely learned of my heresy and escape. But if they discovered my presence and held their tongues they would be complicit, with Brother Gerleys, in the ruse, and would suffer with him the consequences of harboring a heretic if I was discovered. I did not want to think on what those consequences must be.

Did I snore? What man knows if he does or not, unless his wife tells him? Kate has never complained of this, but perhaps she is being kind. A man might toss upon his pallet, cough and wheeze and snore, and know nothing of it, being asleep.

Lads like Osbert and Henry sleep soundly, too youthful to lay awake troubled by conscience or calamity. But certainly if Arthur was snoring above them his thunderous snorts would jolt them awake. Did I do the same in my sleep? Could I remain in the attic and risk discovery and Brother Gerleys' safety?

While I considered these things I heard muted conversation below me. A lay brother had brought bowls of simple pottage for the novices and I had been so deep in thought that I had not heard him open the chamber door. There were indistinct comments about the day's labor and the quality of the ale, which, as I have written, was dreadful.

I heard Brother Gerleys at the wood box, and a moment later heard him tending the chamber fire. Then all became silent as novice-master and pupils departed for compline. When they returned I must somehow attract Brother Gerleys' attention without the novices knowing of it.

I thought briefly of opening the trap door, dropping to the floor, withdrawing the ladder from its slot under the table, replacing the trap door, and then departing for some other hiding place. For three reasons I gave up the idea.

If Brother Gerleys sought me in the attic and did not find me he would likely believe that I had been discovered and taken. He would be affrighted of his safety, for harboring a heretic.

I could do little to discover John Whytyng's murderer alone, while a fugitive. I needed the aid of others, and more even than Arthur I now needed Brother Gerleys.

And if I left the attic, where would I go? I did not know the abbey well, the hidden places found in all such ancient structures. If I could not stay above the sleeping novices there might be other safe locations where I might be hidden. Brother Gerleys would know of these; I would not. I lay upon the pallet and awaited his return.

Monks do not linger in church or cloister after compline, especially on cold November evenings, but seek the dormitory and warm beds. So Brother Gerleys and the novices came straightaway from the church when the office was done. I heard Osbert and Henry bid each other "Good night," and heard Brother Gerleys do the same as he departed for his own sleeping chamber.

An hour or more passed as I considered how I might attract the novice-master's attention without alerting the lads to my presence. I did not need to. I heard the ladder slide from its place under the table and understood that Brother Gerleys' face would soon be at the trap door. Even if in the darkness I could not see it.

A light tap upon the planks told me that Brother Gerleys had ascended the ladder. As quietly as I could I lifted the door and moved it aside. The wood the novice-master had placed upon the hearth before compline had burned down to embers. Only coals glowed there, providing just enough light to see the monk's pale face peering up at me.

"Come down," he whispered. "Replace the boards as you do."

My toes found the top rung of the ladder and I cautiously felt my way down the frail apparatus. When I stood upon the flags Brother Gerleys carefully and silently slid the ladder under the table, then stood silently before me and with an index finger beckoned me to follow. He led me to the chamber door, opened it carefully, motioned me to pass through, then followed. He drew the door closed slowly and when it was shut took my elbow and guided me toward the cloister.

An abbey cloister is a place of silence and meditation, but this night it became a place of whispered conversation and conspiracy.

"Will not the explorators discover us here?" I asked when we were seated in a dark shadow.

"Nay. Your cotehardie is grey and I am all in black. And the cloister is the first place they visit on their rounds. They will have passed through here long since, and will not return 'till after vigils."

"I cannot remain above the novices' chamber," I said.

"I agree. 'Twas the only place which came to mind yesterday, and has served while I found a better. But 'tis too dangerous for Osbert and Henry. If they guess you are in the attic it will place too great a weight upon them... whether or not to keep our secret and put at risk their future at Eynsham Abbey."

"You have found a better place for me?"

"Aye. Well, Abbot Thurstan has. I am to take you there. He has changed his mind, and now wishes to know you safe."

"Where is this refuge?"

"M'lord Abbot has a prayer closet off his chamber, where he seeks solitude for prayer and meditation and permits no other to enter. You are to be hid there."

"Will not Prior Philip and the infirmarer be with Abbot Thurstan?"

"Brother Guibert will visit the abbot, but not Prior Philip."

"Not the prior? Why not?"

"Abbot Thurstan intends to send him away on abbey business."

"What business? Did he say?"

"Nay. Said he would tell us this night, when he had thought it through. Remain here, in the shadows, while I go to the abbot's chamber and see if he is alone. You cannot go there if Brother Theodore or Brother Guibert sits with him."

I was chilled to the bone and thought longingly of the warm novices' chamber. But I did not sit alone in the cloister for long. "Come," Brother Gerleys whispered from the shadows. "M'lord Abbot has sent all others away, but Brother Guibert will visit him before vigils."

We walked silently, carefully, to the abbot's chamber. A cresset was kept lighted upon a stand so that those who came to the chamber in the night could see to be about the matter of providing succor to the dying abbot.

Abbot Thurstan lifted his head from his pillow when our shadows passed between him and the cresset. "Ah, you are come. I did not hear the door open. Must have dozed off. Draw that bench close and sit. We have much to discuss.

"Brother Theodore," he continued, "would sit with me through the night, but I sent him to his bed with a demand that he sleep. He is of no service to me as exhausted as he has become. And he must not guess that you are here."

This speech so taxed the abbot that his head fell back upon his pillow. His eyes closed, and I feared that he might have swooned, but after a moment he spoke again. I was required to lean close to the frail old man, so weak was his voice.

"On the morrow I will send a letter to Bishop Bokyngham. Brother Theodore will write it for me, and I will swear him to silence about its subject. I intend to tell M'lord Bishop that it is my wish that Brother Gerleys follow me as abbot of t his house, if the monks here do willingly choose, as I believe they will.

"I intend to send Prior Philip to Lincoln with the letter, explaining to M'lord Bishop that I did not send it with the archdeacon because I did not yet know my own mind when the archdeacon departed Eynsham."

"Prior Philip will not be pleased to be sent away," I said. "He would rather remain here and seek me, I think."

"Brother Prior will be pleased to travel to Lincoln. I will tell him that my letter concerns him and the future of the abbey. This will be no lie. He desires to be abbot. Prior Philip will believe that the letter nominates him for the office. But I will tell Bishop Bokyngham that he is unsuited for the post, and I will tell him why... that he sent me sprawling down the stairs, thinking to advance to my place in such a manner."

Neither Abbot Thurstan, nor I, nor Brother Gerleys knew yet all of the reasons why the prior was unfitted to be raised to the abbacy.

Brother Gerleys did not speak while the abbot and I conversed. But when we fell silent, he spoke. "'Tis an honor I do not seek," he said.

"And 'tis why, therefore, you are more suited for preferment than Prior Philip. Now, I am weary, and 'tis nearing time for vigils, I think." To Brother Gerleys the abbot said, "Show Master Hugh to my prayer closet. Did you put a pallet and blanket there for him?"

"Aye," the novice-master replied.

I stood and moved the bench away from the bed, so no man would suspect that a visitor had recently sat close to the abbot, then followed Brother Gerleys to a dim corner of the chamber where I saw the dark outline of a door against the grey stone wall.

A glass window in the east wall of the closet allowed some starlight into the space. Enough that I could see the small altar where Abbot Thurstan had knelt in his prayers, and the pallet which would be my bed for the next week. Prior Philip might reach Lincoln in three days of hard travel, but the prior did not seem to me a man who would press on through hardship and roads gone to mud. Four days, then, to Lincoln, four days to return, and a day with the bishop. I would have one more week to find a felon, perhaps a day or two more. If Bishop Bokyngham told the prior what Abbot Thurstan's letter said, Prior Philip might hasten his return so to vent his anger upon the abbot. If Abbot Thurstan yet lived. One week was all I could be sure of.

About a week I had, then, to discover who had slain John Whytyng. Prior Philip had cause, due to his resentment of the novice's mother choosing another husband, and had opportunity. Perhaps he had seen the lad slip from the abbey grounds one night after vigils as he walked the abbey in his capacity as explorator. And he owned a fur coat, from which a tuft might be missing.

Sir Thomas was smitten with Maude atte Pond, and had displayed a violent dislike of competition for the maid's hand. But he was left-handed, and John Whytyng's wounds seemed more likely delivered by a right-handed man.

Simon atte Pond wished his daughter to wed a knight, thereby improving her station. Would he slay John Whytyng to prevent the unraveling of his plans? Whatever those plans might be. Maude said that the voice that she heard the night John Whytyng was slain was not her father's. Would she say so to save him from the gallows?

Or would Maude protect her mother by claiming to have heard a man's voice in the night? Alyce atte Pond was a formidable woman, clearly ready to use violence to advance her designs. And 'tis sure her plans for Maude did not include a novice of Eynsham Abbey.

Osbern Mallory said that he had forsaken pursuit of Maude atte Pond. Did he speak true? Or did Sir Thomas attack the yeoman because he knew of the man's continuing suit for Maude?

Ralph Bigge was said to have an interest in Maude and the lands of her father which would come to her. I must discover some way to meet and take stock of the fellow.

And the ale-house keeper had hinted that Sir Thomas's older brother, Sir Geoffrey, was not so devoted to his wife as he ought to be. How could I learn if this was so, and if it was, if the knight had opportunity to slay John Whytyng?

I lay upon the pallet considering these matters when I heard the door to Abbot Thurstan's chamber open, and Brother Guibert announce his entry.

The abbot must have been asleep. I heard the infirmarer whisper the abbot's name, but could detect no response. Shortly after, I heard the bench creak as Brother Guibert sat himself upon it.

I worried that I might fall to sleep, and move or snore or in some other way make a sound which would announce my presence in the prayer closet. I did not worry thus for long, for in but a few minutes I heard the infirmarer snoring, his back, no doubt, against the wall where I had placed the bench. Certainly 'twas not Abbot Thurstan whose snoring I heard. The abbot could barely raise enough breath to whisper, much less rattle the windows.

The infirmarer's snoring ceased abruptly. The sacrist rang the bell for vigils and caused the slumbering monk to awaken. The pealing apparently awakened Abbot Thurstan as well, for I heard a muffled exchange of conversation before the abbot's chamber door opened and closed. When men order their lives by the ringing of a bell and the chanting of offices it must be that they measure the passage of time even in sleep.

I wrapped the blanket about me and dozed upon the pallet until I heard men enter the abbot's chamber. I could not tell how many men spoke at first, but soon identified Brother Guibert and Prior Philip among the group.

The infirmarer told Abbot Thurstan that he had wine with crushed hemp seeds to aid his sleep, and in my mind's eye I could see him place an arm under the aged abbot's head so as to raise him to drink from the cup.

The abbot's voice was too weak for me to understand his words, but I know what he said next because of the prior's reply.

"Why me? Send a lay brother."

Abbot Thurstan spoke again, and I heard the prior snort in reply. "Important as all that? To send me upon the roads in November when a lay brother could serve as well?"

There followed a long speech from Abbot Thurstan which I could not hear, but which must have convinced Prior Philip that delivering a letter to Bishop Bokyngham was in his best interest.

"I understand," the prior said. "If no other can be entrusted with the letter, then I will do as you wish."

The tone of the prior's voice did not indicate that he was pleased to acquiesce to the abbot's demand, but pleased or not, he would be upon a palfrey come daylight, on his way to Lincoln, with a letter in his pouch which would soon cause him great consternation. This brought me no sorrow, for I had taken a dislike to the man, even if he did not slay John Whytyng, which he may have done, and even if he did not thrust Abbot Thurstan down a flight of stairs, which he did.

I heard Brother Theodore promise to return after lauds. Abbot Thurstan must then have required all those in his chamber to retire for the remainder of the night, for I heard several voices protest that he must not be left alone. I do not know his reply, but an abbot is to be obeyed in his house. His chamber was soon silent, and I heard the door latch fall into place. I could sleep unworried about whether or not I might make some sound which would expose my hiding place.

Chapter 13

Dawn found me rested and eager to find a felon and depart Eynsham Abbey. I would have desired so even was I not required to hide from Prior Philip and his adherents. My Kate grew daily closer to the day of her deliverance. I began to rue the bargain I had made with Abbot Thurstan. Was a Bible worth all of this trouble?

The door to the abbot's chamber opened and closed, and I heard Brother Theodore greet his abbot. I could hear no response. Abbot Thurstan grew weaker each day.

I heard few of the abbot's words as he dictated the letter for Bishop Bokyngham to his clerk. He had said to me that he would explain to the bishop why Prior Philip was not suited to become abbot. I would have liked to know all of that information. Perhaps, I thought, there would be some time while I was alone with Abbot Thurstan when I might ask him. I thought it likely that his objection to the prior's elevation had to do with more than the prior casting him down a flight of stairs.

The letter was not long, for Abbot Thurstan soon fell silent and I heard Brother Theodore moving about in the chamber, no doubt finding wax and the abbot's seal. Shortly after I heard the chamber door open and close again, and the place again became silent. The letter was on its way to Prior Philip, and thence to Lincoln.

I sat upon the pallet and chewed upon my fingernails. I needed Arthur. The longer he took to return from Bampton the more likely, it seemed to me, that he had been delayed because of trouble with men sent to Bampton to seek me. I imagined the villainous things that evil men might do to Kate, and to Arthur could they subdue him, to pry from them my whereabouts. Speculation can be worse than fact.

Someone, likely a lay brother, brought Abbot Thurstan a loaf, and soon after the fellow left the chamber I heard the sacrist ring the church bell for terce. I thought it likely that the abbot would have visitors when the office was done, and was soon proved correct. The chamber door opened, and next I heard Brother Gerleys and Brother Guibert greet the abbot.

I was developing the skill of gaining the sense of a conversation by listening to only one side of it. Abbot Thurstan must have asked the infirmarer of the health of other monks, for Brother Guibert named three who suffered afflictions. The abbot must then have told him to see to their complaints, for the infirmarer said, "I will do so, and return after sext."

The abbot's chamber door opened and closed, and a moment later I heard a hand upon the latch to the door of my closet.

"Your man must have begun his return before dawn," Brother Gerleys said as he opened the door. "He is at the guest house, awaiting instruction."

"Can he come here without raising suspicion?"

"Aye. I have told Brother Guibert that Abbot Thurstan has charged him with concluding the matter of John Whytyng's murder, you having disappeared, and Prior Philip away on another matter, and Arthur privy to what you had discovered before you vanished. Silence is the rule for cloister and refectory, but there are other places where monks may exchange words. I know Brother Guibert. Every monk and lay brother will know of Arthur's commission before nones."

"Send Arthur to me. We have seven days to find a felon, perhaps a few more. Prior Philip will return in little more than a week in a foul mood and opportunity may then be lost."

"Aye... he'll be furious. I do not seek preferment, but better me as abbot of this house than Prior Philip."

Brother Gerleys left me with the promise that Arthur would soon appear, and it was so. I heard the chamber door open and close, but no man greeted the abbot. A moment later I heard Arthur's voice on the other side of the closet door.

"Master Hugh? 'Tis Arthur. You in there?"

I opened the closet door, bade Arthur enter, then closed

the door behind him lest some monk should enter the abbot's chamber unannounced.

"Kate is safe in the castle?" I asked.

"Aye, her an' Mistress Shortnekke. Wasn't much pleased to go, your Kate."

"She is well?"

"Aye. Not pleased that you've got yourself into trouble."

"I'm not pleased about that myself. We think much alike."

"Your Bessie has taken to Mistress Shortnekke, or mayhap 'tis the other way 'round. Whatever, they get on well. The midwife said Bessie was near the age her own lass would be, had the babe not died at birth."

"I was told that men set out from here soon after the infirmarer discovered that his cell was empty. Did they cause you trouble?"

"Not much. I told your Kate that she must not dally, but gather what she would an' hurry to the castle. She did so, an' I told Wilfred to raise the drawbridge once we was safe inside. Four of the abbey's lay brothers rode up not an hour later an' demanded entry.

"Your Kate went to the parapet and called out, asking what it was they sought.

"'Master Hugh de Singleton,' they said, 'bailiff of this manor.'

"Kate told 'em that you were in Eynsham, an' they replied 'twas not so, for they had just come from there and you were gone from the place.

"Kate told 'em that you had intended to travel to Oxford when you left Bampton, an' suggested they seek you there. Then she asked why they sought for you.

"Him what seemed leader of the lay brothers said that the Bishop of Lincoln wished conversation with you. Your Kate would have none of it, an' put the fellows off, so after an hour or so of parley the lay brothers gave up an' rode away.

"I was eager to return here, but Kate thought I should remain in the castle. The lay brothers had not seen me, but Kate said, 'What if these lay brothers come upon you on the road and recognize you? There are four of them, and if you meet on the road they may overpower you, take you to the prior, and he might then use threats against you to force Hugh to give himself up.' So I waited 'till this morn to return. The time at Bampton Castle was not misspent, though," he grinned.

"Since my Cicily perished I am in need of a good wife, an' Mistress Shortnekke, bein' a widow, has need of a husband."

"You and the midwife intend to marry?"

"Aye. Lord Gilbert, him havin' lost Lady Petronilla, will likely understand an' I'll not lose my place."

I thought this prognosis true, and wished him well of his choice.

"We'll be wed as soon as this business is finished," he continued.

"Then you are eager to see a felon brought to justice."

"Aye," he grinned. "An' Agnes also. What will you have me do?"

"There is a gentleman in service to Sir Richard Cyne who is said to look fondly upon Maude atte Pond and her father's lands. Name is Ralph Bigge. Landless, I am told, and handsome. Squire Ralph might be willing to wed a reeve's daughter, 'tis said, if her dowry includes a yardland or two from her prosperous father."

"Ah... I remember. No such fellow would like to see an abbey novice wedge himself between him an' the lass."

"Just so."

"When I find the fellow, what am I to ask of 'im?"

"Do not ask of his interest in Maude. Assume it, and if he protests it is not so, ignore his objection and say all of Eynsham, abbey and village, knows of his desire."

"Sir Richard's house must be a disorderly place," Arthur mused. "What with his son an' a squire in his service both chasin' after the same lass."

"Keep eyes and ears open for conflict," I said.

"Wish you was doin' this," Arthur said. "I've not the wit to see through another man's wiles."

"This abbey is divided, I think. There are those who would report me to Prior Philip if I was seen about the place, and others who would say nothing to betray me."

"Problem bein' you don't know which monks an' lay brothers is which."

"I know of a few who are the prior's adherents. Brother Guibert is surely one. And I know of a few who are not. But no, until this is all sorted out I cannot be seen."

"What did you do to get in such trouble?"

"Some day, when there is time, I will explain it to you."

Arthur cocked an ear toward the door, and I also then heard what had caught his attention. Abbot Thurstan was speaking. I had heard no man enter his chamber. To whom could he be speaking?

I listened at the closet door and heard the abbot call my name. It must have taken all of his remaining strength to raise his voice enough to be heard through the oaken planks of the closet door.

Arthur stood aside and I carefully cracked open the door to be sure that the abbot was alone. Perhaps, I thought, he had become delirious and would reveal my hiding place to Brother Guibert or some other visitor.

Not so. For all of his discomfort and nearness to death Abbot Thurstan was yet in his right mind. I approached his bed, and when he saw me he crooked a finger, requesting me to bend near. Arthur watched from the closet door.

"I am too weak to speak much," the abbot began, "but it takes little strength to hear. I heard you tell your man to seek Squire Ralph. Tell him to take care. Ralph is a pugnacious fellow. Much like his father. He will take offense if he believes he is suspect in a murder, whether or not he is guilty."

Abbot Thurstan had tried to raise himself upon an elbow as he began this warning, but could not remain so and sank back upon his pillow before he was done speaking. He closed his eyes, his admonition at an end.

"Heard 'im," Arthur said. He did not say this with any

concern in his voice. Arthur has dealt with pugnacious men in the past, and usually when the affair was closed such men were much less quarrelsome than when the matter began.

"Return to the guest house for your dinner, then seek Squire Ralph. And wear your dagger. Forewarned may be forearmed, but armed with a blade is better than armed with a warning. Return here after you have spoken to Ralph. Ask of his cloak, if he has one of fur, or fur-lined. He may choose not to answer a mere groom, but refusing to answer may be an answer. Mention Lord Gilbert. Can do no harm."

I retired to the prayer closet, frustrated that I could do nothing but wait while others sought for answers to questions I wished to ask. Abbot Thurstan's dinner arrived, and I heard the infirmarer implore the abbot to eat. His entreaties were at least a little effective, for after a time I heard him praise the abbot upon his consumption of the meal.

Shortly after Brother Guibert departed the abbot's chamber I heard the door open again, and this time the closet latch was next to be raised. When this happened without my hearing a voice so as to know who approached, my heart leaped to my throat for fear that I had been betrayed.

There was no need of worry. The closet door opened and I saw Brother Gerleys with a bowl of pottage, a maslin loaf balanced upon it, and a cup of ale. 'Twas not the fare served to folk in the guest house, but it filled my belly.

Shortly after, the abbey bell rang for nones. I heard the abbot's chamber door once again open and close. I now measured time by the operation of a door. 'Twas not a life I wished to continue, and had been trying and casting aside thoughts of how I might leave the closet yet remain about the abbey to fulfill my commission.

From the other side of the closet door I heard Arthur announce his presence. I opened the door and saw before me a rare sight. Arthur's nose dripped a small trace of blood, and even in the sunless closet I could see that his left eye was turning to purple and would tomorrow be black.

"Right-handed," Arthur said with a wry grin.

"What happened? Is the man as combative as Abbot Thurstan warned?"

"Aye, he is… or was. Perhaps not so much any more. Wears a fur coat, does Squire Ralph."

"You asked this of him?"

"Nay. He was wearin' it when I found 'im."

"Ah. But what of your nose?"

"Caught me unaware."

"What had you said to receive such a blow?"

"Asked 'im if he ever met with Maude atte Pond."

"And he set upon you for that?"

"Not only that. Asked who I was an' why I wanted to know. Told 'im I was groom to Lord Gilbert, an' Abbot Thurstan wanted to know.

"Didn't believe me – about the abbot, that is. I wear Lord Gilbert's livery, so he must have known that much was so.

"Asked why the abbot would care if he courted a maid. I told 'im of the novice bein' slain, an' it bein' the abbot's business to discover who did murder of one of 'is novices."

"That's when he struck you?"

"Aye. Took it personal, like," Arthur said, and tenderly brushed his swelling cheek. "Delivers a solid blow, does Ralph."

"What then?" I could not believe that Arthur, having an eye blackened, would not have responded. "Does Squire Ralph regret his folly?"

"Reckon he does."

"Where did this confrontation take place?"

"In the stables, behind Sir Richard's house. I asked for Squire Ralph at the manor house an' a servant told me he was seein' to 'is horses. I found 'im an' asked of Maude an' told 'im of the abbot seekin' the felon what did for poor John, an' that's when 'e thumped me. Stables is dark. Never saw it comin'."

"What then?"

"Shouldda run."

"What? You?"

156

"Nay. Ralph."

"Why so?"

"I was right dazed for a time, an' he'd a chance to get away. Throws a good punch. But 'e just stood there, waitin' for me to drop, I think. So when I'd gathered me wits I put a fist to 'is belly, an' when 'e doubled over I smacked 'im in back of 'is head."

"Was he yet able to speak, or did you leave him napping in the straw?"

"He come to 'is senses soon enough."

"Was he then willing to speak of Maude atte Pond and John Whytyng?"

"Aye. Put a knee into 'is back and brought an arm up behind 'is shoulder. If 'e hesitated when I asked a question I just shoved 'is arm a bit higher, like."

"Does he yet have the use of it, or was he reluctant to provide answers?"

"Arm should be as good as ever in a few days. Only had to tug on it a few times an' he got the message."

"What did you learn?"

"As folk do say, he's an eye for Maude. Spoke of the lands she'll have of her father."

"Didn't speak of her beauty?"

"Nay. For a landless squire 'er looks is not so important. Beauty fades. Land don't."

"Has he sought Simon atte Pond's assent to pay court to his daughter?"

"Aye. Said the reeve give his consent."

"What of Sir Thomas?" I asked.

"Don't think folks in the manor house are fond of each other. Ralph didn't want to speak of Sir Thomas."

"You persuaded him?"

"Bit of a tug on 'is arm an' more weight on me knee an' he got right gabby. Seems Sir Richard ain't pleased that 'is lad is chasin' a reeve's daughter. Wants 'im to wed a maid of... Didcot, I b'lieve it was. Father's a knight of that place... Sir somethin', didn't catch the name."

"Squire Ralph may have been in some discomfort when he spoke the name."

"Aye," Arthur smiled. "Somethin' like that. Sir Richard is pleased that Ralph is seekin' the maid's hand, so Ralph said. Wishes 'im well, an' is tellin' Sir Thomas regular like to get himself to Didcot, or failin' that back to Swindon, an' find a lass there with lands an' a father with 'sir' before 'is name."

"Did Squire Ralph think that was likely?"

"Don't know. Didn't think to ask. But with 'is arm coiled up behind 'is shoulder 'e was willin' to tell of what I'd not asked."

"Such as?"

"Sir Thomas and 'is brother don't get along."

"Why not? Did he say?"

"He didn't say all, but Maude atte Pond is one of the reasons."

"Sir Geoffrey is wed."

"He is that, but got a wanderin' eye, has Sir Geoffrey. So Ralph says. Sir Thomas knows of it, an' has told 'is brother to leave the maid alone. Many times, if Squire Ralph is to be believed."

"And has Ralph said the same to Sir Geoffrey?"

"Didn't say. But Sir Geoffrey's sure to know what Squire Ralph intends."

"Does Sir Richard know of Sir Geoffrey's improper interest in the lass?" I asked.

"Sir Richard won't care, so says Ralph, what Sir Geoffrey does, as he's already wed to Lady Hawisa. Maude atte Pond's face or lands ain't gonna change that. Sir Richard is only troubled about Sir Thomas."

"With Squire Ralph's face in the straw, did you think to ask of John Whytyng?"

"Aye. Claimed he'd never 'eard of the lad."

"That may be true. Novices don't likely leave the abbey much. Of course, it may also be," I said while thinking aloud, "that he knew of Maude's interest in a novice of the abbey but did not know the lad's name."

"Oh, aye. Shouldda tweaked 'is arm a bit more."

"Perhaps another time."

Arthur pursed his lips. "Another time I'll be more watchful... an' even after all Squire Ralph was willin' to say when I'd got 'is arm behind 'is shoulder, seems like there was more to learn from the fellow. Can't say why. Wish you'd have been there to think of the proper questions to put to 'im."

"You've done well. We know more than before you received your fat lip and purple eye."

"Small price to pay," Arthur smiled crookedly.

The closet door had remained open during this interview, so Abbot Thurstan heard all. I heard him whisper but before I could approach, the chamber door opened and Brother Gerleys entered. I was relieved to see him, as the other frequent visitor to the abbot's chamber was Brother Guibert, and he was surely the prior's man.

The novice-master closed the door behind him, then approached his abbot. "Henry is ready to make his vows and take the tonsure," he said to Abbot Thurstan.

"Prior Philip is away," the abbot replied. "And this is why you speak to me now, is it not?"

"Aye. Prior Philip had no cause to reject him at Corpus Christi. He has been a novice here for more than a year."

"And when Prior Philip returns the cowl will already be Henry's," the abbot murmured.

Brother Gerleys did not reply. It was not required. The abbot spoke what both men knew to be true.

Here was interesting business. Apparently Brother Gerleys had set Henry forward as prepared to take his vows and become a full member of the community, but Prior Philip had rejected the youth. Now, with the prior away, Brother Gerleys sought to see his charge made a monk of the abbey before Prior Philip could return to again veto the lad's advancement.

"Why did Prior Philip oppose Henry?" I asked.

The novice-master jerked his head in my direction, as if he had forgotten my presence. Perhaps he had, being so concerned about Henry taking his vows.

"Don't know," he replied. "Brother Prior seemed to turn against the lad about Easter. All seemed well enough 'till then."

"Have you asked Henry of this? Did the novice do or say something to raise the prior's ire?"

"Henry claims not to know."

"Claims? The word you have chosen tells me that you think otherwise."

"'Tis but a manner of speech. Of course I believe Henry. Would I set him forth as ready to join the community if I thought he was untruthful?"

Here was another question which required no comment.

"I would like to have Arthur speak to the lad... I would speak to him myself, but such a thing is not possible. When will he be received, if Abbot Thurstan agrees?"

"We will begin on the morrow, after terce."

"Three days are required; is this not so?"

"Aye," the novice-master replied.

"And this is why you must begin the process promptly," I said.

Brother Gerleys nodded, and looked to Abbot Thurstan. The frail abbot withdrew a hand, white and trembling, from under his blanket, raised it briefly, and said, "I do approve your recommendation. I never understood Prior Philip's objection to the lad. I cannot attend chapter tomorrow. Brother Wakelin and you must see to the matter."

I learned later that Brother Wakelin was the precentor.

"Why do you wish Arthur to speak to Henry?" asked Brother Gerleys. "He must spend this night in prayer and meditation in the church."

"Does he know that you have approached the abbot on this matter?" I inquired.

"Aye. He awaits the decision in the novices' chamber."

"What is his opinion of Prior Philip?"

"'Tis not meet for a novice to voice an opinion of a superior."

"Of course not, but his behavior will speak when his words will not."

"He was disappointed to be denied."

"Only disappointed? Not angry?"

"You have met the lad. He is of mild temperament."

"Did he not ever ask you why the prior barred his advancement?"

Brother Gerleys thought on this for a moment, then replied: "Strangely enough, he never did so."

"That seems odd, that he would not ask this of you. As if he knew why he was blocked... you think?"

The novice-master pursed his lips, then spoke. "'Tis as I have said. Henry is a calm lad, and not imaginative. That Prior Philip had reasons to reject him may have never entered Henry's mind."

"Perhaps. But I would like to have Arthur speak to the lad before you send him to the church."

Brother Gerleys peered at me with furrowed brow. "This is important to you, I think. Why so?"

"Someone disliked a novice so passionately that they plunged a dagger three times into his back. Now you tell me of another novice who has somehow angered the prior of this abbey."

"You cannot think that Brother Prior did murder? That he opposes Henry completing his vows does not speak of anger. Prior Philip may but believe him unsuited for our life."

"Mayhap."

I turned to Abbot Thurstan and said, "Is it time for Brother Gerleys to know the truth of your fall?"

The abbot looked up at me and nodded imperceptibly.

"Abbot Thurstan did indeed stumble upon the stairs. But when he put out a hand to steady himself Prior Philip grasped it and pushed him down the stairs. Now he lays abed with a broken hip, awaiting death."

The novice-master's eyes grew large, and he turned to the abbot. "This is so?" he asked.

Abbot Thurstan nodded and whispered, "Aye."

"The presbytery stairs are dark," Brother Gerleys said. "A man might grasp the arm of another and no one see. You believe a man who would do such a thing to Abbot Thurstan might slay a novice?"

"It has entered my mind," I replied, "Maude atte Pond heard John Whytyng say, 'I will never do so,' before he was slain. What had been asked of him? Had the same question been asked of Henry? And had he also refused whatever request was made of him?"

"Such a thing is troubling to think upon," Brother Gerleys said. "All know that Prior Philip wishes to become abbot... but to send Father Abbot down a stairway to hasten the day..."

The novice-master did not complete the thought. He had no need to do so. He found it difficult to accept such evil in a place where men were to seek to know the mind of the Lord Christ. But men are sinful creatures, no matter where they spend their days.

"What is it Arthur should ask of Henry?" Brother Gerleys finally said.

"Do not ask him what he may have done to offend the prior. He will likely claim that he does not know, and that may be so. But I doubt it. Rather, ask the lad what Prior Philip wanted of him. He should assume that you know something was required of him. If 'twas the prior who met John Whytyng by the fishpond and asked of him something he would not do, there is a chance that he asked the same question of Henry and received the same answer, and so used his authority to bar Henry."

"If Prior Philip murdered John, why did he not also slay Henry... if the lad refused him about some matter?" Brother Gerleys asked.

"Perhaps he had no opportunity. Or whatever John refused him he also threatened to make known," I said, "whereas Henry did not."

"'Twould be best, I think, if you did not accompany Arthur to this interview," I said to Brother Gerleys. To Arthur I said, "Return to the guest house. Brother Gerleys will send Henry to you. The lad may speak more freely if he knows that no other monk will hear his tale, and he will join the community regardless of what he may say."

"If Henry feared the prior at Eastertide, will he not yet fear him, and so refuse to answer?" Arthur asked. "Prior Philip may yet be his next abbot. Surely he will worry that it may be so."

"Tell the lad that Abbot Thurstan has this day sent a letter to Bishop Bokyngham, recommending Brother Gerleys be elevated to the post," I replied. "The news may loosen his tongue."

Chapter 14

Arthur and Brother Gerleys departed the abbot's chamber. I do not know if Abbot Thurstan heard this discussion or not. I looked down upon him when the others were away, and saw that his eyes were closed. Perhaps he slept. If so, I would not disturb him.

I trusted Arthur, but would have preferred to speak to Henry myself. I waited impatiently for Arthur to return, and had nothing much left of my fingernails when he did.

'Twas nearly time for vespers when Arthur reappeared. As before, I heard the abbot's chamber door open and close, and waited silently to learn who might have entered. Through the closet door I heard Arthur greet the abbot and announce his presence. I bade him enter the closet.

The small window in the abbot's prayer closet was nearly black, so the only light was from the cresset Abbot Thurstan had in the past used to light his devotions. Arthur's purple eye was visible, dark against his pale cheek and forehead.

"What have you learned?" I asked.

"Not sure," he replied, "not bein' a scholar. But there's much amiss in this abbey."

"You learned this from a novice?"

"Aye. 'Twas like 'e was carryin' a great burden, an' when 'e knew there was some matter between 'im and the prior what was near to discovery, decided to tell all. 'Course, I don't know what it all means... but what I do understand is trouble enough."

"So my guess was correct? Prior Philip asked something of Henry, the novice refused, and for that the prior barred his taking the cowl?"

"Aye, think so."

"What was it the lad refused to do?"

"Join some secret body."

"Here? At the abbey?"

"Must be."

"Did the prior name this group?"

"Henry said 'twas called the Brotherhood of the Free Spirit. Never heard of 'em."

I had, and told Arthur so.

"Why did Henry not report this to Brother Gerleys, or to Abbot Thurstan?"

"Said Prior Philip told 'im if he did so he'd not be believed. The prior said none would believe a novice rather than a prior, an' did Henry speak of this he'd tell the abbot 'twas Henry an' Osbert who was the heretics."

Heretics may hang, or burn, and many Free Spirits had had their charred corpses left chained to posts as a warning to folk who were intended to see the result of heresy and abjure such errors so as to avoid a similar fate. Not all that Holy Church calls heresy is so, but some is. The Brotherhood of the Free Spirit is, but I thought the teaching had died away, and was much surprised to hear it named as present in Eynsham Abbey.

"Who are the Free Spirits?" Arthur asked.

"Heretics," I replied.

"What is it they believe?"

"It would take all night to explain. But, in a nutshell, they follow the teaching of Amaury de Bene, a teacher at the University of Paris."

"Frenchman," Arthur scoffed. "What did 'e say that vexed the bishops?"

"God is in all... His spirit is in all things."

Arthur stared at me, silent, his forehead furrowed.

"That got 'em burnt?" he finally said.

"Aye. If their teaching is believed, then original sin is nonsense, and redemption is unnecessary, and all men will see heaven."

"How so?"

"If God's spirit lives in all things, in all men, how can God's spirit be evil or sent to hell?"

"Oh," Arthur said. I believe he was yet unsure of the matter.

"So there can be no such thing as eternal punishment for sinners," I said. "In fact, the only sin those of the Free Spirit recognize is a man's failure to understand his own divinity, and so to wrongly believe that other forms of sin exist."

"You spoke true," Arthur said. "'Twould take all night for me to understand. But," he said thoughtfully, "if there's no sins, what's to stop them folk from doin' all sorts of mischief?"

"Nothing. Rather, they teach that sins and felonies and suchlike are good things. Doing evil is a step toward freedom of a man's spirit. Only foolish folk live by obedience to Holy Writ."

Arthur scratched his head in wonder. "So the more wickedness a man does, the better, an' them who submit to kings an' bishops an' such is wrong?"

"Aye. Men who succeed in perverting virtue and persuading others to do likewise are called 'adepts,' and followers are to obey them."

"Like I'm to obey a bishop if 'e tells me to do a thing, or not do some other?"

"Aye. I heard it said that followers would do murder, or fornication, if an adept demanded it of them."

"You think Prior Philip might be one of them adepts?"

"I don't know what to think. When I learned of the Brotherhood of the Free Spirit while a student at Baliol College I was assured that the heresy was most often discovered in France and the Low Countries, and had died out. It seems this may not be so."

Arthur and I were speechless for a moment, considering what each had learned from the other. During the silence I heard a soft rapping sound coming from the abbot's chamber. I looked through the open closet doorway and saw Abbot Thurstan hitting the side of his bed with his knuckles. He was so weak that he had been unable to make himself heard over our conversation, but when it ceased the tapping could be heard.

I approached the abbot's bed, and when he saw me he beckoned with a bony finger for me to bend low. He began to speak, but 'twas all he could do to gather breath enough to be heard.

"I heard your man," he said. "Prior Philip has been a puzzle to me since he came here as a novice. Now much is clear. His words and behavior were often mystifying."

"How so?" I asked.

"In chapter he would never confess any but the most trivial sin. A monk who confesses to no sin in chapter is considered guilty of two sins: that which he will not confess, and the sin of refusing to admit to sin." Here Abbot Thurstan fell silent, gathering his waning strength.

"So," he continued, "Prior Philip always confessed to something in chapter... he once confessed to desiring flesh in the refectory. But I do not remember him ever disclosing any but venial sins. He never spoke of lust or theft or fornication or the temptation of such things."

"Other monks did?" I asked.

"Sometimes," the abbot whispered. "Monks are but men. Prior Philip, if he truly is of the Brotherhood of the Free Spirit, owns to no sin, so his confession at chapter was another sin. A lie."

"What will you have me do?" I asked.

Abbot Thurstan was silent, his eyes closed. I looked closely at his blanket to see if it yet rose and fell. I thought for a moment that Arthur's report might have dispatched the aged monk, shocking him from this life to the next.

The blanket moved, and shortly he opened his eyes and spoke. "The heresy must be rooted out of Eynsham Abbey," he said, with as much force as he was able. "This may be my last service to the Lord Christ while I yet live... but so long as I live I will see it done."

My mind went back to the interview with John Thorpe, and the words of his wife which he abruptly stifled. Was this what the woman was about to say? Would Sir John protect his brother from a charge of heresy?

"When did Philip become prior?" I asked.

"Four years past. The year the French king died. He was sub-prior before that."

"Does a sub-prior have power to reject a novice?"

"Nay. Not at this house. Only an abbot or prior may do so."

"Has Prior Philip disallowed any novice, other than Henry, since he assumed the office?" I asked.

Abbot Thurstan lay silent for a moment. "Martin," he said. "Martin Glover."

"What reason did Prior Philip give for spurning the fellow?"

"'Twas three years past. Not long after Philip was made prior. I don't remember his objection."

"What became of Martin? Did Prior Philip eventually relent?"

"Nay. Martin's father sent him to Winchester. To St. Swithin's Priory. He is a brother there."

"St. Swithin's saw no reason to reject the novice?"

"Nay. His father's a prosperous merchant of London. St. Swithin's was pleased to receive a plump endowment, I'm sure."

"Did the lad's father settle an endowment upon Eynsham Abbey?"

"Aye, he did."

"Were you required to return it?"

"Nay," Abbot Thurstan said. "We did not force Martin away. He chose to depart after Prior Philip rejected him."

"If you had sent him away you would then also have had to return his father's coin?"

"Not if we had good cause. Such a dispute, when it occurs, always provides employment for the lawyers."

"How many novices have taken vows since Philip became prior, and are now brothers of Eynsham Abbey?"

"Three. Not so many as should be, but all abbeys, unless they are wealthy and of great renown, suffer as we here at Eynsham for a lack of new brothers."

"Is the infirmarer one of these?"

"Brother Guibert? Aye, so he is. He took his vows but a few months after Philip became prior. Was much interested in the well-being of his brother monks, so I made him assistant to Brother Anselm, infirmarer at the time. Brother Anselm was full of years and of wisdom. When he died last year 'twas Brother Guibert who was best suited for the obedience."

Abbot Thurstan again fell silent. Whether from fatigue or thought I knew not.

"Why did you conclude that Brother Guibert was new to the abbey, since Brother Philip became prior?" he said finally.

"He shows the prior much deference," I said.

"Aye. Many of the younger brothers do so. Philip is a scholar, and with wit like a bodkin. He is ever ready to puncture youthful notions."

"Only youthful opinions? Does the prior never dispute with older brothers?"

"Rarely. There is little time for idle chatter here. All must be silent in cloister, refectory, and during Holy Office."

"What of Brother Gerleys?"

"He came to us as a novice but a few years after the great pestilence first struck. Has been novice-master for ten years or so. The obedience requires a man of patience, with the wisdom age does impart."

"You said three novices have taken vows since Brother Philip became prior. Who are the other two?"

"Brother Adam and Brother Herbert."

"Do these show deference to Prior Philip as does Brother Guibert?"

"Surely. But 'tis as should be," Abbot Thurstan said.

"Aye," I agreed. "Any young man should show honor to his superior. But do these venerate Prior Philip more than might be needful?"

The abbot was again silent. Arthur shifted uneasily upon his feet. Finally the abbot answered.

"You believe Prior Philip may be their adept? Brother Guibert and Brother Adam and Brother Herbert?"

"There must be some reason that the prior accepted those three but disallowed..."

"Martin," the abbot whispered.

"Aye, Martin. Perhaps Prior Philip's reasons were laudable, but perhaps not."

"As with young Henry," Abbot Thurstan said softly.

"Has Prior Philip a fur-lined coat?" I asked.

"Aye, he has. Why do you ask?" the abbot said.

I told him of finding a tuft of fur upon a thorn between the abbey and the place where Arthur and I had discovered John Whytyng's corpse.

"Does any other brother own such a garment?" I asked.

"Nay. We have strayed far from the Rule, I fear, we who are abbots and priors. 'Tis why the Cistercians view us so reproachfully. But the sainted Benedict did not live where winters are so severe. Abbots and priors are often aged men, and the cold settles in our bones. 'Tis no great sin, I think, to be warm, nor a virtue to be cold, else we should all remove to Scotland."

I was becoming convinced of Prior Philip's guilt in the matter of John Whytyng's murder. He resented the novice's family; the mother for rejecting him, and the father for succeeding where he had failed. Henry Fuller was not already a brother because he had refused the prior's requirement that he join the Brotherhood of the Free Spirit – if Henry was to be believed. Maude atte Pond had heard John Whytyng say, "I will never do so," to some man. Then, a few moments later, the novice was struck down. Did he say these words to Prior Philip? Was this his reply to an invitation to enter the Brotherhood of the Free Spirit?

Prior Philip, with a monk named Eustace, was responsible for seeing the abbey secure each night. Maude said that she had met with John Whytyng in the night several times. Did the prior see John let himself out of the abbey using the key he had fashioned? This seemed likely. The novice would find himself in a compromised position, there by the fishpond, at midnight. Prior Philip may have thought that this was a lever he could use to pry John to his will. If the novice would not become his disciple in the Brotherhood of the Free Spirit, the prior would tell the chapter of John's meeting Maude in the night and his dismissal from the abbey would be sure.

What the prior did not know was that John Whytyng had already purposed to abandon a monastic life, so the prior's threat would have been hollow.

Maude had said that most of the conversation in the night there by the fishpond had been whispered. She had heard only what was said when voices were raised in anger. Had Prior Philip threatened John Whytyng with discovery in this hushed discourse? If so, John might then have disclosed his intent to return to his father. He might even have threatened Prior Philip, to inform Abbot Thurstan against him. The prior would then understand that he had no hold over John, and 'twas the novice who held the upper hand over him. All monks own a knife, but would a prior own a dagger? And would he think to take it with him to such an encounter? Surely he would not think himself threatened in the night.

All of these thoughts passed through my mind, and another also. "I would like to speak to Brother Eustace," I said to Abbot Thurstan.

The abbot's brow furrowed in puzzlement.

I explained. "He serves with Prior Philip as explorator, does he not?"

"Aye," the abbot whispered, and I saw understanding in his eyes. His body might be near to death, but his wit was unimpaired. "Perhaps Brother Eustace knows of matters he has kept concealed... seen things of which he has not spoken."

"For fear of Prior Philip," I suggested.

"Just so. But if you face Brother Eustace you will place upon him a great burden. The brothers all know that you stand accused of heresy, have escaped Brother Guibert's cell, and are now being sought."

"Who will Brother Eustace tell?"

"Ah, he would come to me. I sent Prior Philip away," he smiled. "Speak to him here, in my chamber, before me. I will demand of him that he tell no other of your presence, or of what matters you ask of him."

"Will he obey, do you think, or is he the prior's man?"

Abbot Thurstan thought on this for a few moments before he replied.

"I chose him for the duty. Prior Philip did not, nor did he seem much pleased with my choice. Brother Godfrey had served as explorator with Prior Philip and the priors who served before him, but he was advanced in years, and often stumbled in the night, so asked to be relieved of the obedience."

"Why did you choose Brother Eustace, when the prior might have desired another to assist him on his rounds?"

Abbot Thurstan pursed his lips. "'Twas not that Prior Philip said that he preferred another. And before my selection the two seemed to live in harmony... as they do yet. But when I told Prior Philip of my choice there was a brief scowl which flashed across his face. I wondered at this at the time. But nothing came of it. I thought 'twas perhaps my imagination.

"'Tis nearly time for vespers," he continued. "Brother Guibert will visit before the office with wine and herbs to help me sleep. I will tell him to send Brother Eustace to me after vespers. You should return to the closet. Brother Guibert may appear soon."

I motioned to Arthur to follow me to the closet, and when I shut the door behind us I extinguished the cresset so that the infirmarer would see no glimmer of light escaping from under the door. The closet was dark, only starlight from the window and a sliver of illumination under the door from the cressets lighting the abbot's chamber gave faint light to the place.

We had not long to wait before the abbot's chamber door opened and we heard Brother Guibert greet his abbot. As before we could hear no response from Abbot Thurstan, but through the infirmarer's words could follow the conversation.

Brother Guibert offered wine and crushed hemp seeds, and silence followed as the abbot consumed the draught. When he had finished he must then have asked a question of Brother Guibert, for I heard the monk say, "All of the brothers esteem Prior Philip, I think."

Silence followed, in which the abbot must have asked another question. I heard the infirmarer say, "Nay, he has never done so." More silence, then with some agitation Brother Guibert said, "Nay, M'lord Abbot, there is nothing hidden in the abbey. You have surely been deceived."

Another silence. Then, "I will do so. But you must not trouble yourself," the infirmarer said, "with worry of apostasy among the brothers."

There was no more conversation. I heard the chamber door open and close, and but a few heartbeats later I heard the sacrist ring the bell for vespers.

Chapter 15

bbot Thurstan must have asked a pointed question of Brother Guibert about the faithfulness of his brother monks. When I heard the infirmarer's denial I was at first displeased that the abbot had given Brother Guibert cause for suspicion if he was of the Brotherhood of the Free Spirit, and Prior Philip was his adept.

But as I thought on the matter I decided that perhaps 'twas a good thing to poke the hornets' nest and see what might flee from it. I tapped Arthur upon the shoulder, squeezed past the bulky fellow – the closet was tiny – and opened the door. No need to fear discovery. The monks were at their office.

Brother Eustace would likely prefer to see to his duties as explorator, then crawl under his blanket 'till vigils, rather than attend his abbot. I waited, with Arthur, upon a bench in a dark corner of the abbot's chamber. One of the cressets which lighted the room was extinguished, its oil consumed. Brother Eustace was prompt.

And he was not alone. The chamber door opened and two monks entered. The first I did not recognize, the second was Brother Guibert. I had not expected the infirmarer to appear with Brother Eustace, else I would have awaited the explorator in the closet.

The infirmarer closed the chamber door behind him and with the first monk approached the abbot's bed. Neither man peered into the dark corner where Arthur and I sat, nor made any sign that they had noticed our presence. But if either of us moved we would surely be seen. I remained still.

"I am come," said Brother Eustace, "as you asked. How may I serve you?"

Abbot Thurstan struggled to raise himself upon an elbow, failed, then spoke. "Brother Guibert, I wish to speak to Brother Eustace alone."

The infirmarer turned, saw our shadows in the corner, and stopped, peering into the dark to see who it was in the abbot's chamber. "You!" he said, and I knew I was found out.

"Brother Guibert," the abbot said, "you must tell no man who is here this night. I expect your obedience."

Then, to Brother Eustace, Abbot Thurstan said, "Here is a man who wishes to speak to you of grave matters. I am your abbot, and I command you to answer truthfully all that he asks of you."

The abbot then twisted so as to turn his gaze toward me. Brother Guibert backed away, as if to make for the door, intending, perhaps, to seek some brawny lay brothers to remove me again to his cell.

Abbot Thurstan saw this, and with as much volume as he could muster, cried, "Halt!" Brother Guibert obeyed.

"'Twas not my wish," the abbot whispered, "that you return with Brother Eustace. But as you are here you must remain 'till Master Hugh has done with you."

I have learned in similar circumstances in the past that altitude can be an advantage in prodding answers from those who might otherwise be reluctant to satisfy my curiosity. I told Arthur to bring forward the bench upon which we had recently sat, told the two monks to sit upon it, then requested of Arthur that he stand before the chamber door.

Brother Guibert sat with his arms folded, in an attitude of hostility, but Brother Eustace seemed more curious than antagonistic, wondering what this encounter was about. I began with him.

"How many times, when you made your rounds to secure the abbey for the night, did you see John Whytyng leaving through the north porch of the church?"

Brother Eustace's mouth dropped, and even though their habits were black and the chamber was dark I saw Brother Guibert extend an elbow into the explorator's ribs.

"John...?" Brother Eustace stammered. "The novice?"

"Was there another John Whytyng about in Eynsham?" I said.

"Uh... novices retire to their beds after compline," he said quickly, "and are not required to rise for vigils."

"That I know. I did not ask you of a novice's schedule."

I waited, and the room fell silent. This allowed the explorator time to consider what I might know. I wished for the monk to believe that I knew more than I did. Abbot Thurstan finally spoke, his whisper easily heard in the stillness.

"Answer Master Hugh," the abbot commanded.

"Thrice," the monk said softly. I saw a look of scorn pass across Brother Guibert's face.

"Why did you not report these transgressions to your abbot?" I said.

"Prior Philip was present. We together saw the lad. He said he would report to M'lord Abbot. Did he do so?"

"He did not," Abbot Thurstan said. "It is surely time for me to meet the Lord Christ. I have failed to rule the abbey as I should have done. My wit has been as clouded as my eyes. Truly, even had I not plunged down a stairway, I would no longer wish to live, to see daily the failure of my duty."

"Not so, M'lord Abbot," Brother Eustace said with muted vehemence. "You have governed us wisely and well."

"There are matters about which you, I think, are ignorant," Abbot Thurstan replied. "And for this you should be thankful."

Brother Eustace's only response was a puzzled expression, but I saw alarm in Brother Guibert's eyes.

"John Whytyng went missing in the night nearly two weeks past," I said. "'Twas a Wednesday evening he was last seen. Did you and Brother Prior see him leave the church through the north porch that night?"

Brother Eustace was silent – considering, I think, which reply, truth or falsehood, would do him most harm.

"Aye, we did so. Brother Prior said we should wait in the shadows to see if he came that night."

"What hour of the night was this?"

"Soon after vigils."

"And the other times that you saw him leave through the

door in the north porch, was it the same hour?"

"Aye."

"Had you and Prior Philip lain in wait for the novice on other nights, or was Wednesday the first time?"

"After the second time we saw the novice leave the abbey we waited in the porch to see would he do so again. Prior Philip said that before he told M'lord Abbot of this he wished to know where the novice went after leaving the abbey precincts."

"When the novice left the church, what then?"

"Brother Prior told me to complete the rounds alone. I was to leave the door to the north porch of the church unlocked, so Prior Philip could re-enter after he had followed John Whytyng."

"You did so?"

"Aye."

"Did you again see Prior Philip that night?"

"Nay. Not 'till I left my bed for lauds."

"The prior was then in his accustomed place? He had not sought you in the night?"

"All was as customary. Prior Philip said nothing of following John Whytyng. I had no opportunity to ask of him."

"When the novice was discovered missing, did you not then wonder what Prior Philip had learned in the night as he followed the lad?"

Brother Eustace was silent for a time, then said, "I thought that if Brother Prior wanted me to know what he had found he would tell me. 'Tis unwise to meddle in Prior Philip's business."

"Even when you did rounds to secure the abbey for the night in the days after the novice disappeared, you asked nothing of Prior Philip? Not even after John's corpse was found?"

"Nay."

"And you told no one, not even Abbot Thurstan, that the last monk to see John Whytyng alive was the prior?"

"Nay."

"Why not?" I asked. If he had done so my work at the abbey would already be completed and I would not be sought as a heretic. So I thought.

Brother Eustace looked to the bed where his abbot lay, listening. "All know that M'lord Abbot is near death, and Prior Philip may succeed him."

The monk said no more, so I finished his thought. "You wished to save yourself the embarrassment of asking awkward questions of the next abbot of Eynsham Abbey?"

Brother Eustace dropped his gaze and replied, "Aye."

All this time Brother Guibert had sat immobile, arms crossed, lips drawn tight. Now he spoke.

"Do you accuse Prior Philip of doing murder?"

"Someone did murder," I replied, "and if Brother Eustace speaks true the prior was the last abbey resident to see John Whytyng alive."

"Bah. Why would Prior Philip slay a novice?"

"Because of what the novice knew," I said.

Brother Guibert did not immediately reply. He was startled, I believe. Men may die for what they know as well as for what they do.

"What could a novice know which would cause Brother Prior, or any monk, to slay him?"

Then, to Abbot Thurstan, Brother Guibert said, "I accompanied Brother Eustace to see that you were comfortable for the night. If there is nothing you need I wish to seek my bed. Vigils will come swiftly. I suppose when Prior Philip returns he may then deal with this heretic as you are unable to do so."

"I am well able to deal with heretics," the abbot whispered, "and I will do so when I encounter them."

Brother Guibert stood and glanced askance at his abbot but said no more.

"Master Hugh," the abbot continued, "is in my service. You know now that he remains in the abbey, but no others do. I wish his presence here to remain hidden. If others learn he is within the abbey it must be because one of you has told. This I forbid. I command your silence. Winter will be a poor time to be upon a road to Scotland, but if you speak of this interview to any man you will find yourself transferred to Dunfermline Abbey."

Then, to me, with what remained of his strength, Abbot Thurstan said, "Have you done with these brothers?"

"Aye, for now. I would like for Brother Eustace to seek the dormitory and send Brother Adam and Brother Herbert to us."

"Now?" Brother Eustace asked. "They will not be pleased to leave their beds."

"I will do so," Brother Guibert said. "Brother Eustace has already been delayed upon his rounds."

"Nay," I said. Then looking to Abbot Thurstan, I said, "I do not wish for Brother Guibert to have words with Brother Adam or Brother Herbert."

The abbot seemed to gather himself for the exertion of speech. "Do as Master Hugh requires," he said. "And remember, say nothing of his presence here."

"What am I to tell Brother Adam and Brother Herbert?" Brother Eustace asked.

"Nothing," I replied, "but that their abbot wishes to speak to them of an urgent matter."

"All matters," the abbot whispered, "are urgent for a dying man."

I nodded toward the door. Brother Eustace stood and with the infirmarer departed the chamber. When they were away I knelt beside Abbot Thurstan's bed.

"Are you in pain?" I asked. "There are other herbs which may be added to your physic. Lettuce seeds will help you sleep."

"I will soon sleep long enough. A month past I was content to die. Now I wish to live... long enough to see apostasy rooted from this abbey."

I sat upon the bench and Arthur joined me. "Want I should seek the novice-master an' get oil for the other cressets? Reckon he'll have some," he said.

"Nay. You'll wake him and perhaps the novices. Darkness can be intimidating. A man cannot see where danger lies, so believes it might approach from any source."

"Oh, aye," Arthur agreed.

Perhaps Brother Adam and Brother Herbert slept soundly.

They did not soon appear in the abbot's chamber. Of course, the dormitory is opposite the cloister from the abbot's chamber and they traveled the space in the dark. But 'tis a space they knew well. I believe they paused to consider why Abbot Thurstan wished their presence in his chamber on a cold November night.

But monks obey their abbot, even one who is near death, so perhaps their arrival was not so tardy as I thought. I was impatient to learn what I could from these brothers.

The abbot's chamber door opened slowly, as if the man who pushed against it was unsure of his purpose. The single cresset provided little illumination, and when the monks entered the chamber I did not recognize either of them.

Arthur and I did not await Brother Adam and Brother Herbert in a dark corner, but in the center of the chamber, near to the cresset. The monks looked from Abbot Thurstan to me and back to the abbot. I had not before seen these monks, but they knew me. One stared at me open-mouthed. Now four monks and the novice-master knew of my presence in the abbey. The secret would be impossible to keep. But with Prior Philip away perhaps concealment was no longer necessary – so long as I could prove a felon before he returned, and Abbot Thurstan lived a few more days.

"Master Hugh," the abbot said, "has been wrongly charged with heresy. I have examined him and find no substance to the accusation. He has questions for you. It is my command that you answer truthfully."

Abbot Thurstan had raised his head for these words, but now fell back upon the pillow. The speech had exhausted him. I wondered how many more times he could compel his weakening body to perform before it would fail him.

The two young monks looked from their abbot to me, and as with Brother Eustace and Brother Guibert, I invited them to sit upon the bench. Arthur stood, arms folded, before the chamber door, assuming a grim countenance, which he likely thought would help wring truth from those who might otherwise think to deceive.

Whoso had slain John Whytyng had, if Maude atte Pond spoke true, returned with another and the two had taken the novice's corpse to the verge of the wood where Arthur and I and the birds had found him.

I needed to question these monks, as I was then sure that Prior Philip had done murder, for he had reason and opportunity. I was also convinced that there must be others in the abbey who were of the Brotherhood of the Free Spirit and that one or more of these had helped remove John Whytyng from the pond.

It seemed also that a monk recently given the tonsure, and therefore acceptable to the prior, might be the assistant who aided in moving the slain novice to a vacant corner of the abbey grounds.

"Nearly two weeks past, early upon a Thursday morn," I began, "Prior Philip sought one, or perhaps both of you, to aid him in a private matter. 'Twas soon after vigils, I think. Which of you did he seek? Or was it both?"

The monks turned to look at each other and even though the chamber was dim I could see in their faces that the question startled them. Here was an unwelcome discovery. At least one of the monks should not have been much surprised by the question.

Brother Adam and Brother Herbert studied each other for a moment, then, finding no answer in each other's eyes, Brother Adam turned to me and spoke.

"Why is it Brother Prior is supposed to have needed our aid in the night? He did not seek me. I am under my blanket every night 'till lauds."

As Brother Adam concluded his protest he turned and faced Brother Herbert, as if challenging his brother monk to admit rising in the night at his prior's request. Brother Herbert did not delay his reply.

"Prior Philip has not sought me in the night. Why would he do so...? Ah, I see. 'Twas then John Whytyng disappeared from the abbey. You and your man found him. You believe Brother Prior had to do with John's disappearance and death. That is what this question is about, is it not?"

Both monks protested innocence in the matter and I had no way to demonstrate otherwise. I had, however, another weapon which might cause one or the other to reconsider their denial.

"You have heard," I said, "that there is heresy in Eynsham Abbey."

"Aye," Brother Herbert replied. "Brother Guibert, 'tis said, heard you denying purgatory."

"That is not the heresy of which I speak. There is, among the brothers, an adept of the Brotherhood of the Free Spirit."

Chapter 16

The reaction I sought, and did not find, when I asked the monks which of them had been called to assist Prior Philip in the night, I now saw. Alarm flashed briefly across Brother Adam's face and I saw him clench the plank of the bench so that, had there been light enough to see, his knuckles would surely have been white.

Brother Herbert did not seem so troubled. Perhaps he was more skilled at deception, or it could be that the cresset flame did not cast as much of its glow upon his face as upon Brother Adam's. But I knew that my arrow had struck home, and so thought to unloose another.

"You have heard of the Brotherhood of the Free Spirit," I continued. "'Twas thought that the heresy was confined to France and the Low Countries, and that sufficient of its adherents burned that the heresy died out... as would be expected of those who went to the stake.

"But there is evidence that the heresy yet has followers." As I spoke I glared at the monks with as much choler in my gaze as I could muster.

"What has that to do with us?" Brother Herbert replied.

"You know well, and matters will go better for you if you confess all to Abbot Thurstan and beg mercy of him."

I glanced from Brother Herbert to Brother Adam, and saw again Adam's death grip upon the bench.

"Do not think that Holy Church will not send a monk to the sheriff for him to work his justice," Abbot Thurstan whispered.

I said no more, but waited. The chamber was dark and silent but for the abbot's labored breathing. The rattle in his chest seemed louder than I remembered. I was not alone in thinking so. All four in the chamber turned to the abbot's bed.

He saw this, and spoke again. "Aye, 'tis true. I may see the Lord Christ before lauds. But you must not think to keep silent until then, and assume all will then go well for you. Prior Philip has taken a letter..." Abbot Thurstan fell silent, too weak to continue. He waved a hand weakly to me, indicating that I should come close. I did.

"I am too weak to explain matters," he whispered. "You must do so."

"Prior Philip," I said, "has taken Abbot Thurstan's letter to Bishop Bokyngham. In the letter your abbot has nominated Brother Gerleys to succeed him, and gives cause why Prior Philip should not do so. Although, when the letter was written, Abbot Thurstan did not know of the full reason the prior should not be made abbot."

"But Prior Philip is second here only to M'lord Abbot," Brother Herbert protested, "and of right must have the position."

"He has forfeited it," I said.

"How so?" Brother Herbert snapped. "And why does a heretic stand here in M'lord Abbot's chamber and repudiate Brother Prior's claim?"

"Tell them," Abbot Thurstan whispered. His words were faint, like a gasp, and then nothing more but the wheezing of his chest as it rose and fell.

"I think I need not tell you why the prior is unfit to become your abbot," I said. "It is for the same reason you are likely unfit to be brothers of Eynsham Abbey."

I knew that this was a leap, to impute apostasy where there was small evidence of the sin. I watched the monks intently as I spoke the accusation. Would guilt cloud their faces, or fear of the gallows did they not recant the heresy?

The monks glanced toward each other again. Brother Herbert scowled darkly at his companion, and Brother Adam looked away, peering into a dark corner of the chamber as if seeking there some escape from this examination. He found none, and opened his mouth to speak.

"Brother Prior..." he said, but before he could say more Brother Herbert delivered a smart blow with an elbow into Brother Adam's ribs. Brother Adam nearly toppled from the bench.

"Say no more!" Brother Herbert commanded, and stood, glaring down at his companion.

"Why must he be silent?" I asked. What confession was he about to make? What was he about to tell us of Prior Philip?

"Nothing a heretic need know," Brother Herbert said.

The monk's fists were in tight balls. I thought him ready to strike, either me or Brother Adam. Arthur saw this also and stepped toward the angry monk.

To Arthur I said, "Take Brother Herbert to the guest house and see he remains there while Abbot Thurstan and I hear what Brother Adam would tell us of the prior."

Arthur took Brother Herbert's arm gently, but the monk twisted from his grasp. "Keep silence!" he shouted to his companion, and turned to the chamber door as if to flee.

The bench was his undoing. He tripped over it and fell headlong. Arthur was upon him in an instant, while Brother Adam stood open-mouthed.

Arthur hauled the protesting monk to his feet with one hand firm upon Brother Herbert's arm, and the fingers of his other hand squeezing the tender place between the monk's neck and shoulder. Brother Herbert's belligerent attitude vanished. He gasped in pain, and when Arthur shoved him toward the chamber door he stumbled to the opening with no further protest.

When Arthur and Brother Herbert were away, and the chamber door shut, I turned to Brother Adam and sat in Brother Herbert's place upon the bench. 'Twas a time to befriend, not intimidate.

"You said that Prior Philip did not seek you in the night a fortnight past. Do you wish to amend your reply?"

"Nay, he did not do so."

"Did any other man wake you, to aid him or Prior Philip?"

"Nay. No man has awakened me from my rest."

The monk seemed sincere. I could see no deception in his eyes or manner, nor hear falsehood in his speech. I have served Lord Gilbert Talbot as his bailiff at Bampton for three years. From this duty I have become skilled at discovering deception and falsehood. Perhaps Brother Adam was more proficient at prevarication than I thought, or it was too dark in the chamber to see what would be obvious in daylight. Or perhaps he spoke the truth.

"What of Brother Herbert?" I said. "Has he spoken of being called to assist the prior in the night?"

"Nay."

"What other friends does Brother Herbert have among the monks of this abbey? Who else might he tell of being summoned in the night for some task?"

Brother Adam was silent for a few moments. "We took the cowl at the same time," he finally said, "and were novices together before that. Brother Herbert has no closer friend than me, I think."

"If he would not tell a secret to you, you say, he would tell no other?"

"Aye."

Here was more disquieting news. If Prior Philip had not sought one of these monks, who then had assisted him in removing a corpse from the fishpond and carrying it away? Were there other adherents of the Brotherhood of the Free Spirit among the monks? Or was Henry Fuller wrong? Was Prior Philip opposed to Henry's tonsure for some other reason? Was the presence of the cult here at Eynsham Abbey but my imagination?

No. There was evidence enough that the heresy was here, and that the prior was a part of it. But if neither Brother Adam nor Brother Herbert had risen from a bed to help move a corpse in the night, who had done so?

Could it be that Prior Philip did not slay John Whytyng? No, I was sure that he had done so. But to prove it so I must find the man who had helped the prior dispose of the novice's corpse. If I could not, I would not likely see justice done for John Whytyng.

"Have you ever burned a finger?" I asked the monk, changing the subject.

Brother Adam's brow furrowed as he attempted to follow this new path. "Aye," he said. "Most men have done so."

"Indeed," I replied. "The pain is great, even if but a small blister is raised. After such a mishap I have often wondered at the agony suffered by those wretches who are burned for their heresies. Some recant, but most go to the stake unrepentant. Such folk must be zealous in their error, to endure the torment they know is to come."

I watched Brother Adam carefully as I spoke, to see if there was in his expression some confession of the fear I hoped was in his soul. There was. I saw his adam's apple rise and fall as he swallowed the bile which I suspect rose in his throat as he considered flames and faggots and chains and ill-mannered observers of such spectacles.

"Why do you speak of this to me?" Brother Adam said between gulps.

"I am troubled. You are in some danger of the gallows or the stake if what I have learned this day is true. We in England generally hang our heretics, but there are some who would prefer dealing with apostasy as the French do, with flames."

"What? Me? What man has betrayed me?"

"Betrayed? Why do you speak of betrayal? An interesting word for you to choose. Is there some matter involving your deeds or opinions you wish to keep obscure?"

"All men have such," the monk said softly.

"Aye, but if they are monks they confess such sins and do the penance assigned them. What have you failed to confess?"

From the corner of my eye I saw Abbot Thurstan turn his head upon the pillow and gaze intently at the young monk. Brother Adam saw this also and quickly looked away.

"Henry Fuller was denied the cowl some months past," I said.

The monk looked at me, puzzled at this new direction. "Prior Philip rejected him," I said. "A few years past, when Brother Gerleys announced that you and Brother Herbert were ready to become brothers, he made no objection. Will you tell me why this was so? Do you know of the prior's objection to Henry Fuller? Can you think of a reason for Prior Philip accepting you but not Henry?"

"What has this to do with John Whytyng and heresy and men being led to the stake?"

"I believe you know. And 'tis also my belief that Abbot Thurstan will require less penance from you if you speak of how all of these things are connected, than if I must explain all to you and him."

"What did Henry Fuller say?" Brother Adam said.

"Why do you suggest that the novice might have had something to tell me?"

Brother Adam did not reply.

"Perhaps," I said softly, "Henry told what you should have told, when Prior Philip gave you similar reason to speak."

"I could not," the monk said suddenly, and his words were nearly a sob. "If Eynsham refused me I had nowhere else to go. My father is not wealthy. He was sorely taxed to provide a place for me here. There was no coin to find me another abbey if Brother Prior would not accept me here."

"Even though most abbeys see declining numbers in their dormitories?"

"Even so. Prior Philip demanded I do his will or he would see that no other house would have me. What was I to do? I was to have no lands. My brother has received all."

"What did Prior Philip demand of you?"

"I think you know," Brother Adam sighed.

"I would hear it from you, as would Abbot Thurstan."

The monk was silent for a few moments, then spoke. "Prior Philip required that I give obedience to him rather than M'lord Abbot."

"Did he ask that you do sinful things?"

"Aye."

"To release your spirit from bondage?"

"Aye."

"Did he say a name for this heresy?"

"He did... we are of a brotherhood, he said. The Brotherhood of the Free Spirit."

"Is your spirit indeed free?" I asked.

"It does not feel so," the monk admitted.

"Brother Herbert and Brother Guibert are of this cult also – is this not so?"

"Aye."

"Who else of the monks?"

"None other, but three of the lay brothers are so."

A worrisome thought entered my mind. "Did any of these accompany Prior Philip to Lincoln?"

"Aye, all three, and one other not of us."

I pushed the concern to the back of my mind, to be dealt with later, and asked again of the night John Whytyng was slain.

"You said that Prior Philip did not call you from your bed a fortnight past. Do you wish to amend your denial?"

"Nay, I spoke true. Brother Prior has never come to me in the night."

"Nor to Brother Herbert?"

"He has never spoken of it."

It must be, I thought, that the prior had sought one of the lay brothers to help him draw John Whytyng from the pond and carry him off. But how could I discover if this was so when the lay brothers who owed obedience to the prior now accompanied him on the road to Lincoln? What snares might they now be devising to seat the prior in Abbot Thurstan's chair?

The letter to Bishop Bokyngham had been sealed with wax and imprinted with Abbot Thurstan's seal. Prior Philip would not open and read it before he reached Lincoln. But if the bishop told him of the letter's contents he might hasten to return and on the way invent some means to thwart the abbot's wishes. I must make all haste.

Brother Guibert and Brother Herbert should join Brother Adam in the abbey cell, but I had not the authority to make this happen, and I wondered if, in his weakened condition, Abbot Thurstan did either. Brother Eustace did not concern me. He was no heretic. But the other three knew I was yet in the abbey and even those monks not infected with apostasy knew I was accused of heresy. What if the three of the Brotherhood of the Free Spirit should incite their brother monks against me and their abbot? They had been told to keep silence about my presence, but their cult awarded no honor to obedience. Rather, respect came to those who embraced evil and forsook piety. If the monks of Eynsham Abbey did not now know I was in the abbot's chamber they likely would by lauds.

"Will you remain an adherent of this odious faction, and hang or burn, or renounce it, seek absolution of your abbot, and live?" I said.

Whether or not the monk might die was not for me to say, but Brother Adam did not consider that. Flames were much upon his mind, and perhaps had been for many months.

"I forswear the Brotherhood," the monk said, "and do seek absolution for my sin."

Abbot Thurstan had watched and listened as Brother Adam confessed his sin. Now he waved a hand over his blanket, inviting the monk to approach his bed.

"Do you truly repent your sin?" the abbot whispered.

"Aye."

"Why did you not tell me of this heresy, and so lift the sin of silence from your shoulders?"

"At first Brother Prior persuaded me of his practices. I could not counter his wit. When I began to doubt his opinion I remembered his warning, that no new monk would be believed against his prior."

"Your penalty must be severe," the abbot said.

"My guilt has encompassed me," Brother Adam replied. "I seek a rigorous penance to make me pure again."

"Very well. It is your due, and you shall have it," Abbot Thurstan whispered, then fell silent.

The abbot did not speak for some time, whether considering Brother Adam's punishment or harboring his strength I could not tell.

"You will be excluded until Ascension Day, and receive only

bread and water during that time. Each Friday, before chapter, you will confess your sin anew and receive twenty stripes upon your back."

I thought the monk might rebel at this severe chastisement. He did not. He knelt beside the abbot's bed.

"I do not resent this discipline. It will purge my sin. I welcome the correction."

Brother Adam had barely finished this affirmation when Abbot Thurstan wheezed and shuddered. His back stiffened, and his breath seemed to stop. His mouth fell open, his eyes closed, then his chest began to rise and fall again.

Brother Adam stood and looked to me. "He is near to death," he said. There was panic in his voice. "You heard the penance he required of me."

"Aye, I did."

"You must make it known to my brothers. I must be cleansed of my sin."

"I will do so... but I have a demand of you also. I cannot pardon you of any sin, but the Lord Christ will surely look with favor upon a man who assists those who seek to see justice done."

"What is it you wish?"

Before I could reply Abbot Thurstan coughed and his body trembled under the blanket. The monk and I gave our attention to the dying man, his question and my need both forgotten.

"He spoke true," I said. "He may see the Lord Christ before lauds."

"The brothers must be assembled," Brother Adam said, "to keep vigil and read from the psalter."

"I dismiss you. Call the monks from their slumber."

I soon discovered how approaching death in a monastery is announced. A few moments after Brother Adam departed the chamber I heard a series of loud, rapid blows seemingly delivered against some door. I learned later that Brother Adam had taken a staff and pounded with it upon the cloister door, this being the accustomed method of making approaching death known to all who reside in an abbey.

A few moments later I heard numerous footsteps shuffling in the corridor outside the abbot's chamber door, which, in haste, Brother Adam had neglected to close after his departure. I thought briefly of retreating to the abbot's closet, but decided such evasion would be only a temporary escape from discovery. Of the monks who knew of my presence in the abbey at least one would likely tell others.

Monks crowded into the chamber. Most looked to the abbot's bed first when they entered, but soon turned to see who it was who stood against a wall in a dark corner. If these brothers were surprised by my attendance upon their abbot they hid it well. None stared openly at me. Rather, they returned their silent gaze to Abbot Thurstan.

When all were present I heard a monk speak. This was, I learned later, the precentor. With Prior Philip away and his abbot near death, responsibility for shepherding his abbot from this world to the next now devolved upon this monk.

He directed his fellows to leave the chamber, explaining that Abbot Thurstan must be shriven, and that he would call them back when the work was done. I retreated to the closet and shut the door. This was evidently distant enough for the precentor, for he watched me enter the closet and said nothing. After a brief time I heard him go to the chamber door and recall his brothers. I left the closet and rejoined the monks.

The precentor assigned two monks to sit with Abbot Thurstan and read to him from the psalter. Two others were appointed to replace these in two hours, and two others would perform the task after lauds.

The bench was conveniently near to the abbot's bed, so the monks assigned to read to Abbot Thurstan sat upon it to carry out the duty assigned to them. The single cresset was moved close upon a stand, and one by one the other monks left the chamber, awaiting recall when Abbot Thurstan died. I remained in the dark corner, watching. No monk paid me heed. More important considerations occupied their minds. This would aid my search for evidence, but after Abbot Thurstan was buried their thoughts would drift back to a heretical bailiff. By that time I must have evidence of the prior's guilt, or it was likely I would never have such proof.

The precentor was last to leave the chamber. Abbot Thurstan had recovered his wit enough that he saw and knew what was his condition. I heard him whisper for Brother Wakelin. Although his voice was weak, the precentor also heard this, since the readers had not yet begun the solace of the psalter.

He returned to Abbot Thurstan's bed and bent low until his ear was a hand's breadth from the abbot's lips. I could not hear what he was told, but when his abbot was done speaking I heard him say, "I will do so." And then he left the chamber.

I remained. 'Twas pleasant to hear the words read from the psalter, until I recalled the reason for the readers' presence. I began to grow drowsy. I decided that no one would be much troubled if I sat in the abbot's chair and rested my head upon his desk. And indeed, the monks who read to Abbot Thurstan paid me no heed.

I must have fallen to sleep. The next thing I knew, one of the monks had stood and opened the chamber door. Its hinges awakened me. The remaining monk continued to read.

A few moments later, through the open chamber door, I again heard the vigorous thumping of a staff upon the cloister door. A short time earlier the din had called the monks to their dying abbot. I thought it likely it would do so again, and that it would be best not to be found with my feet under the abbot's desk, even if he had no further need of it. So when the monks again entered the chamber I had resumed my place in the dark corner.

I am half a head taller than most men, so could see over the monks who were crowding into the chamber. The precentor motioned to a monk who carried a wooden bucket, and the fellow proceeded to empty the bucket's contents upon the planks of the chamber floor. Cold ashes poured from the bucket.

Another monk then laid sackcloth upon the ashes, then two others drew back Abbot Thurstan's blanket and lifted his frail body from the bed. They placed him upon the sackcloth, then two other monks began to read from the psalter again. But I believe the words did Abbot Thurstan no comfort. He yet lived, but was no longer sensible. I heard the death rattle in his throat.

The grey light of a November dawn was becoming visible through the chamber windows when Abbot Thurstan died. I could see nothing of this, for the monks of the house crowded near to him, and he was upon the floor. The precentor had knelt, then I saw him stand and announce the death.

He then called Brother Theodore and bid him approach the cresset. To the assembled monks he said, "Abbot Thurstan required of me this night that a copy of his letter to Bishop Bokyngham be read to you upon his departure from this life. Brother Theodore has it."

The monks turned as one to the abbot's clerk, and there was silence but for the shuffling of feet upon planks as monks shifted their place the better to see and hear Brother Theodore.

Before the clerk could speak the church bell began to ring. The sacrist had departed the chamber to announce to the lay brothers and the village that there was this night a death at Eynsham Abbey.

When the bell fell silent Brother Theodore explained that he held in his hand a copy of the letter which even then Prior Philip was delivering to Bishop Bokyngham.

Mouths opened in astonishment as the clerk read of Prior Philip's part in Abbot Thurstan's injury. When the letter concluded with the abbot's nomination of Brother Gerleys to the abbacy all heads turned to a far wall and there I saw the novice-master and his charges. The chamber had been so crowded that I had not before noticed them. The application of a stout staff against the cloister door had awakened even those who slept far from the door, in the novices' chamber.

In such circumstances 'tis common for a dying abbot to nominate several possible successors and allow the brothers to choose among them. I saw a few of the monks whisper to each other, but most heard the nomination with little expression that I could see, as if the proposal was expected and acceptable.

"Now 'tis time for lauds," the precentor said. "Brother Jocelyn, Brother William, remain here with Abbot Thurstan."

The monks filed from the chamber but for the two who had been assigned to keep vigil over their abbot's corpse. They abandoned the bench and sat cross-legged upon the floor in a sign of respect for Abbot Thurstan.

When the celebration of lauds was completed some monks, I knew, would, upon the precentor's command, return to the chamber to prepare Abbot Thurstan for burial. This would include washing the corpse. I had no wish to be present for this. It seemed a sacrilege that I should look upon the abbot's naked, shrunken body. And I had questions for Brother Herbert. I silently left the chamber and walked in the half light of dawn to the guest house.

Chapter 17

I found Arthur seated before the hearth, enjoying the blaze, and Brother Herbert stretched out upon my bed. To my questioning frown Arthur said, "Has a headache."

"Rise," I said to the monk. He did so slowly, and as he did the firelight revealed the cause of his discomfort. His left cheek was puffy, his upper lip split and bloody, and his left eye was soon to be swollen shut. His visage resembled Arthur's after his confrontation with Squire Ralph.

"Didn't fancy stayin' here 'till you'd had words with 'im," Arthur said.

"What happened?"

"Brought 'im in here, as you said to do. Didn't much want to come. Fire had burned low, so we'd been 'ere but a short while when I put more logs on the fire. Whilst I did so 'e come up behind me, seized yon poker, an' would've whacked me aside of me 'ead had I not been too quick for 'im.

"First blow missed, but 'e swung again an' caught me in the ribs. Made me angry, that did. I smacked 'im, an' 'e dropped the poker an' took to your bed."

"Sleep long, did he?"

"Should be well rested," Arthur said.

"Did he take to the bed, or did you take him?"

"Little of both."

"Brother Adam," I said to the swaying monk, "has told all. You, he, Brother Guibert, and several lay brothers are of the Brotherhood of the Free Spirit, and Prior Philip is your adept."

Brother Herbert opened his mouth as if to speak.

"Do not deny it," I said. "Brother Adam has confessed his sin and welcomes the penance assigned him to cleanse his soul."

The monk's mouth closed, as nearly as could be with half of his upper lip swollen the size of an onion.

"There are yet some matters about which I am unclear," I said.

"Ask Brother Adam," Brother Herbert mumbled.

"I have. His remorse for his sin weighs heavily upon him, but there are a few things I need to know which he could not tell me. Perhaps you will be able to do so."

"Why should I speak to you of abbey matters?"

"Because your abbot assigned me the work of discovering who murdered John Whytyng, and because you would prefer not to hang or burn."

This caught his attention, but he was not yet cowed. "The novice's death has naught to do with me or Prior Philip or any other you imagine to be of some brotherhood. And Abbot Thurstan no longer governs here. I heard the bell toll for his death. Prior Philip now rules Eynsham Abbey."

"He might, but for two things," I said. "He is on the road to Lincoln, and the letter he carries tells Bishop Bokyngham of the reasons he should not be made abbot, and nominates Brother Gerleys to the post."

The monk seemed ready to spit to show his disdain at this information, and perhaps would have, but the condition of his lips allowed only a drooling rivulet down his chin. 'Twas most unseemly.

"Few of the obedientiaries are among the heretics of the abbey," I continued. "So Brother Adam says. Not the sacrist nor the precentor nor the cellarer. Only the infirmarer. You should consider your position. Brother Adam regrets his past allegiance. If Brother Gerleys is confirmed as abbot of this house, and the bishop's court turns you over to the Sheriff of Oxford to receive the king's justice, you will likely hang. A prior might escape, but a common monk has little influence."

I said no more, but allowed Brother Herbert to consider my words in silence. 'Twas not the first time I had threatened the monk, but when I first spoke of the penalty he gave such peril little credence. Now, I believe that he did, and the thought caused his shoulders to droop and his attitude to soften. The thought of hempen rope will often work such a change.

When the monk had had enough time to consider a possible future in the hands of the Sheriff of Oxford, I again spoke.

"Brother Adam said that Prior Philip did not seek him in the night a fortnight or so past. The prior had some man's aid. If not Brother Adam, then you or Brother Guibert. If Brother Gerleys is confirmed as your new abbot 'twill go easier for you if you confess all."

The monk sat silently, weighing the implications of my words. "Brother Prior has never awakened me in the night," he said, "not a fortnight past nor any other time."

"Have you heard Brother Guibert speak of such?"

"Nay... will you indeed send me to the bishop's court and the sheriff?"

Brother Herbert had seemed immune to threats, but I saw now 'twas not so. Perhaps his imagination was lacking, and unlike Brother Adam he could not readily visualize himself being led to a scaffold. Until now.

"That will be your new abbot's decision," I replied. "And his choice will depend upon your abandoning heresy and giving aid in rooting it out of the abbey."

"Prior Philip said we would soon be numerous enough that we would rule the abbey. Henry and Osbert and John would join our brotherhood, he said. But John is dead. We must seek more novices, the prior said, and be patient. Perhaps in five years, sooner if he became abbot, we might possess the abbey."

"And what then? The bishop and his archdeacon would yet oversee Eynsham Abbey."

"Bishop Bokyngham has never visited the abbey, and archdeacons can be bribed."

This was no doubt true, but if the monks of St. Mary's Abbey of Eynsham elected Brother Gerleys their new abbot, Prior Philip's scheme would fail. A prior may have enough influence that he will not hang for his heresy, but for doing murder even Holy Church will demand some penalty.

"Your brothers are preparing for Abbot Thurstan's funeral," I said. "Go to the precentor and explain your absence at lauds, then seek Brother Gerleys and beg his pardon for your heresy. When he is made abbot he will assign your penance. Now go."

Brother Herbert did not hesitate, although he did seem unsteady as he walked to the guest house door and passed from view.

"That prior may 'ave done for the novice on 'is own," Arthur said, "but someone helped haul the corpse to the wood. Think it was the infirmarer, then?"

"Him, or a lay brother."

Before the sacrist rang the bell for terce I questioned Brother Guibert. I examined the infirmarer sharply, but although I left him also with the hint of rope about his neck, and gained an admission of knowledge of the Brotherhood of the Free Spirit, he was adamant that he had never left the dormitory in the night to assist Prior Philip. I had no way to prove otherwise.

Lay brothers of the abbey reside in their own dormitory. When Eynsham Abbey was larger this must have been a crowded space. Even now a lay brother who stretched upon awakening might give his neighbor a knock. It seemed likely that if Prior Philip roused any of his three followers among the lay brothers some others would know of it.

Prime was well past when I sought the lay brothers' dormitory, so most were about their day's work. But as I entered the room an ancient lay brother tottered to his feet and began a wavering path toward a door at the far end of the narrow chamber.

He must have been afflicted with the disease of the ears, for although I scuffed my feet against the rushes and coughed loudly, yet the old man continued his halting pace, paying no heed to the noisy fellow behind him.

I tapped the feeble lay brother upon a shoulder to gain his attention and nearly caused him to collapse upon an adjacent bed. Had I not caught and steadied him I think he might have done so, or pitched headlong upon the rushes.

Cots lined the narrow dormitory and I guided the lay brother to one of these and invited him to sit upon it.

"Eh?" he replied.

I pointed to the bed, sat upon it, and patted the blanket next to me. He understood the gesture and collapsed beside me.

"Three lay brothers," I said loudly, "accompanied Prior Philip to Lincoln. Where are their cots? Can you show me?"

"Cats?" he said. "No cats 'ere. Some in stables. Catch mice an' rats there."

"Cots," I repeated, louder.

"Cots? Whose cots?"

I repeated the question, and the fellow pointed a wizened finger toward the far corner of the chamber.

"The three who travel with Prior Philip, their beds adjoin each other?"

"Aye."

"Where do you sleep?"

I knew that unless I wished to ask each question twice, I must speak forcefully. The old man heard, but so did another who entered the dormitory as I spoke.

The elderly lay brother pointed to the bed where I had first seen him upon entering the chamber and said, "Just there. Who are you, an' why do you ask who sleeps where?"

"Aye," the newcomer said in a hostile tone. "Why do you trouble Aylmer?"

"I am Hugh de Singleton, bailiff to Lord Gilbert Talbot at Bampton. Abbot Thurstan assigned me to discover who murdered the novice John Whytyng."

"Oh… 'eard about you. Too bad about the lad. But how can Aylmer help you?"

"The novice was slain in the night, near to the east fishpond. Some man, from village or abbey, found him there and did murder."

This lay brother could hear my questions without my being required to shout in his ear. For this I was much pleased.

"Aylmer," I said, "sleeps there," and I pointed to his bed. "Who sleeps in the far corner?"

I pointed to the bed next to those Aylmer had indicated as the sleeping spaces of the lay brothers now accompanying Prior Philip on his way to Lincoln.

"So happens," the newcomer said, "I do. What is that to you?" The hostile tone had returned to the man's voice.

"The three who sleep near and across from your bed, did any man come to them, one or all three, in the night, a fortnight past?"

"Don't know. I'd be asleep myself, wouldn't I?"

"You never heard any of these three leave his bed in the night?"

"Well... some do. To seek the privy. Need to meself, usually."

"And is a cresset kept burning here, as in the monks' dormitory, so that a man can see his way?"

"Aye."

"But none of the three who travel this day to Lincoln have risen in the night because some other man came to them and awakened them?"

"If so, the fellow did not awaken me."

If the lay brother whose bed was closest to those who were of the Brotherhood of the Free Spirit did not hear any of the three rise in the night, it was unlikely that any other lay brother whose cot was more distant from the three would have done so. I was thwarted. My design had been to find the man who aided Prior Philip, monk or lay brother, in transporting John Whytyng's corpse to a distant corner of the abbey grounds, and threaten him with the king's justice until he told of the prior's felony. I had failed.

In a few days the incensed prior would return to Eynsham Abbey. He would soon after learn that a heretic bailiff was partly responsible for his troubles. Abbot Thurstan was dead. Who of the monks would believe a bailiff over their prior – and a bailiff accused of heresy by Brother Guibert – that the prior had cast

Abbot Thurstan down the stairs? The abbot had written of this to Bishop Bokyngham, and Brother Theodore had read a copy of the letter to the monks, but I had no doubt that Prior Philip had wit enough to explain how Abbot Thurstan had been mistaken, and would likely blame me for the abbot's error.

And if I accused the prior of the heresy of the Brotherhood of the Free Spirit, who then would believe me? Would Henry Fuller summon enough courage to testify of Prior Philip's demand, when the prior might control his destiny? Would the monks of Eynsham Abbey abide by Abbot Thurstan's wishes and select Brother Gerleys as their next abbot? Prior Philip would disavow knowledge of the Brotherhood of the Free Spirit, which would be no sin, according to the heresy.

Prior Philip had his own private chamber on the upper level of the west range, near to the abbot's chamber, where rank permitted him to sleep undisturbed by the snores of other monks. I was so baffled that I decided to enter the chamber while the monks were assembled in the church for terce. Perhaps I might find some incriminating evidence there. I returned to the guest house, told Arthur of this desperate plan, and sat upon my bed to await the bell calling the monks to the office.

We did not wait long, and when the tolling ceased we walked through the empty refectory to the stairs leading to the upper level of the west range.

Monks have no need of locks, for they are to own no private possessions. Yet the door to the prior's chamber was locked. Perhaps this was a clue. Was there something within his chamber that Prior Philip did not want other men to know of? Or was the lock there because, like many Benedictines, he had strayed far from the Rule and owned goods valuable enough to be worth stealing?

I was ready to turn away from the prior's door, secured as it was against entry, when Arthur placed a hand upon my arm, grinned, and drew his dagger. Arthur is a man of many skills. I learn of more of them each day. He inserted the point of his dagger into the lock, twisted it about until he heard a click, then turned the latch and pushed open the door.

Prior Philip's chamber was not so large or well furnished as the abbot's chamber, but was equipped with a bed with a thick mattress and a large chest. I wondered when I saw the chest what possessions a Benedictine would own which would require such a box.

I opened the unlocked chest and investigated its contents. Two black habits of finest wool were there, three cowls, and three silver objects: a spoon, a platter, and a small salver. What use these might be to a monk I know not. Over all of these was laid a fur-lined coat.

I had yet in my pouch the tuft of fur I had plucked from a thorn a fortnight past. I set this bit of pelt upon the fur lining of the prior's coat and was dismayed. The fur I had found near to the place where John Whytyng's corpse had lain was chestnut brown in color, perhaps from a fox. A rabbit's grey fur had kept the prior warm. The fur patch from my pouch was surely not torn from this coat.

Arthur saw me staring disconsolately at the open chest and peered into it from behind me. "Silver?" he said, assuming that my dismay was due to discovering that a Benedictine, and a prior at that, refused to live in harmony with the Rule.

"Aye, silver, and a fur-lined coat."

"We have our man, then," Arthur said.

I did not reply, but pointed to the reddish-brown tuft I had laid upon the grey rabbit fur.

"Oh. That the fur what you found?"

"Aye."

"Didn't come from that cloak, then, did it?"

"Nay."

"Suppose the prior owns two fur coats? Cold business, to travel to Lincoln in November. He might be wearin' one fur coat, if he owns two, an' the one keepin' 'im warm on his journey might be the one that scrap o' fur come from."

Arthur's suggestion was possible, and I grasped it eagerly. If it was not so, I had even less reason to accuse the prior of murder than I had an hour before. The mismatched fur did not mean that Prior Philip was innocent of John Whytyng's death. It meant only that I was yet unable to prove his guilt, and with no thought of how to proceed against the man. I had better find something new against him, for in a few days he would return, threatening retribution against all who opposed him. I would likely be first upon his list.

I replaced the tuft of incriminating fur – it might yet incriminate someone – in my pouch, closed the chest, and bid Arthur follow me from the chamber. It would be well if Arthur could relock the prior's door, else when he returned he would suspect his chamber was entered while he was away. But try as he might, Arthur could not lock what he had unlocked. We soon heard the footsteps of monks leaving the church, so I told Arthur to abandon the effort and come with me.

We walked quickly to the novices' chamber, and were seated there, innocent of mien, when Osbert and Brother Gerleys entered. Brother Gerleys saw me glance at Osbert and read my thoughts.

"Henry remains in the church," he said, "to pray and meditate. The chapter will vote tomorrow to admit him."

"Will he be accepted?"

"Aye. Some believe 'tis not meet to make such a decision before Abbot Thurstan's funeral, but even these would accept him. Since the pestilence our numbers shrink. We cannot cast off one who is so minded to join us."

"What of Prior Philip?"

"He is not here to object. And even should he become abbot he cannot undo what chapter has done."

"Will he be chosen abbot over you? Even after the brothers heard Abbot Thurstan's charge against him?"

"Maybe so. Some believe a prior must not be passed over, others that Abbot Thurstan must have been mistaken about what happened the night he fell... that the blow to his head addled his brain."

"Does Prior Philip own two fur-lined coats?"

The novice-master frowned, puzzled by this change of subject.

"Nay. But one, I believe."

"Did you see him depart for Lincoln?"

"Aye. All of the brothers gathered to bid him 'God-speed.'"

"Did he wear his fur coat?"

Brother Gerleys frowned as he thought back to the event. "Nay, he did not, as I remember. He wore a thick woolen cloak. Probably did not wish to return with his fine cloak spattered with mud."

Arthur's suggestion was wrong. Prior Philip owned but one furred coat, and its lining did not match the fragment I had found fixed to a thorn. Perhaps this wayward scrap in my pouch was indeed from some incautious wild animal and not from some man's garment. The color and texture seemed to be that of a fox. Perhaps Reynard had caught his tail upon the brambles while pouncing upon a coney.

"What do the brothers say of my presence in the abbot's chamber?" I asked.

Brother Gerleys shrugged. "Nothing."

"None wish to see me back in Brother Guibert's cell? Do not some wonder aloud how I came to escape the cell?"

"If so, they do not speak of it. Gossip is forbidden. We who have lived many years in a cloister learn to master our curiosity... most of us."

"I wonder if Prior Philip has also learned to subdue his curiosity?" I said. "When he returns he will have many questions about events while he was absent."

"Aye, he will so. And likely will not be pleased by the answers. But why did you ask if Prior Philip owned two fur coats? You are here to seek who has slain John Whytyng. What have the prior's cloaks to do with that?"

"Nothing, it seems."

"But you once thought so?"

"Aye. But this is not the first time I've been mistaken."

"You think Brother Prior had some knowledge of John's death do you not? If the novice left the abbey in the night Prior Philip would be most likely to know of it, being explorator. But," Brother Gerleys said after some hesitation, "why would he not confront John if he knew he had slipped from the abbey? Or try to defend the lad if he saw him attacked in the night? He asked me soon after Michaelmas if John was ready to take his vows."

"What did you reply?"

"I told him that all three lads were ready, and but for his thwarting him, Henry would be tonsured already. Osbert will not be eighteen 'till after Easter, so he is too young."

"Did you know that John was prepared to leave the abbey?"

"He was not happy here, but where would he go? His father wished him here."

"He spoke of Oxford, and studying law."

"He did? Not to me... perhaps to Osbert, or Henry."

The novice-master looked to Osbert. The novice replied with a shrug and said, "John never seemed eager to be about God's work, but he did not speak of Oxford. Not to me, nor to Henry, I think, or Henry would have told me."

"How do you know this?" Brother Gerleys asked me. "Did you learn of it from his father?"

"Nay. For now you must be content with understanding that it is so. John Whytyng did not wish to continue here."

"Could that be why he was slain? Would Prior Philip have done murder to prevent him leaving? Is that your thought?"

"I know not what to think," I replied. "But if I cannot solve a murder in five or six more days we both may see disagreeable days to come... But Henry will be a brother of this abbey, you said, and the prior cannot undo what chapter has done?"

"Aye. Tomorrow the vote, and all brothers will be in the chapter house. When he has been accepted the sacrist will give him the tonsure, then all will go to the church, where the mass will be celebrated and Henry will take vows of poverty and chastity and obedience. Then for three days he will live alone, having last place in church, cloister, and chapter house. He will remain behind in the church after matins to meditate or to sing the psalmody, and he will be required to sleep with his hood up. Of course, in November, this is no great trial.

"At the end of three days Henry will receive the Kiss of Peace at mass, and then his head will be uncovered, making of him a member of our community. 'Tis the abbot who is to do this, but we have none. Perhaps the precentor will perform the ritual. I will not. 'Twould seem presumptuous."

Chapter 18

I missed my Kate. And Bessie. When I accepted Abbot Thurstan's commission I thought the exchange of a few days to seek a felon in return for a Bible to be an excellent trade. But as days passed I was less sure of the bargain. And if I did not discover who had slain John Whytyng the failure would gnaw at me for months to come. I would awaken in the night and bemoan my defeat.

Unless in the next five or six days I discovered some new evidence pointing to a murderer, Prior Philip would return and set all for naught. Even if he was not chosen abbot he would yet be prior, and rule the abbey until a new abbot was chosen. And when Brother Gerleys, or some other which Bishop Bokyngham might have in mind, became abbot and was called away on abbey business, the prior would be left in charge. Who could know what mischief he might cause the abbey? Or the mischief he might cause me?

For three days I retraced my steps, questioning those to whom I had spoken in the past, and was not well received for my trouble, but for Osbern Mallory, who was pleased that I pronounced his wound healing well. The others – Squire Ralph, Sir Thomas, Sir Geoffrey, whom I had not earlier questioned, and Simon atte Pond – could not add to my search. Or would not. Indeed, but for the yeoman of Cumnor these men were resolute in sending me from their presence as ignorant of John Whytyng's death as ever. By this time village gossip had told the folks of Eynsham why I was prowling about the village and abbey, and it required little wit for a man to guess that if I sought him with questions, it must be that I thought him a possible felon. Or that I thought he knew of a possible felon. Were it not for Arthur standing behind me during these interviews with arms crossed and a grim expression upon his partly purpled face, I believe the gentlemen, and even the reeve, might have produced a dagger and bid me be gone. A youth was dead, but no man of Eynsham seemed much troubled.

Abbot Thurstan's funeral was upon Sunday. On Wednesday, near to terce, Prior Philip returned. I did not know of this for an hour or more, for Arthur and I were at the time in the guest house awaiting the lay brother who would bring loaves with which we might break our fast. He brought also the news of the prior's return. The report did not improve my appetite.

We had but finished the maslin loaves and ale a few minutes earlier when the door to the guest house crashed open and two men entered with resolute expressions upon their faces. Neither could be described as handsome, and ill humor did not improve their appearance.

Arthur did not appreciate this unannounced intrusion, and leaped to his feet, scowling, with his right hand on the hilt of his dagger. I was immediately upon my feet also, but when the two men halted but a step inside the chamber door 'twas not my appearance which halted their advance.

Before I could ask the meaning of their abrupt arrival the first of the fellows spoke. "Prior Philip wishes to speak to you. You are to come with us."

"Where?" I asked.

"His chamber. He awaits you."

"Tell the prior that I have much to discuss with him, but would prefer to entertain him here, in the guest chamber. I have no other pressing business, so will await his visit this morning. Your chauces and cotehardies are mud-spattered. Did you accompany Prior Philip to Lincoln?"

"Aye. But you are to come with us." The lay brother also rested a hand upon the hilt of his dagger. I did not wish for conflict with these fellows, but I thought it likely that if I appeared before the prior our conversation would be brief and both Arthur and I would leave his chamber securely bound. And this time Brother Gerleys might find it more difficult to free us. I decided to give the men a cause for alarm.

"Tell the prior that I have prepared a letter" – this was not completely a lie, for I had composed a message in my mind – "to send to Bishop Bokyngham regarding a heretical brotherhood which has contaminated this abbey, and wish to discuss the business with him as a matter of great urgency. I have discovered that monks, and some lay brothers also, have succumbed to this heresy, and, unless they repent, are in danger of the scaffold."

I said these last words with a solemn visage, frowning into the eyes of first one man, then the other.

"It will be best if Prior Philip appears alone. The heresy is widespread. Who can know which of the brothers may be infected?"

"We'll find 'em," Arthur added. "An' when we do they'll 'ave more to fear than this dagger." And as he spoke he drew his blade from its sheath.

I do not know which was most effective, my words or Arthur's dagger. One or the other caused the lay brothers to back through the door, then turn on their heels and flee across the kitchen garden toward the refectory.

The Eynsham Abbey guest house is not grand, as it would be in greater monasteries. There were no separate accommodations for those of great estate but for a partition which divided the chamber. Early in our stay at the abbey I had opened the door to see what lay beyond the divider. Night had come when I did this, so I saw little of the unlit space. Now I went again to the partition door, and opened it, and peered into this unused area.

Furnishings there were of higher quality, the beds equipped with thicker mattresses. It was clear that when some baron wished lodging at Eynsham Abbey, he and his lady would be housed in this more elegant chamber while his retainers slept where Arthur and I resided.

The rear of this better half of the guest house abutted the dormitory. No door was there, which was good. We could not be overwhelmed by men coming for us from two directions. If the prior decided to force a way into the guest house, there was but one door through which men could enter, and to do this they must pass Arthur. No easy task when only one man at a time could occupy the doorway.

The word "brotherhood," when I used it, seemed to concentrate the minds of the lay brothers whom Prior Philip had sent for me. I thought they might use it when reporting to the prior, and was sure that if they did, he would deny his dignity enough to appear at the guest house to learn what I knew and if the knowledge could be used against him.

The prior did not come to the guest house alone, as I had asked, but when Brother Guibert attempted to enter with him I denied him. I thought that Prior Philip might then depart also, but he waved a hand toward the infirmarer, indicating that he should go, and walked to the center of the chamber. He wore yet the long, mud-spattered black cloak which had warmed him upon his journey. I motioned to Arthur to shut the guest house door, and as he did so the prior turned and, with hands upon his hips, gazed imperiously at me.

I believe the prior was accustomed to intimidating others by looking down upon them, as he is taller than most. He could not do so with me, as I am also tall. I looked him in the eye, but he did not look away.

Neither of us had spoken. I waited for Prior Philip to begin the conversation. This he hesitated to do, but when the silence became onerous he finally spoke.

"How is it you defy me? I am lord of this abbey. You refused to attend me."

"You are temporarily lord of Eynsham Abbey, I think. Abbot Thurstan told me of what was in the letter you took to Bishop Bokyngham."

"Bah. Doddering old fool. I told the bishop his accusation was baseless."

"There are other matters. If your only concern was that of Abbot Thurstan's accusation that you shoved him down the presbytery stairs, you would not have come here as I asked. But when your lay brothers spoke the word 'brotherhood' you decided to have conversation with me, to learn what it may

211

be that I have discovered whilst you were upon the road. You would not be here in the guest house if you were not uneasy, I think."

"Bah." (This seemed one of the prior's favorite expressions.) "I care little for what you may have learned in my absence."

"Even who has done murder?"

I watched the prior intently as I said this, to see if he would react to my claim (untrue, but he would not know that) that I knew who had slain John Whytyng.

"You have discovered who has slayed the novice?" he asked.

There was no indication that such knowledge on my part gave the prior any anxiety. Of course, I thought, an adept of the Brotherhood of the Free Spirit would be experienced in lying and therefore skilled at it. If forced to leave the abbey, perhaps he might take up the law.

"Who is the killer?" he asked.

"We must first discuss another matter," I said. "I have discovered heresy within Eynsham Abbey."

"You have discovered?" the prior said incredulously. "How does a heretic discover his own heresy? The archdeacon has reported all to Bishop Bokyngham."

"Not all, I think. The man who reported my words to Abbot Thurstan is himself a heretic. Will the bishop believe the testimony of such a man?"

"Who is this heretic?"

"The infirmarer, Brother Guibert."

"What evidence have you for such a charge?"

I thought I detected just the beginning of concern in the prior's words.

"The testimony of others who shared the heresy, but have repented their error, and of some who were invited to join the heresy but refused."

"So you will condemn a man as a heretic upon the word of other heretics?"

"The word of those who are heretics no longer."

"What heresy has supposedly infected this house? Tell me,

that I may root it out. 'Tis a prior's duty, in the absence of his abbot, to do so."

"The brothers will soon choose a new abbot. He will deal with apostasy."

"I surely will."

"The brothers know the contents of the letter Abbot Thurstan sent with you to Bishop Bokyngham. Some may believe the accusation against you false, but those are few. Brother Gerleys will be the next abbot of this house, and unless Bishop Bokyngham has some other candidate in mind he will approve him. Either way, you will not be abbot of Eynsham Abbey."

Prior Philip's marred countenance reddened as I spoke. "So you claim," he growled.

"You asked of the heresy I have found. There are in Eynsham Abbey members of the Brotherhood of the Free Spirit."

"The Free Spirit? That heresy died away a century past," the prior said. "And 'twas never great here in England. Who has told you this nonsense?"

"I told you, those who now repent their foolishness and sin. In every such company of heretics there is an adept, a leader, whose commands the others must obey."

"Who is this man?"

"You, as you well know."

"I have served as monk and prior for many years with no blemish upon my reputation. Do you expect that you, a mere bailiff, will be believed if you make this charge known?"

"You do not deny it, then?"

"Nay. To what purpose? I am proud of my enlightenment and the hidden secrets I have brought to others."

"You do not fear the hangman?"

"Nay. Who would believe you, did you accuse me?"

"I told you, there are others: Brother Adam, and Brother Herbert. Brother Henry…"

"Brother Henry? Was the novice made a brother in my absence?" The prior's face reddened again.

"Aye. You thought he would succumb to your demand, as did Brother Adam and Brother Herbert, but he would not, as Martin Glover and John Whytyng would not. Martin Glover left Eynsham Abbey and joined another monastery. But when you required John Whytyng to join the heresy he refused, and you learned then, in the night beside the fishpond, that he intended to forsake a vocation and leave the monastery. You would then have no hold over him. If he told of your heresy there was danger that he might be believed, so you silenced him with a dagger in the back."

Prior Philip's mouth dropped open as I made the accusation. I thought this to be evidence of his guilt. The bishop's court would not accept an open mouth as evidence, but I thought I could find other proofs. Brother Eustace had seen the prior go out in the night to follow the novice, and no other saw the lad alive after.

"You believe I murdered the novice?"

"You were there with him in the night. There are witnesses."

"Who says so?"

"Brother Eustace has told me that you followed John from the church after he let himself from the abbey with his key. And there is another who hid near the pond and overheard the novice refuse your demand. You saw no other course to save yourself. A novice might not send a heretic prior to the scaffold upon his witness alone, but you knew that John's testimony would cause others, especially Abbot Thurstan, to watch you more closely to see if some part of his accusation might be true."

"I did not slay him," the prior said. His attitude had deflated like a sheep's bladder kicked too hard.

"If not you, who did? You admit that you were there. 'Tis why you urged Abbot Thurstan to discharge me... you feared I might learn of your felony."

"I did not slay him," he said again. "I know not who did."

"Why should I believe you?"

"'Tis the truth," he shrugged.

"There is no truth for an adept of the Brotherhood of the Free Spirit. That which is false is as acceptable, nay more acceptable, than truth."

The prior did not respond. Nothing he said could be believed. But he finally spoke.

"I left the novice beside the fishpond," he said. "If he left the abbey he could do me little harm. I had no need to slay him. He said that he planned to tell Brother Gerleys of his choice, then depart. He would not speak to Abbot Thurstan, he said."

"Why should I believe this?"

"Because as I returned to the north porch of the church I saw the man who must have slain the novice."

"Who was it?"

"'Twas dark, and had he not moved I would not have seen him. But I was all in black, so he did not see me and hide himself. Don't know who it was, and paid the man no attention."

"It did not trouble you that he was about after curfew without a light?"

"That's a beadle's worry, not mine."

"Next day, when John Whytyng was discovered missing, why did you not speak?"

"Foolish question. How could I know these things without implicating myself in his disappearance? I thought he had changed his mind. Decided not to tell Brother Gerleys he was leaving the abbey, and chose to depart in the night. He'd no possessions in the novices' chamber to reclaim. I was pleased that he was away. When you found him dead I congratulated myself that I had held my tongue."

"When I found the novice dead, why did you not then speak of the man you saw in the night?"

"And say what? That I had followed John to the fishpond in the night? Abbot Thurstan might have assumed that we had planned to meet there. I had no desire to be sent to Scotland or Norway."

"You may yet go to some such place. 'Twill be better than the alternative."

"You think a bishop will turn a prior over to the sheriff for punishment?"

"I do not know the mind of Bishop Bokyngham, but the archdeacon seemed eager to root out heresy."

"'Tis a prior's word against a bailiff's."

"A bailiff, four monks, one not of this house, and several lay brothers."

"Lay brothers? But they were with me on the road to Lincoln."

"Aye, they were. But when pressed 'tis my belief they will abjure your heresy rather than face a noose. Do you trust that they will remain loyal to the Brotherhood of the Free Spirit, even to death?"

The prior hesitated, and I saw in the pause an admission that he could not be sure of his followers. And even if they remained loyal to the Brotherhood, 'twould be no betrayal of the order to lie, for that was the conceit upon which the organization had been founded. Would they betray him, the prior must have thought, to save themselves? Of course. He faced the ruin of his plan, and he knew it.

"I did not slay John Whytyng," he said again.

"You follow a heresy which admires falsehood," I said. "Why should I, or any man, believe you?"

The prior had no answer, caught in a web of his own devising. But foolish as it seemed at the time, I believed him. His fur coat did not match the tuft in my pouch, he had evidently roused no man in the night to help him draw John Whytyng's corpse from the pond and carry it away, and he spoke true: he had small motive, for he would surely be believed over a novice if John had accused him of heresy.

"We will go to the north porch. Show me where you stood when you saw the man the night John Whytyng was slain."

Prior Philip was not eager to do this, or cooperate with a mere bailiff in any way. He would not have, I think, if he could have discovered some way of escaping the hold, tenuous as it was, which I had over him. I motioned to the guest house door. He walked through it and Arthur and I followed. He said not one word, nor looked behind to see if we came after.

The prior did not lead us through the west range or the cloister to the church, but circled around the kitchen and the abbot's lodging, past the west front of the church, and stopped when he reached its north porch. Only then did he speak.

"I stood here, with my hand upon the latch, when movement in the street caught my eye. The moon was near to full, and the night nearly cloudless."

"Where was the man when you first saw him?"

"Just there," the prior said, and pointed toward Simon atte Pond's barn.

"Which way did he travel?"

"Don't know. He passed behind those bushes yonder by the road, and I saw no more of him. He did not make for the abbey so I paid him no heed."

If this shadowy fellow, skulking about in the night, was the felon I sought, he had already slain the novice when Prior Philip saw him, for if the prior was to be believed, he was seen walking from the abbey fishpond, not toward it. Such would agree with Maude atte Pond's assertion that John Whytyng was slain but a few moments after his conversation ended. That conversation, 'twas now clear, was with Prior Philip.

Had this fellow seen the prior leave the church and followed? Why would he do so? What interest could some curfew-violator have in a monk's nocturnal business? If not the prior, had the man followed John Whytyng? If so, how could he know that the novice would leave the abbey and be waiting to follow him? Or was this shadowy presence mere coincidence?

There was no sun to warm this day, but even had there been, the north porch would have been in shadow, and cold. Again I wished for my fur coat, and shivered.

"Did the fellow walk slowly, or did he seem in a hurry?" I asked.

"He was hurried," the prior replied. "He knew his path, even in moonlight, and was quick to follow it and vanish beyond yon bushes."

The foliage toward which the prior pointed was bare of leaves, but the thicket of intertwined stems was dense enough that even in daylight a man walking behind the hedge might not be seen. And if he continued on that course he would pass from the road to the forecourt of Sir Richard Cyne's manor house.

"Come with me," I said, and walked toward the road and the place where the prior had seen a man leave Simon atte Pond's toft. I did not look behind to see if Prior Philip followed. Arthur would see that he did. The prior's presence behind me would help guarantee truthful answers at the house I intended to visit.

Chapter 19

A few paces along the road and we came to Sir Richard's manor house. I waited 'till we had passed beyond the bushes which fringed the road, then turned my head quickly toward the house, so that if any man peered from an upper window, my glance would be too quick for him to hide himself from view.

A man did. Sir Thomas looked down upon us. Did the knight ever do anything but stare from that window? When he saw my eyes upon him he disappeared.

A few more strides and we came to the path which led to the reeve's house. I turned toward the door, and heard Prior Philip and Arthur follow. The prior had not spoken as we passed the manor house. Whether or not he followed my gaze and saw Sir Thomas at his window I know not.

But when I approached the reeve's door he spoke. "Why do we come here?" he asked. "And what has this place to do with a man seen in the night? You believe I saw Simon atte Pond, and that he did murder?"

"Nay. Wait, and listen."

I rapped my knuckles upon the sturdy door, and a few moments later the old washerwoman who had entered the abbey with Maude appeared, drying her hands upon an apron.

The woman had visited the abbey many times and recognized the prior. Her hands flew to her face and she stepped back in surprise.

"I'll fetch Alyce," she stammered, and turned to leave us standing in the doorway.

"Not necessary," I said. "You may speak as well as any who may enter this house."

When I had earlier stood at this door I had seen that it opened to a large chamber. This hall was furnished with benches, chairs, chests, and a table. At the left end a fireplace warmed the room. To the right was a partition, and two doors. Simon atte

Pond's prosperity had allowed him to enlarge his house with a bay for private rooms. I had thought it likely that these doors led to bedchambers, and this now prompted my visit.

I pointed toward the first door, which opened to a room lit by a small window of glass, another sign of the reeve's prosperity. This window looked out upon the road before the house, and across the road to Sir Richard's manor house. From the manor house, of course, a man might also look upon this window.

"Who sleeps in this bedchamber?" I asked. The question so startled the servant, and the prior's presence behind me had so unsettled her, that she did not think to dissemble.

"The lasses," she said. "Maude an' Isobel."

The door to the house had no lock, which I thought odd for so prosperous a household. I peered around the open door and saw an upright fixture fastened to a vertical beam between the hinges. Another like it was fixed to the latch side of the jamb, and propped in the corner I saw small oaken beams which, when dropped in place, would bar the door. If the hinges were greased, the bar could be lifted and Maude could pass from the house silently, with no rasping of key in lock.

"And whose chamber is that?" I asked, pointing to the second door.

"Simon an' Alyce sleeps there."

"And you and the other servants? Where do you sleep?"

The woman nodded over her shoulder to a ladder which led up to a loft over the far bay of the large chamber. "In the loft," she said. "The lad sleeps in the stable, with the beasts."

To leave the house in the night Maude would need either to open this front door, or to silently pass the chamber where her parents slept to depart the house through a rear door. Then she must creep past the barn, where slept another of the household. I thought it likely she would choose the front door. The night John Whytyng was slain was well lit. 'Twas nearly a full moon, and skies had been cloudless, the weather dry, for some days before the murder. Could it be that Sir Thomas Cyne had stood at his window that night and watched the lass steal from the house to meet her novice at the fishpond?

Maude told me that she had crept from her parents' house several times before the night John Whytyng was slain. Had Sir Thomas seen one of these earlier escapes and watched for another? In my mind's eye I saw him at his window, watching, then following the lass as she made her way to the pond. Where did he think she was going, and what did he expect to find there? Whatever the answers, it was unlikely he anticipated the presence of Prior Philip. Perhaps he heard Maude and the novice speak before the prior came upon them, and knew his pursuit of the maid doomed. Then, from the shadows, he would have heard Prior Philip and John in dispute.

When the prior stalked off in disgust Sir Thomas saw opportunity to do away with this rival. He would have known that Maude was somewhere near. But could she identify him in the moonlight? Perhaps he struck in passion, without considering that he might be identified. Then, in fear of discovery, he fled, to return with another who would help him move the novice's corpse to some far place. He should have known that the novice would be missed and eventually found, but those who act out of fury and passion do not likely consider the consequences of their impulsiveness.

I bid the servant "Good day," and motioned to Arthur and Prior Philip that 'twas time to leave. My mind was as fixed now upon proving that Sir Thomas Cyne had done murder, as a day earlier I was convinced that Prior Philip was the felon. But the prior's thoughts were on other matters.

"No one will believe you," he said as we set foot upon the road. "I will claim that 'tis you and Brother Gerleys and the novices who are of the Brotherhood of the Free Spirit. That Brother Gerleys is your adept. All who have heard of the Brotherhood know that members hold truth to be irrelevant, so when you protest 'tis not so, your repudiation will be expected and disbelieved."

This thought had occurred to me. An accomplished liar is more readily believed than the maladroit truthful.

"What of Brother Adam? And Brother Herbert?"

"Brother Guibert will say that they followed Brother Gerleys. Their confession is to protect him, and is false, to save themselves from their due penalty."

The prior thought that he had firm ground again beneath his feet. Eventually Bishop Bokyngham and his archdeacon would be required to decide which faction within Eynsham Abbey spoke the truth. My testimony would do no good. The archdeacon already thought me a heretic. If I pointed to Prior Philip as the apostate he would likely believe the opposite.

The prior guessed my thoughts. "The archdeacon will see you hang for two heresies," he chuckled. "Which will make the noose tighter, I wonder?"

Arthur heard this conversation while following from the reeve's house. He inserted another thought into the conversation.

"Lord Gilbert is at Goodrich Castle. He thinks right well of Master Hugh. An' the Sheriff of Oxford an' Lord Gilbert is close friends, Sir Roger an' Lord Gilbert havin' gone off to war with the French together. In five days I can be to Goodrich an' back with Lord Gilbert. You think Lord Gilbert, an' Sir Roger will allow some wart-faced prior to send Master Hugh to the scaffold? An' 'ere's another reason you should think afore you speak such lies." Arthur circled around before the prior as he spoke, and concluded his words by lifting an imposing fist before Prior Philip's widening eyes.

"You would not strike a monk and risk the wrath of Holy Church," the prior said hopefully.

"The wrath of the Church don't trouble me none. Won't be nobody to tell the archdeacon what happened anyway."

"I'll tell him."

"No, you won't," Arthur said. He spoke softly, but there was menace in his voice. "If Lord Gilbert an' the sheriff can't persuade you to steer away from falsehood, I'll do so."

Arthur left no doubt as to the means of persuasion he would employ. The bruise upon his cheek told Prior Philip that he was accustomed to the occasional brawl and his demeanor spoke that he would cheerfully accept another. Prior Philip might have been an adept, but I thought it unlikely the title would also apply to his ability in a fight.

The prior fell silent, and with Arthur standing resolute before him, he stood still. He had thought his opposition limited to me and a few monks. Now he understood that he must overcome a great lord and the king's Sheriff of Oxford. His shoulders began to droop and I pressed my advantage.

"Scotland or Norway? Which would you prefer? When Brother Gerleys is confirmed as abbot I'm sure he will give you your choice. And if the bishop puts some other monk in place as abbot you will have the same option. I and Lord Gilbert will see to it. Now, let us return to the abbey and meet with Brother Gerleys."

"Meek" is not a word which in past days I would have used to describe Prior Philip, but as we walked to the abbey precincts, and he considered the opposition of Lord Gilbert and Sheriff Roger de Elmerugg, he became crestfallen and subdued. I believe he saw a difficult journey to Scotland in his future.

We passed the manor house and I stole a quick glance toward the window where I had often seen Sir Thomas. He was not there. Or was that a fleeting shape I saw standing back from the window and moving quickly aside?

I led Prior Philip past the church to the west range, then to the novices' classroom. I hoped to find Brother Gerleys there, but he was away. Osbert was bent over a desk, quill in hand, ink and cheap paper before him, practicing his hand. I asked for Brother Gerleys.

"In the chapter house, meeting with Brother Precenter and Brother Sacrist," he said.

"Run quickly and fetch them, all three. Tell them Prior Philip has an important announcement."

The prior's subdued manner had been gradually replaced by a scowl. His mind was considering, I knew, how he might escape his dilemma and turn it to his advantage. Osbert set his quill beside his work and trotted off upon his errand. I pointed to a bench and told the prior to sit. He remained standing.

There was a brief silence, then Prior Philip opened his mouth to speak. But before he could do so Arthur said, "Master Hugh said 'Sit.'"

The prior decided that if he did not sit of his own accord Arthur would require him to do so unwillingly. After a moment given to considering the method Arthur might use to convince him to sit, he did so. The words he was preparing to say he swallowed.

A few moments later the precentor and the sacrist followed Brother Gerleys into the chamber. Osbert also entered.

"'Twould be best," I said to Brother Gerleys, "if Osbert was sent upon other duties."

The novice-master looked down upon the ink, quill, and paper, and told the lad to take his work to the cloister and finish it there before the light failed.

Osbert knew some matter of great import was to be raised, and was abashed that the business was thought to be too distressing for his tender years. When the lad was away and the chamber door closed I turned to the seated prior and spoke.

"To avoid great unpleasantness, it would be proper for you to announce to these, your brothers, that you withdraw your name from consideration for the office of abbot and do endorse Brother Gerleys for the post, as Abbot Thurstan desired. Furthermore, tell them of your desire to be assigned to Dunfermline Abbey."

Precentor, sacrist, and novice-master exchanged astonished glances. The precentor finally spoke.

"Is this so?"

Prior Philip's wit had left him. He nodded dumbly, eyes downcast, which was surely a new and novel posture for him. Later, on the road to Scotland, he would think of many words he might have said. But for the moment he was silent.

"Do you wish to address the chapter?" Brother Gerleys said.

The prior shook his head. He wished for no more humiliation than he now endured.

"When will you depart?" the sacrist asked.

"Tomorrow, at first light," he said. "I have no wish to remain where I am not wanted."

I thought that if such was the case, he would not remain long at Dunfermline Abbey, but held my tongue.

Brother Gerleys felt himself sufficiently empowered that he now spoke. "Brother Prior, I will write a letter to Dunfermline's abbot, requesting him to welcome you to his house. I will not relate your heresies while here, but you should know that if you continue in your wickedness you will be found out there, as you were here. Tomorrow in chapter we will pray for your safe journey. Now you must prepare for travel. Go to the church, and pray there for your soul."

Five men stood silent, no other words spoken or needed. Prior Philip stood slowly and left the chamber. He faced the ruin of his plot and a journey which would have been arduous even in mid summer.

And I faced the ruin of my explanation for John Whytyng's murder. The prior was guilty of many sins, and I had wished murder to be among them, but this was not so. The novice had been dead for three weeks. For more than a fortnight I had sought his killer. Too many of those days, I now knew, had been wasted trying to prove the guilt of an innocent man. Well, innocent of murder, anyway.

But as prior, precentor, and sacrist left the chamber, another solution to the puzzle of John Whytyng's murder was taking form in my mind.

"You set out to discover a felon," Brother Gerleys said, "and found rather a heretic. Will you continue to seek a murderer, or is the trail too cold?"

"I had thought 'twas cold, but perhaps it has become warmer."

Both Arthur and the novice-master looked at me with puzzled expressions. I explained to Brother Gerleys that the prior had seen a man walking from the pond after his argument with John Whytyng, and that this shadowy figure had disappeared in the direction of Sir Richard's manor house.

"An hour past I required Prior Philip to go with me to Simon atte Pond's house, where I sought information, and saw Sir Thomas gazing down upon us and the reeve's house from an upper window."

Brother Gerleys said nothing. I explained. "Arthur and I have seen the knight often as we pass on the road, peering from that window. What could he hope to see which is not already familiar to him?"

The novice-master's eyes opened in understanding. "The maid... Maude?"

"Aye. Her bedchamber is at the front of the reeve's house. 'Twould have been a simple matter for the lass to unbar the door when all are asleep and sneak off in the night to meet John Whytyng.

"'Twas nearly a full moon the night the novice was slain. Sir Thomas, at his window, could have seen Maude steal away and followed. He might have heard Prior Philip and John in dispute, knew that Maude was somewhere close by, and when the novice told the prior he intended to leave the abbey, Sir Thomas guessed that Maude and her lands were lost to him."

"Sir Thomas is the murderer, then?" Brother Gerleys asked.

"I believe so. I once thought 'twas the prior, but no longer do... even though his words are not to be trusted without corroboration."

"But Sir Thomas is left-handed," Arthur reminded me. "You said, from the wounds in the novice's back, that his killer would be right-handed."

"Aye, so I thought. But it may be that John heard his assailant approach and began to turn to see who was there, so that Sir Thomas's dagger pierced him on his right side."

"How can this be proven, if so?" Brother Gerleys asked.

"Sir Thomas ain't gonna' admit to murder an' put 'is neck in a noose," Arthur said.

"We must trap him."

"How?" the monk asked.

"I intend to spread gossip, and see how he responds."

226

"What gossip?"

"Simon atte Pond opposed the suit of a tenant of Cumnor, although the fellow is nearly as prosperous as the reeve. I intend to tell some folk that he has changed his mind, and now looks with favor upon the suit. Sir Thomas is eager for the lass and the land she will inherit, and may decide to remove another rival."

"This will put Osbern Mallory in some danger," Arthur said.

"Aye. We will go to Cumnor and stay under his roof for a few days, to see if Sir Thomas can be caught."

"How will you put this gossip abroad?" Brother Gerleys asked.

"The ale house," I said.

"Will you tell Simon what you intend?"

"I must. He favors Sir Thomas, I've heard, but I think no man of the commons wants a murderer for a son-in-law, even be he a knight."

"What if he protests?"

"We must pray that he will not, for I have no other trap devised."

"When will you do this?" Brother Gerleys asked.

"Now, this day. I will seek Adam Skyllyng's ale. He knows why I am in Eynsham, and I will allow him to pry the gossip from me."

"An' then we seek the reeve an' tell 'im what's been said," Arthur said. "Be too late for 'im to object."

"What of Osbern Mallory?" Brother Gerleys asked.

"We will go to Cumnor this day to see he is safe. And I think he will not be opposed to the scheme. We must act with haste; the day is far gone."

I asked the novice-master to see that our palfreys were saddled and ready, then told Arthur to follow. 'Tis no more than a hundred paces from the abbey gatehouse to the ale house, and before I had consumed half a cup of the man's ale I had allowed him to draw inference that Osbern Mallory of Cumnor was likely to wed Maude atte Pond.

I declined a second cup of ale, which disappointed Arthur, and hastened to the reeve's house. It was yet light, and I feared

227

he would be about his work and I would need to take time to find him. But he was at home. The man was not pleased to learn of his part in my plot. I could see that he hoped 'twould fail. He did not want to lose a knight for a son-in-law. I was somewhat worried that he might cross the road and divulge the scheme to Sir Thomas, but he promised that he would not. Sir Thomas had not been at his window when we walked to the reeve's house, but upon our return to the abbey I saw him there again, barely visible in the dying light.

I hurried to the guest house for my sack of instruments. There was, I thought, a reasonable chance that I might have need of them before many days passed.

It would not do for the knight to see Arthur and me ride past on our way to Swinford and Cumnor. So when we departed the abbey we led our beasts past the fishponds, behind the reeve's dwelling, past the wood, and joined the road to Swinford two hundred paces east of Sir Thomas and his window.

'Twas nearly dark when we splashed across the Thames at Swinford, and two miles beyond, at what remained of the plague-ravaged village, we entered Cumnor. Several houses showed light gleaming through oiled-skin windows. Osbern Mallory's was one of these. I left the palfreys with Arthur, in the road, approached the house and called out my name. I thought an unannounced knock upon Mallory's door, given recent events, might cause the man to greet a caller with a blade rather than a welcome.

I heard a bar lifted from the door and a moment later Mallory's shadow filled the opening. My supposition was correct. I saw a dagger in the man's hand – a legitimate caution.

The yeoman was surely surprised to see me, or any caller, at his door at such an hour. I apologized for the intrusion and explained that an urgent matter brought me to Cumnor.

"Me arm's doin' well," he said, misunderstanding my explanation. "But come in. See for yourself."

"Arthur has our palfreys in the road. It is important," I said, "that they be hidden in your barn. I will explain in a moment. Have you place for them, and a cresset to light his way?"

Mallory's brow furrowed, but he trusted me enough that he asked no questions. He turned from me, found an unlit cresset, touched its wick to one which was lighted, and brought it to me. This I took to Arthur, pointed to the shadow of the barn in the toft behind the house, and told him to join us in the dwelling when the beasts were cared for.

"I have put you in some danger," I began, when I returned to the house. This news did not seem to trouble him much. He did not ask how this was so, assuming that I would explain. I did.

"Gossip in Eynsham will say that Simon atte Pond has changed his mind and now favors your suit for Maude." Mallory's puzzled frown immediately became a broad smile.

"'Tis but gossip," I said, "and not true." The grin faded. "At least, not yet. Who can tell? It may yet be so."

"How did this rumor begin?" Mallory asked. I explained events in Eynsham of the past few days, and told him that I expected Sir Thomas to soon learn of Mallory's rise in Simon atte Pond's estimation.

"You think he'll try to slay me as he did the novice?"

"Aye. Mayhap as soon as this night, 'though I think the morrow or a day or so after more likely. I and my man will keep watch with you through the night. Perhaps 'twould be best if your lass was elsewhere. Is there a family in the village who will care for her for a few days?"

"Jaket an' Anne live just across the way. Got a lass same age as my Maggie. They'll keep 'er."

"Take her immediately. Tell them you will explain the need on the morrow."

He might as well have taken time to explain the need then, for Arthur, Osbern, and I took in turn sleeping and waking all through the night, but no man came near to Mallory's toft. Perhaps tales did not travel so rapidly in Eynsham as I had thought.

Chapter 20

The next night also was quiet. By the third night I began to despair of my trickery, and to worry that the Lord Christ disapproved of deceit, even when intended to good purpose. Whether or not He approved I cannot say, but if He opposed my stratagem He did nothing to subvert it.

'Twas well past midnight, a slender crescent of moon just rising above village roofs, when Arthur put an elbow into my ribs. Mallory and I were slumbering while Arthur kept watch. I started to wakefulness and felt Arthur put a finger across my lips to indicate silence. I was alert enough to take his meaning, and whispered for an explanation.

"Heard a horse whinny... quiet-like, an' some distance off. Nobody ought to be about this hour of the night."

I silently shook Mallory by the arm – his good arm – and he awakened with enough wit that he understood the cause for my taking his arm must be that some man approached.

We listened silently for some time, but heard nothing. I began to think that Arthur had heard the wind sighing through bare branches of trees behind Mallory's barn. Arthur read my mind.

"Not my imagination," he whispered. "There's a beast out there somewhere, an' where there's a beast there'll be a man."

His point was well taken, and I wished that Mallory had glass in his windows rather than skins. Sir Thomas, I thought, did not know that we lay in wait for him, but we did not know how he approached or what he intended.

"Are your hinges greased?" I said. "If I draw open a door, will the squeal alert whoso may be about in the night?"

"Put goose grease on 'em near to Lammastide, front an' back."

"Silently as can be, open your rear door a crack, no more, so we may see if the scoundrel approaches, or hear him should he tread upon a twig. I'll do the same at the front door. Just a crack, mind, so he doesn't see in the moonlight and flee."

Mallory stepped silently through the rushes and vanished in the gloom. I turned to the front of the house and delicately raised the bar and then turned the latch. The hinges were silent as I drew the door open to the width of my hand and peered out. I saw only a village sleeping under a starlit night, a crescent moon rising over the church tower.

I remained motionless at the door awaiting the appearance, if Arthur's ears were reliable, of some man abroad after curfew, when no honest fellow would be.

The house was silent, as should be if all within were asleep, so he who approached in the night was heard before he was seen. I heard a metallic "click," and then another. Arthur soon stood at my shoulder. He said nothing, but touched my shoulder. He had also heard the sound.

We heard it again, and a moment later a soft puffing sound. I knew then what I had heard: the sound of flint against steel. The next sound seemed like a man blowing upon tinder to urge it to flames. But where was the fellow?

Any man attempting to set tinder ablaze in the night will tell his place by the sparks and flame. I saw neither. Did my ears mislead me? The sounds I heard surely did not conform to a normal autumn night.

If some man did not attempt to start a blaze, what then did I hear? What else might a man do in the night which sounded like flint striking steel?

I did not need to answer my question. Arthur tapped me upon my left shoulder while I was peering into the darkness to my right. I turned and followed the direction of Arthur's arm as he pointed silently to the left of Mallory's door. Behind a leafless hedge, just across the road, no more than fifteen or twenty paces away, I saw a faint orange glimmer, and then another. These brief flashes became a steady glow. I heard no more sound of flint against steel, or breath upon tinder. Sir Thomas had lit his fire. Or so I thought.

I guessed what he intended. Some rain had fallen in the past week, but the past fortnight and more had been unusually dry. I supposed that Sir Thomas purposed to toss a brand to the thatch of Osbern Mallory's roof and burn the house down upon him. If so, his approach to the dwelling would be clearly visible, and any flame he carried would blind him with its light and obscure we who might appear from the darkened house to frustrate his plan.

And then the orange glow disappeared, as if it was a candle snuffed out. One instant it was there, the next, gone.

"What...?" I heard Arthur whisper in my ear.

And then I saw it again, nearly invisible, but a glimmer of light appeared, and as I watched, it began to move, first to the right, then it seemed to come straight toward me. Here was a mystery, but the puzzle was solved soon enough. The dim light briefly flickered, then flashed into full flame. 'Twas no more than five or six paces from me, and so bright that my eyes were dazzled. I saw only the brilliant flame and the black night surrounding it. Whoso approached the house had hidden his fire under some shroud.

I hesitated. Too long, as happened. Before my wit returned the blaze before my eyes described a circle and then flew through the air to bounce against the thatch of the roof.

Arthur saw this also, and made to push past me. This he could not do, for I had already launched myself in the direction of the man who thought to burn Osbern Mallory's house. I could not see the fellow, my eyes yet disordered by darkness, the light, then darkness again. But the man I sought suffered from the same loss of vision. Surely he heard my approach, but could not, I think, see from whence the threat came.

I stumbled in the darkness, flung my hands before me to catch my fall, and found my arms entangled in two legs. I knew whose these must be, so wrapped my arms tightly about the ankles so the felon could not escape.

Arthur did not stumble. He was running nearly full apace when he struck his quarry. The man could not step back to absorb the blow. I had him by the ankles.

He had been so intent upon his attack, I think, that he gave no heed to defending himself. That suddenly, out of the night, two men might be upon him, was a thing for which he was unprepared. He did not have long to consider this. He went down flat upon his back with Arthur dropping upon his belly. The fellow gasped, twitched, and lay silent, the breath driven from his lungs.

"Got 'im," Arthur said triumphantly.

"Hold him here," I said, "while I see what damage his brand has done. If he awakens and tries to escape, put him to sleep again."

Osbern had heard the tumult at the front of his dwelling, and arrived at the scene as I stood to seek whatever blaze might be upon his roof. I saw none. The torch had bounced from the roof and lay sputtering in Mallory's toft. The thatch had been too damp to catch, and the flame had not alighted upon the thatching and remained, but had rolled to the eave and fallen to the ground.

"What has happened?" Mallory asked.

"We have caught Sir Thomas trying to set your roof ablaze. We'll take him inside, light a cresset, and see what he has to say for himself."

We did so. Arthur had to help the fellow to his feet. If Arthur, in full flight, struck a horse he would leave the beast reeling. Our captive staggered across the threshold into the dark interior of the house. A moment later Mallory lit a cresset from a live coal on the hearth and set it before... Squire Ralph Bigge. I was stunned to silence.

Arthur may also have been surprised, but this did not lead to inaction. He gave Squire Ralph a vigorous shove and the stupefied squire staggered back before collapsing upon a bench against the wall.

"Get a cord to bind him," I said to Mallory. The fellow was nearly as robust as Arthur. It would be well to have him restrained before he gathered his wits.

Squire Ralph may have heard these words, but if so he made no response. He remained bent double, arms pressed against his affronted belly. I thought a rib or two might be broken, but there is little a surgeon can do for broken ribs, and where he was likely to be by Candlemas 'twould make no difference to him whether his ribs were whole or shattered.

Mallory disappeared through the rear door of his house. A few moments later he returned with a length of hempen cord stout enough to restrain a bull. He and Arthur bound Squire Ralph's wrists behind him, which seemed to increase the pain he felt in his gut, and then bound his ankles together.

The fellow was by this time regaining his senses, looking about as if to discover some way to escape his predicament. I had been wrong again. First I thought 'twas Prior Philip who had slain John Whytyng. Then my suspicion fell upon Sir Thomas Cyne. But my trap had caught Ralph Bigge.

The squire ceased his searching about the house and looked to me.

"Tell me why you wished to burn Osbern Mallory's house," I began. I thought I knew the answer, but wished to hear it from Squire Ralph. Wishing will not make a thing so. Squire Ralph said nothing.

This displeased Arthur. He sat beside the knight, thrust an elbow into his aching ribs, and said, "Master Hugh asked you a question."

Squire Ralph gasped and bent double. A cracked rib or two, surely. I shook my head to discourage Arthur from trying any further incentive to make Squire Ralph speak. Another such poke in the ribs and the fellow might swoon. What then could I learn from him?

When Squire Ralph was able to draw himself upright I again asked him why he cast a torch upon Osbern Mallory's roof. He did not immediately reply, but then looked from the corner of his eye and saw Arthur seemingly poised to deliver another jab to his offended ribs. He had not seen my wordless instruction to Arthur that such goading should be discontinued, so must have thought another thrust likely.

"Paid me," he said.

"Who? Someone paid you to set this house ablaze?"

"Aye."

"Who?"

The squire hesitated, considered Arthur's elbow, then said, "Sir Thomas."

I was wrong again, perhaps – if Squire Ralph spoke true. I began to wonder if Eynsham village and abbey were overrun by members of the Brotherhood of the Free Spirit, in whom no truth could be found. But if I could not believe a man with broken ribs, who believes the brawny fellow beside him is about to strike him again if he speaks false, who could I believe?

"How much were you promised?"

"Twenty shillings."

I had been wrong so many times in the past days that I had no fear of once more being mistaken.

"And this is to buy your silence about the death of the novice, as well? 'Twas you who helped carry the lad's corpse from the fishpond, was it not?"

Squire Ralph eyed Arthur's elbow and replied, "Aye."

"And you will so testify to the King's Eyre in Oxford?"

"Aye," he replied softly.

"Does Sir Thomas own a fur coat?" I asked.

Here was not a question the knight expected, and his eyes opened wide.

"Answer," Arthur said. There was no Christian charity in his voice, which was likely explained by the discoloration of his cheek which Squire Ralph's fist had caused.

"Aye," Squire Ralph said.

"Lined with fox, or rabbit?"

"Fox."

"When dawn comes we will return to Eynsham and see what Sir Thomas has to say of this matter," I said.

Arthur, Osbern, and I took it by turns watching Squire Ralph, but bound and in pain as he was, there was little to fear of him escaping us. Arthur saddled our palfreys, and we untied Squire Ralph's ankles so he could walk the road between us. His horse, he said, was tied to a sapling at the entrance to the village, and when we came upon it we lifted the grimacing fellow to its back and so returned to Eynsham.

While yet a distance from the village it occurred to me that Sir Thomas might again be at his window, see us approach with Squire Ralph bound between us, comprehend his danger, and flee. We turned from the road and entered Sir Richard's holdings from a fallow meadow behind his barn. The horses we left with a wide-eyed stable boy. The lad had likely seen Squire Ralph depart some hours past and did not expect him to return with his wrists bound behind his back.

Nor did Sir Thomas. We found him at a table, breaking his fast with a fresh loaf and ale. A servant stood nearby, preparing a pot for the fire. Sir Thomas leaped to his feet when he saw how Squire Ralph was restrained. He was wearing a fur-lined coat to ward off the morning chill.

"You were too cowardly to attack Mallory again," I said, "so sent another to do your felony. Mallory, even though you wounded him, might fight, unlike an unarmed novice."

"What? Why have you trussed up Squire Ralph like a goose for the roasting?"

"'Tis not his goose that's cooked," Arthur said, "but yours."

"Twenty shillings," I said, "to buy silence and a murder. No doubt you thought it a fine bargain, supposing the return of the investment would be Maude atte Pond and her father's lands."

"You speak foolishness," Sir Thomas said.

"Take off your coat," I said.

"What? No man tells me what to do in my own house."

Sir Thomas's hand went to his dagger, but Arthur was quicker, having already seen the likelihood that Sir Thomas would not cooperate. Arthur held the point of his blade to Sir Thomas's throat, then lifted the man's dagger from its sheath and tucked it into his own belt.

"Master Hugh wishes for you to remove your coat," he said softly, but with malice.

I believe Sir Thomas saw no compelling reason why he should not comply. Men do not often examine the hems of their coats.

"Lay it upon the table," I said. Then, to Arthur, "Watch him. See that he does not attempt to flee."

I withdrew the tuft of fox fur from my pouch and held it before me, as if studying it for the first time. Sir Thomas's expression changed from one of anger to one of concern. He did not understand the importance of the bit of fur. He soon did.

With the fine fur coat spread upon the table, I lifted the hem and a moment later discovered a place where the fur lining was shredded. I placed the tuft in my hand upon the bare spot. The color and size were a match.

I turned to Squire Ralph, who had watched this intently. "Did Sir Thomas wear this coat the night he asked your aid in moving John Whytyng's corpse?"

The knight looked from me to the coat to Sir Thomas before he spoke. "Aye," he finally said.

I was prepared for Sir Thomas to explain his damaged coat and disparage my insinuation. I was not prepared for what he did. He bolted, pushing past a surprised Arthur and leaping for the door. To reach the door he must pass me. I had time only to extend a foot. He tripped and staggered and at that instant his father opened the door to enter. Father and son crashed to the threshold, a tangle of arms and legs and shouted curses.

Arthur and I pulled Sir Thomas and Sir Richard apart. Arthur pushed Sir Thomas back into the chamber and with the point of his dagger convinced the knight to sit upon the bench beside Squire Ralph.

Sir Richard, meanwhile, patted the dust from his cotehardie, looked about, saw his son with a dagger at his throat, and discharged a stream of questions, demands, and curses. When he had exhausted his vocabulary I explained why Arthur and I were in his kitchen, what his son and Squire Ralph had done, and what I intended to do.

Evidently my explanation was clear. Sir Richard spluttered in dismay, but made no attempt to deny my assertions. Perhaps he had known the truth of John Whytyng's death for many days. I was unlikely to be able to prove that, and there would be little to be done even if it was so.

My intention was to take Sir Thomas and Squire Ralph to the abbey cell. This I told Sir Richard. Next day was Sunday. On Monday Arthur, I, and a half-dozen lay brothers would take knight and squire to the Sheriff of Oxford. Sir Roger would hold them in Oxford Castle dungeon 'till next the King's Eyre met and they were tried for their crimes. Arthur and I would have to travel winter roads to give witness to their felonies. This was not a pleasing prospect.

Arthur removed his belt, grasped Sir Thomas's arms and pinioned them behind him, then using the belt tied the knight's wrists together behind his back.

I did not believe that Sir Richard would defile the abbey and attempt to free his son, but nevertheless advised Brother Gerleys that trusted lay brothers be assigned to guard the cell door. This was done.

'Tis but six miles from Eynsham to Oxford. Sir Thomas and Squire Ralph were delivered to the sheriff on Monday and charged before noon. Sir Roger keeps a fine table, so when he invited me to dine I did not hesitate to accept. Arthur and the lay brothers ate with Sir Roger's sergeants and I heard no complaints about their meal while we rode back to Eynsham.

Next morn Arthur and I departed early for Bampton. Brother Gerleys, soon to be Abbot Gerleys, bid us "Fare well," and assured me that the Bible Abbot Thurstan had promised would be completed by St. John's Day.

I found my Kate well, and Bessie also, residing yet in the castle. Kate had been unsure of my instructions and so decided to remain within stone walls, with valets and grooms about, rather than risk she knew not what at home. I believe she was pleased to leave the drafty stone pile and return to Galen House.

Arthur and Agnes wished to wed, but could not. 'Twas Advent, when no marriages are permitted. But on Tuesday, the twenty-sixth day of December, they wed in the Church of St.

Beornwald's porch and took up residence in an empty chamber along the castle north wall. Lord Gilbert may find a more suitable place when he returns to Bampton.

On January 8 my Kate gave birth to our second daughter. We named her Sybil, my mother's name. She had promised a son and thought me disappointed. Kate knows me well, but she is mistaken. The lass was strong and hale, Kate and I are young. There will be opportunity yet for sons.

The King's Eyre met three days after Candlemas. Arthur, I, and Abbot Gerleys gave testimony. Squire Ralph, whose ribs seemed healed, was fined ten shillings and released. He knew 'twould be folly to seek to retain his place with Sir Richard, so did not return to Eynsham. I have heard that he now serves a knight near to Durham, where reivers come down from Scotland to steal cattle and coin, and men skilled with a sword may always find employment and perhaps, eventually, a knighthood.

Sir Thomas was sentenced to hang for his murder of John Whytyng. Arthur, I, and Abbot Gerleys did not remain in Oxford to see the man upon a scaffold, but returned to Eynsham the same day. There I learned that, his other options now vanished, Simon atte Pond had granted Osbern Mallory permission to pay court to Maude. I suspect that she will be amenable to his suit. 'Twould mean no more raw and blistered hands from doing the monks' laundry.

I spent the spring of the year enjoying my Kate and Bessie and Sybil, and looking toward the day when I would own a Bible.

Afterword

The village of Eynsham has provided a walking tour of the locations associated with the medieval abbey. St. Leonard's Church, located to the north of the abbey precincts, dates to the thirteenth century.

The Brotherhood of the Free Spirit was not a monolithic belief. Some adherents were no more heretical than the Lollards, with whom they shared some opinions. Others of the Free Spirit, as described in *The Abbot's Agreement*, were genuinely heretical. There is some evidence that the heresy did not completely disappear until the fifteenth century.

Many readers have asked about medieval remains and tourist facilities in the Bampton area. St. Mary's Church is little changed from the fourteenth century, when it was known as the Church of St. Beornwald. Visitors to Bampton will enjoy staying at Wheelgate House, a B&B in the center of the town.

Village scenes in the popular television series *Downton Abbey* were filmed on Church View Street, and St. Mary's Church appears in several episodes. Bampton also hosts a large Morris dancing festival on the Monday Bank Holiday in late May.

Ashes to Ashes

**An extract from the eighth chronicle of
Hugh de Singleton, surgeon**

Chapter 1

I had told my Kate for several days that St. John's Day should not be considered midsummer. Roger Bacon, the great scholar of an earlier century, and Robert Grosseteste before him, showed how the calendar has gone awry. Bacon told all who would listen that an extra day is added to the calendar every one hundred and thirty years or so, and so in the year of our Lord 1369 we are ten days displaced. Kate laughed.

"What difference," she asked, "even if 'tis so?"

"Easter, and such moveable feasts," I replied, "are out of joint. What of Lent? How does a man know when he may consume meat and when he may not, if the day of the Lord Christ's crucifixion is ten days misplaced?"

"Oh... aye." But she was yet unconvinced, I think, so when men of Bampton began gathering wood for the Midsummer's Eve fire I said no more. We would make merry with others of the town and castle, and celebrate the warm days of summer, regardless of the calendar. I have been wed three years and more. I know when to hold my peace.

The great pile of fallen branches from Lord Gilbert Talbot's forest was raised in a fallow field to the north of the Church of St. Beornwald. For three days fuel was added. I watched the pile grow each day, little suspecting that the daily increase would soon bring me much consternation.

Kate had tied green birch twigs above our door in honor of the summer, so when we departed Galen House at dusk to watch the lighting of the St. John's Day fire I had to duck my head to avoid entangling my cap in the greenery.

I am Hugh de Singleton, surgeon, and bailiff to Lord Gilbert Talbot at his manor of Bampton. I thought that Lord Gilbert might, with some of his knights, attend the Midsummer's Eve blaze. The Lady Petronilla died a year past, when the great pestilence returned, and Lord Gilbert was much distressed. But when he returned to Bampton in the spring, after spending the winter at Goodrich Castle, I thought he seemed somewhat recovered from his great sorrow.

Lord Gilbert did not attend, but several of his retainers – knights, gentlemen and their ladies, valets and grooms – did so. I am not much given to capering about like a pup chasing its tail, so stood aside and lifted my Bessie to my shoulder so that she could better see as others danced about and played the fool, aided in their efforts, no doubt, by great quantities of ale.

Bessie had discovered speech, and exercised her vocabulary as the flames reached into the sky as high as the roof of Father Thomas's vicarage, which stood a safe distance to the east. Kate held Sybil in her arms. The babe was but five months old, was unimpressed by anything inedible, and so slept through the shouts and singing and garish illumination.

Bessie also soon became limp against my shoulder. The merry-making would continue without us. Kate and I returned to Galen House, put our daughters to bed, and fell to sleep with the raucous sound of celebration entering our chamber through the open window.

I was breaking my fast next morning with a loaf and ale when I heard the church bell ring in a solemn cadence. The passing bell. The Angelus Bell had sounded an hour before. Someone in Bampton or the Weald had died in the night. At nearly the same moment a hammering upon Galen House door jolted me from my semi-comatose condition. The pounding ceased and a man shouted, "Master Hugh!" in a voice which might have awakened half the residents of Church View Street. It did awaken Sybil, who instantly realized that she was hungry and began to wail. Kate hastened to the stairs to deal with our daughter while I stumbled to the door to learn who was awake so early after such a night.

Father Thomas's clerk, Bertrand Pecock, stood before me, his fist ready to again strike against the Galen House door if I had not opened it.

"Master Hugh, Father Thomas would have you attend him. There are bones."

"Bones?" I replied stupidly. I am not at my best until an hour or so has passed since Kate's cockerel has announced the dawn.

"Men gathering the ashes found them."

"Ashes?"

"Aye… from the St. John's Day fire. To spread upon a pea field. They came to the vicarage to tell Father Thomas. He has sent me to tell you of this foul discovery and to fetch the coroner."

"The bones are human?"

"Aye. There is a skull. I have just come from the place."

In past years men would often pitch the bones of swine into a St. John's Day fire so as to ward off sickness in cattle and men. 'Twas thought to do so would prevent aerial dragons from poisoning streams and ponds of a night with their foul froth. But I had not heard of this being done at Bampton since I came to the village. Of course, men might toss a few bones into the pile of wood as a precaution, I suppose, and none know of it. But human bones are a different matter.

Kate descended the stairs from our chamber carrying Sybil, with Bessie holding tight to her mother's cotehardie. I told my wife of the discovery and set off for the field while Bertrand hastened to tell Hubert Shillside, Bampton's coroner, of the bones, and request that he assemble his coroner's jury.

Father Thomas had notified Father Ralph and Father Simon of the discovery. The three vicars of the Church of St. Beornwald stood staring at the ash pile, their arms folded across their chests as if deep in thought. Who knows? Perhaps they were. But knowing Father Ralph, I doubt it so.

Four villagers stood opposite the priests, leaning upon rakes and shovels. A wheelbarrow half filled with ashes stood beside the four.

"Ah, you have come," Father Thomas said. This was obvious to all, so I did not reply. As I drew near the ash pile I saw some white object gleam in the morning sun and crossed myself. Being forewarned, I knew what this must be.

"Bertrand will fetch the coroner," the vicar continued, "but I think Hubert will need your advice."

246

I did not ask what advice Father Thomas thought I might supply. Surgeons do deal with bones, but when called to do so the bones are generally clothed with flesh. Shillside and his coroner's jury would put their heads together, cluck over some fellow's misfortune, then leave the matter to me. 'Tis what bailiffs are to do; find and punish miscreants. I knew this when I accepted Lord Gilbert Talbot's offer to serve him at his Bampton manor. Good and decent folk prefer to have little to do with a bailiff. So also felons. Most bailiffs have few friends.

I walked slowly about the pile of blackened ashes and felt yet some warmth from what had been six or so hours before a great conflagration. The men scooping the ashes had come early to the work, to gather them before others might think to do so. But they had ceased their labor when they found the skull. This was clear, for the rounded cranium was yet half-buried, eye sockets peering blankly at me from an upturned face. Well, it was a face at one time.

I saw a few other bones protruding from the ashes; enough that I was convinced that whoso was consumed in the flames went into the fire whole. But to discover if this was truly so I would need to sweep away the ashes and learn what bones were here and how they lay. I would await Hubert Shillside and his jury for that. And the ashes would cool while I waited.

Bampton's coroner did not soon appear. Most of his jurymen had attended the St. John's Day fire the night before, drunk too much ale, and cavorted about the blaze 'till near dawn, so they would likely have to be roused from sleep to attend to their duty. A sour-looking band of fellows eventually shuffled into view beyond the church.

When they had approached close enough to see the skull, one and all crossed themselves, then bent low to better examine the reason for being called from their beds.

I stood aside as Shillside collected the jury after each had circled the ash pile. I could have predicted their decision. There was, they decided, no reason to raise the hue and cry, as they could not know if a felony had been done, and even if 'twas so, there was no evidence to follow which might lead to a murderer. A man, or perhaps a woman, was dead. The coroner's jury could discover nothing more. They would leave further investigation to me. So said Hubert Shillside as his jury departed to seek their homes and break their fast.

Before the coroner left the place I drew him to where the three vicars of the Church of St. Beornwald stood. I asked the four men if any man or woman had gone missing from Bampton or the Weald in the past few days. They shrugged, glanced toward one another, and shook their heads.

"Perhaps some fellow had too much ale last night, before he came to the fire, and danced too close," Father Simon suggested.

"Odd that no one would see him fall into the flames," Father Thomas said. "Most of the village was here, and in the light of the blaze he would surely have been seen."

"Would've cried out, too," Shillside said. "No man burns in silence, I think."

"Or woman, either," I added.

"What will you do with the bones?" Father Ralph asked. "We should bury them in the churchyard, but must not do so 'till we know that the dead man was baptized."

"And was not a suicide," Father Simon said.

Were there any corpses to be found in England unbaptized, and therefore ineligible to be interred in hallowed ground? I thought not. And I could think of a dozen more acceptable ways to take one's life than to dive into the flames of a St. John's Day fire.

The vicars and coroner fell silent, staring at me. They wanted to know who had died, and whether or not he had perished in Bampton's Midsummer's Eve blaze. I needed to know how the man, or woman, had died, and, if possible, where. If the four men gazing at me expected me to provide answers to these questions, I had best begin the search.

The first thing must be to gather all of the bones. Mayhap there would be the mark of a blade across a rib to tell how death came.

But I had no wish to go down on hands and knees in the still-warm ashes to inspect bones. I turned to the men who had found the bones, and instructed them to sift carefully through the ashes, and place all bones into their wheelbarrow.

These fellows were not pleased to be assigned the task, but knew that their lord's bailiff could make life disagreeable if they balked.

Unpleasant tasks are best accomplished quickly, and so after a moment of hesitation Lord Gilbert's tenants emptied the ashes from their partly filled wheelbarrow and set to work with spades and rakes to uncover bones. I was required to caution them several times to use less haste and more care. The vicars and Hubert Shillside watched from across the ash pile as the stack of bones in the wheelbarrow grew.

Only a few minutes were required to discover and retrieve the bones. The men continued the work, however, finding nothing more, until I bade them desist. I assigned one fellow to follow me to Galen House with the wheelbarrow and told the others to watch for any bones they might have missed when they continued the work of recovering ashes for use upon their fields.

When Kate agreed to wed a bailiff she did not consider, I think, that her husband would use her table to inspect a skeleton. Marriage may bring many surprises.

I told Roger, for so the villager who accompanied me with the wheelbarrow of bones was named, to take his burden to the toft behind Galen House. Kate looked up from a pot in which she was preparing our dinner, and her mouth dropped open in surprise as I propped open the door to the toft and began to drag our table through it.

"There is better light in the toft," I explained.

"For what?" she asked.

"Examining bones... human bones."

Kate's hand rose to her mouth. "On my table?"

"They have been through last night's fire," I said.

"You will place roasted flesh upon our table?"

"Nay. There is little flesh. Nearly all has been consumed. Bones remain. No man knows who it was that was in the blaze. I hope to discover some mark upon the bones which will tell who has died, and how."

"Oh. You believe murder may have been done?"

"I have considered why a man, or woman, should be in a Midsummer's Eve fire. Would they place themselves there? I cannot believe it so. Then why would some other lodge a corpse there? The only explanation I can imagine is that the person who did so thought the flames would consume all, flesh and bones, and so hide an unnatural death."

Kate's hens scattered as I dragged the table from the door and Osbern set his wheelbarrow beside it. In a few minutes I had emptied the wheelbarrow, heaped the ash-covered bones upon the table, and set Osbern free to return to his work at the ash pile.

Bessie, I believe, understood something of the nature of the business her father was about, for she stood in the doorway with her mother, clutching Kate's cotehardie and staring wide-eyed at the pile of bones. Kate soon tired of watching me scratch my head and returned to her pot.

I intended to assemble the bones as they would have been a few days past when they held some man upright. As I did so I discovered that most of the small bones of feet and hands were missing. Either they had been consumed in the fire or were overlooked when the tenants recovered the larger bones from the ash pile.

Several years past, when I was new-come to Bampton, I had stood in my toft over a table like this covered with bones. Those had been found in the castle cesspit, and in pursuit of a felon I had nearly sent an innocent man to the gallows. I breathed a silent prayer that the Lord Christ would turn me from error if I blundered so again.

When I had arranged the bones properly I began my inspection with the skull, and here the examination might have ended. Behind the right ear was a concave fracture. A few small fragments of the skull were missing, and those that remained showed a depression deeper than the width of my thumb. There was no indication of the injury beginning to knit. The victim had surely died soon after the blow was delivered which made this dent. The stroke had killed him, or rendered him senseless so that a blade could be used to end his life, perhaps with a slash to the throat, or a thrust into his heart.

I studied the remainder of the bones, but found no other marks upon them. I did not search these for a cause of death. I believed I had found that. I hoped to discover some anomaly which would help to identify the corpse. A broken arm, perhaps, which had healed, so that some friend or relative of a missing man who knew of a past injury might tell me whose bones lay upon my table.

I turned the skull and examined the teeth. Only one was missing, and the others had few flaws. Here, I thought, was the skull of a young man. I took a femur from the table and held it aside my leg. I am somewhat taller than most men, so did not expect the bone to match mine in length, but was surprised how short the femur was when compared to my own. 'Twas perhaps a woman, I thought, who burned in the fire, or a very short man. How to know?

I puzzled over this as I stood over the bones, and remembered a lecture from my year as a student of surgery at the University of Paris. The instructor had placed before his students two pelvic bones: one male, one female. That of the man appeared larger. Then he placed before us a plaster imitation of the skull of a newborn infant, and showed how a babe's head would pass through the female pelvis, but would not do so through the opening in a man's pelvis, even though the male pelvis seemed the greater.

A movement in the door of Galen House caught my eye. Kate had left her fire to watch my examination of the bones. She held Sybil in her arms.

I called to Kate to bring the babe to me. At five months old her head was larger than when newly born, but not much.

I spread my hands about her head to measure, then went to a corner of the toft where mud from recent rain had not yet dried. I fashioned a sphere of the proper size from the mire, then returned to Kate and Sybil and the table of bones.

Kate drew back as I approached with the muddy ball. "What are you about?" she asked.

"Watch," I said.

I held out the muddy orb to compare it in size to Sybil's head. It was somewhat smaller, which was as I intended. I turned to the pelvic bone upon the table and tried to pass the mud ball through it. I could not do so. The opening was far too small. 'Twas the bones of a man which lay in the sun upon our table. A small man, who had lost one tooth.